FIELDS OF
BLOOD

Other books in the AMERICAN VAMPIRE SERIES

THE AMERICAN VAMPIRE SERIES

FIELDS of BLOOD

VAMPIRE STORIES
FROM THE
AMERICAN MIDWEST

LAWRENCE SCHIMEL AND MARTIN H. GREENBERG

CUMBERLAND HOUSE
NASHVILLE, TENNESSEE

Published by Cumberland House Publishing, Inc., 431 Harding Industrial Park Drive, Nashville, TN 37211.

Cover and interior design by Joel Wright.

Library of Congress Cataloging-in-Publication Data
Fields of blood : vampire stories from the American Midwest /
    [edited by] Lawrence Schimel and Martin H. Greenberg.
        p. cm. — (The American vampire series)
    ISBN 1-888952-79-2 (alk. paper)
    1. Vampires—Middle West—Fiction. 2. Horror tales, American-
Middle West. I. Schimel, Lawrence. II. Greenberg, Martin Harry.
III. Series.
PS648.V35F54 1998
813'.0873808375'0977—dc21   98-5222
                                                         CIP

Printed in the United States of America
1 2 3 4 5 6 7—04 03 02 01 00 99 98

For Ron McCutchan,
something to sink your teeth into!

—L. S.

Contents

Introduction

The vampire is less interested in the amber waves of grain for which our country is famous than in the crimson waves of blood coursing through the veins of the men and women who tend those fields.

While most fiction about vampires tends to center on the urban experience, and expecially on coastal cities like Los Angeles and New York, the American heartland is also a home for these creatures of the night. The wide open skies of the Midwest provide an enticing expanse of night in which a vampire might fly in search of prey. And once a victim has been located—solitary, having left the sanctuary of home to step out into the dark—it is usually easy prey. In less populated regions the vampire has less to fear from others coming to his intended meal's defense.

Small-town life poses some different problems than urban existence for the vampire: In a town where everyone knows one another, the newcomer is immediately suspect—even if innocent.

Even though we are all relatively new to these lands, we have put down roots fast and firmly and, in the struggle to keep body and soul together, do not often welcome interlopers. But as some of the characters in these stories learn, it is important not to be too disdainful of outsiders because sometimes these immigrants will be our salvation, coming to our aid when the veil of night has unleashed a vampire within our midst.

Of course, sometimes these strangers are not friends, and we struggle to save our families and ourselves from the vampire's fang.

The Midwest does have its major cities—Chicago, Minneapolis, Milwaukee, Indianapolis, Detroit, and many others. But it also has wide stretches of open road across open field, with the occasional abandoned farmhouse that seems a perfect refuge from the storm—until you learn, as night falls, that it's not as deserted as it appears. . . .

The stories in *Fields of Blood* will take you to both the heartland's cities and its fields, in tales that range from the old glory days of prohibition to modern-day agricultural farming techniques. You will find vampires full of malice and dark intent and others who have "seen the light" and wish to reform their bloodthirsty ways. You will read stories that make you afraid of the dark and the creatures who lurk within its folds and stories that make you laugh at your own fears.

But always they will be stories of vampires in the vital heartland of our country, hunting for the blood and emotion that pulses through the human heart.

—Lawrence Schimel

Acknowledgments

This book would not exist without the assistance of Stefan Dziemianowicz, which is greatly appreciated by both editors.

John Helfers also provided invaluable help in compiling and processing this project.

Thanks are also due to many others for suggestions and other help in tracking down some of the stories included, but especially to: Keith Kahla, Greg Cox and his Transylvanian Library, Ellen Datlow, and Margaret L. Carter.

FIELDS OF
BLOOD

A cop faces many dangers, but he never thinks he'd end up like this!

Undercover

BY NANCY HOLDER

It was a November night in Chicago, and the sleet stabbed Stan's shoulders like daggers—or in his case, incisors—as he ducked into the station house and crammed his umbrella into a stand inside a wire cage.

"Hey, Detective Stepanek," the desk sergeant greeted him. "Man, what a night, eh? It's enough to . . . kill . . . you." His voice trailed off and he went back to his paperwork. His face was a purple blush of embarrassment.

Stan sighed and began peeling off his gloves. Yeah, well, some guys never got used to him.

Neither did some women.

He scowled at everyone and no one as he unbuttoned his coat. Twelve months now since his Change. And Leslie wouldn't come near him. Some day he would find the fiend who'd done this to him and pay him back in spades.

Or stakes.

Man.

He ran a hand through his hair and pushed through the double doors past the sergeant's desk, and strode down the hall. A couple of beat cops, clad in dripping rain gear, saw him and nodded, but shifted their gazes as soon as they politely could. Fragging cowards.

His teeth hurt. He was hungry.

The black letters on the glass door read, "JACK ZIRES." That was his boss. He rapped hard, waited for the grunt, got it, and went into the small cubbyhole jammed with file cabinets and paper.

Tall and bald, Jack was eating a salad out of a Styrofoam container. Six months ago, he had become a vegetarian and ever since then, his cholesterol tap-danced near the danger zone and he couldn't bring it back down. It made him cranky.

"Hey." Jack gestured to a seat. He had heavy black eyebrows and a perpetual five o'clock shadow; was bitter about the lack of hair on his head. Took a lot of ribbing for it. Before he became a vegetarian.

"How you tonight?" he asked between bites of salad. Stan had forgotten what lettuce tasted like. Not, he recalled, that it had ever tasted like much. Steak, he missed. Chocolate. Pizza. Not lettuce.

"I'm okay," Stan muttered, straddling the chair.

"Leslie again?" They were close enough to talk about things like that.

"Is it ever anything else?" Stan wiped the raindrops off his head and straightened out his legs. His shoes were soaked.

"Well, yeah, sometimes it is." Jack stabbed a carrot, picked it of fthe fork, and ate it with his fingers. "Sometimes it's your kids. Sometimes it's your parents. Sometimes it's your fellow detectives and other persons in uniform." As Jack, an unreconstructed chauvinist, referred to the women on the force.

"Jeez, Jack, I'm not a complainer."

"I know." Jack patted Stan's forearm. He was one of the few people Stan knew who would actually touch him. "Listen. Listen hard, I've got something for you, and I'm going to give it to you and you alone. Okay?" He nudged something in his salad, sneered at it, and put down his fork. "Some of these vegetables. I don't know." He touched a paper napkin to his lips and dropped it onto his cluttered desk.

"Okay," he said, and opened a drawer. He reached in and withdrew a plastic bag that contained the remains of a lady's black wallet.

He dropped the bag in front of Stan. Nodded at it.

"Check it out."

Stan eyed him, dropped his gaze. Opened the bag and fished out the wallet. "So?" he said, and then saw the fragment of a picture in the inside window, where ordinarily you might slip a driver's license. He gasped and almost dropped the wallet, then held it close and leaned into the beam of light from the crookneck lamp on Jack's desk.

It was part of a face, but it was a face he suddenly remembered with the force of a roundhouse right. Huge brown eyes, a long thin nose, and a beautiful red mouth that hid her cruel surprise. Yes, he knew it now: it'd been a woman, or something pretending to be one. Dear God.

"How—how did you get this?" He could barely speak.

"Stoolie Bob brought it in. Said he found some broad lying dead on the street. Or so he thought. Took her purse and he was going through it when she stood up and tried to kill him. That's all he said, but he hasn't been himself since. I thought of you." Jack winced. "No offense."

"None taken." Stan hadn't been the same since. "Why'd he bring it to you?"

"Wanted me to lock him up for theft."

Stan's heart beat faster. "Got anything else?"

"Put that new guy on finding out where the purse was bought, if possible. I dunno. It's a long shot. Could be somebody else's purse. I mean, does your wife carry pictures of herself in her own handbag?"

"I don't remember," Stan said morosely.

"Aw, man. Women can be so cold." Jack stared down at the remains of his salad and shut the Styrofoam container. "I need a hamburger injection, damn it."

"So," Stan pressed.

"So. I didn't hold Stoolie Bob, and he's waiting for you at The Old Same Place. Wants to talk."

Stan inclined his head. "Thanks, Jack."

"I ain't telling anybody else about this. You got enough problems. Anybody asks you what you're working on, tell 'em special detail, and if they have any more questions to come to me."

Stan reverently put the wallet back in the bag and slipped the whole thing into the pocket of his jacket. "Thank you. If I ever crack this, Jack, I'm buying you a steak."

Jack regarded Stan with sad eyes. "Wish you could eat one with me, buddy."

Stan said nothing.

There was nothing to say.

◊◊◊

He took his own car to the South Side. The windshield wipers sluiced the gray rain away just in time for more gray rain to take its place. There was hardly anyone on the street; steam rose from the grates. Electric lights were muted, as if the bulbs had filled up with water.

It was not a fit night for man, beast, or those stuck somewhere in between.

But there was one highlight. He pulled into an alley, turned off the engine, and got out, rapped twice on a bright blue door. It opened and a handsome Hispanic woman appeared on the threshold. She was wearing a large, ornate crucifix that bothered Stan not at all.

"Buenos Noches." He handed her a twenty.

"A usted," she replied. She was a nurse, worked for the university. She left for a moment, returned with something in a brown paper bag.

"O positive."

He took it. *"Gracias."*

With a barely suppressed shudder, she shut the door.

He ripped open the plastic container and scarfed down dinner.

◊◊◊

About twenty minutes later, he parked in another alley, behind a Harley, and turned off the engine. Sat for a moment behind the wheel and calmed himself. Stoolie Bob was a real squirrel. He didn't want to spook him, have him clam up. Anything he could tell him about the woman, anything at all, would be the best news he'd had in a year.

He got out and walked around the corner. The Old Same Place was such a dive it didn't even have a nicely hand-lettered sign, much less an electric one. Its clientele consisted of those a buck or two away from homelessness, and looking to make that buck inside The Old Same Place by peddling drugs or other assorted good times, or hustling pool.

Used to be it was okay he went in there. But now, as he pushed open the wooden door, conversation died away for a moment before it resumed at a higher, more nervous pitch.

He wished he knew what he looked like. But of course, he cast no reflection in the mirror behind the bar.

The floor was cracked linoleum and the barstools and booths were covered in extremely distressed burgundy. Smoke that cast purple cobwebs hung motionless in the air. The place reeked of old cigarettes, mildew, sweat, and cheap perfume.

"G'evenin'," he said, and bellied up to the bar.

John Joseph, the grizzled old black proprietor, was washing a glass. A cigar hung out of his mouth. He nodded his reply.

"Stoolie Bob in?"

John Joseph jerked his head toward the back corner booth. Sure enough, Bob's signature navy-blue watch cap bobbed up and down like a puppet on *Sesame Street.*

The bartender poured Stan a drink, any drink; it was nice of him to do it when he knew Stan couldn't properly exploit it. Still, Stan blended in better with a fistful to carry around. He guessed. He took the glass and ambled over to Stoolie Bob's booth and stood there.

Stoolie Bob was talking to a young man with scars on his face and neck. Especially his neck. They both saw Stan and the young man whistled through his broken, brown teeth.

"It's true," he murmured, awed.

"You mind?" Stan asked harshly.

The man glanced at Stoolie Bob. "Later," he said, scooted to the end of the booth, hesitated, then got up and around Stan as fast as he could.

"I knew you'd come," Stoolie Bob gushed. He made to reach for Stan's hand, stopped himself. "Ya gotta help me. I'm marked now. She'll come back for me."

Stan slid back in his seat and feigned nonchalance. You got more out of Bob if he figured he wasn't going to get much out of you.

"She's like you, Mr. Detective!"

"Oh?" Stan yawned.

"Yeah! She's all white, and she's got these teeth!" Stoolie Bob lowered his voice. A vein pulsed below his jaw line like it was sending out a distress call. "I need your help. You gotta tell her to leave me alone. Tell her I'm your friend. That I help you solve cases, alla time. Please." Now Stoolie Bob did grab Stan's hands. His fingers were dry and papery.

"That so."

"Yeah!" Stoolie Bob gripped his fingers.

"And you made her acquaintance at?"

"I was down to the Loop. I was near Hyatt. I know I'm not supposed to be there, Mr. Detective. But I was hungry."

And the pickpocket pickings were pretty good down in yuppieland, Stan finished silently.

"And she was wearing?"

"I thought she was dead! I wasn't stealing from her!"

"And she was wearing?" Stan repeated.

"Black. All black. Black sweater. Black pants. Black coat." He paused. "Black boots."

Stan sighed. "Where's the rest of her purse? Was her wallet just lying beside her? Was it in her pocket?"

Stoolie Bob hesitated. He let go of Stan and dropped his hands under the table. Stared at the Formica.

"Bo-ob, yoo-hoo."

"I thought she was dead." He thrust out his lower lip.

"I'm not going to bust you." Stan folded his hands and leaned forward. "I want to help you. 'Cause you're right, Bob. She'll come back for you unless I can talk her out of it." A damn lie—well, maybe, how the hell should he know?—but what did it matter?

"Okay, okay." Stoolie Bob squared his shoulders. "It was in her pocket."

"Okay, Bob. That's okay. Now, this is important. Was there anything else in her pocket? Think about it. Anything else?"

Bob nodded. "Yeah. Yeah, there was. Book of matches."

Stan's eyes flickered. "Did you keep them? Do you have them?"

Stoolie Bob shook his head. "No. But I read 'em," he said hopefully. "They was from a restaurant. Called something funny. The Zigooner, something like that."

Zigooner. Stan thought. He called to John Joseph, "You got a Yellow Pages?"

John Joseph ducked his head under the bar, straightened, and showed him the phone book. Brought it over to the table.

"Thanks." Stan began to flip through it to the restaurant section. Zigooner. Zig.

Zigeuner. Bingo. Had to be.

Stan flipped the book shut. He rose, took out his wallet, and gave Stoolie Bob his usual fee of ten bucks.

"Night," John Joseph called, but Stan was already out the door.

"Tell her I'm your partner!" Stoolie Bob called out desperately.

Someone else muttered, "J. J. why you let that pasteface in here? He makes me sick."

Pasteface. Damn.

◊◊◊

The Zigeuner was a Rumanian restaurant near the Hyatt.

Bingo. Oh, yes, double bingo and it was all on red, baby.

Blood red.

Stan showed the photo to the waiters in white, open-throated Gypsy shirts, trying to keep his voice below the violin music, and they all acted so blind, deaf, and orally challenged that he knew he had the right place. Oh, he'd had people freeze up around him—such as his wife—but this was different; this was freezing with a purpose. This was freezing because they knew something.

But they sure didn't want to tell him what it was.

"Listen, I'll leave my card," he told a dark, husky man who kept opening the cash register, counting the money, and shutting it again. "I can be reached here on the night shift." He thought for a moment. "Here's my home phone too. It's very urgent. If anyone remembers seeing this woman"—and here he held out her picture again, and the man flinched again—"I would really appreciate hearing about it. Really, I would."

He left, more hopeful than frustrated. And praying she wouldn't, or hadn't, left town.

◊◊◊

Leslie was asleep when he got home. He tried not to wake her, but she had become a light sleeper since his Change.

He hadn't touched her in a year. Not even a kiss.

"Hi," she said, as he made sure the curtains were drawn against the windows. "How'd it go?"

"I have a lead." Her expression said she understood what he meant.

"Good."

"Maybe she . . . maybe I can be . . ." Changed back, he wanted to say, but he was afraid to.

Leslie took a deep breath. "Stan, I filed the papers today. This isn't fair to the kids. I . . ." She looked away.

"I love you," he whispered. "I would do anything . . ."

"You can't."

"I have a lead."

She wiped a tear from her eye. Her Adams apple bobbed. "It's just that, I, Stan . . ." She looked at him full on. "I can't help thinking about what you are. What you do to stay . . . alive." Her voice broke on that last work.

"Please sleep on the couch from now on." She looked away.

Why tonight? he thought. Why, when he finally had a clue?

"I haven't hurt anybody," he said.

"You might." She pulled the covers over herself.

He started to say more, sensed the futility of it.

Grabbing a pillow and a blanket, he trudged into the living room. Considered. The kids would try to wake him up. She hadn't thought of that. They would see him lying there, staring up at the ceiling like a zombie. Or like what he was.

He got back in his car and drove to a motel. Which was, he suspected, what she wanted all along.

He hoped no one at the restaurant called his home phone. Because all of a sudden, it wasn't home any more.

◊◊◊

Sundown, and his eyes popped open.

He called Leslie when he woke up, and a man answered the phone. Depressed, he paid a visit to the owner of a pretty shady mortuary and had a snack. So let the guy overcharge on embalming, cut a few other funeral corners.

Man, police work was a dirty job sometimes. Or make that survival. But he had never hurt a soul; Leslie knew that. He had never touched a single living being in the entire hellish year.

He showed up for work at ten, as always. Jack had bent a lot of arms to keep him from rotating shifts; hell, he *had* broken some arms to keep Stan on the force.

The desk sergeant said, "Some woman called you. Wouldn't leave her name. Did leave a number."

Stan grabbed the slip of paper and ran to his office. Slammed the door. Yes, yes. He screwed up the number and had to punch it in again. Yes, baby, yes.

Jack ducked his head in, brows raised, with a look of eagerness of his sallow, underfed face. Evidently he knew about the call.

Stan looked up at him while the phone rang. Jack was a good friend.

"Hello?" Yes. It was a woman's voice, deep and sexy, very nervous. Stan hunched forward. Jack shut the door, leaving Stan in privacy.

"It's Stan Stepanek."

"Ah." A sigh of relief. "Ah, yes. Meet me now. Please, meet me. Alone. Tell no one."

Jeesh, so she could finish the job? He said, "Where are you?"

"No, not here. I can't trust . . ." She caught her breath. "Meet me in front of the aquarium in twenty minutes."

Dial tone.

Stan closed his eyes for a second. The room was whirling. He licked his lips and rose.

The door opened. Jack poked his head in.

"You got any silver bullets?" It was supposed to be a joke, but it fell flat.

Jack replied, very soberly, "No, but I was thinking you could use the tip of your umbrella, if you pushed hard enough. Was it her?"

"Maybe." Better have been.

"What's she want?"

"I don't know." But he knew what *he* wanted: revenge, an explanation, some help.

"You want backup?" Jack smiled grimly. "Guess not."

Without thinking, Stan checked the revolver in his shoulder, felt for his badge. What, was he going to Mirandize her? Bring her in for violating the laws of nature?

"Well," he said, and Jack shook his head. Swallowed hard.

"Good luck, buddy."

Stan nodded, said nothing. Left.

◊◊◊

The moon hung low in the sky, casting a silvery glow over the river, and beyond, the vast expanse of Lake Michigan. Over the tall figure who stood on the knoll, watching him advance.

Her face was cast in darkness. He tensed, wishing he had some protection. None of that Bela Lugosi stuff worked—crosses and holy water, no help at all. And he knew what he was talking about.

"Detective Stepanek?" she asked, in that deep, rich voice. It was heavily accented, some kind of East Europe thing.

"Yes. And you?"

She came forward, into the soft fuzz of a streetlamp. He was taken aback. Despite the fact that she was white as chalk, she was the most beautiful woman he had ever seen in his life. Her eyes were huge and deep velvet brown; her cheekbones, her nose, her large red lips blended into a dream that just couldn't be real. Her hair tumbled around her shoulders in soft curls and kissed her neck. Her long, pale, slender neck.

Her photo had not done her justice.

"And you?" he repeated, his voice shaking, maybe not so much with terror as he had expected it to. Maybe with . . . wow, with he didn't know what—

She jerked. "I'm . . ." She looked away. "I was Natasha Boranova." When she looked back, tears glittered on her cheeks. "I'm sorry. I didn't know what I was doing. I'm . . . I'm a stranger here." The tears came in earnest now. They made her look so helpless, so vulnerable.

"Hey," he said softly, walking closer. She was shaking, probably just as . . . scared . . . as he was.

"We were here illegally."

"Yeah, I'll bet," he tried to joke. "I don't think Immigration has a quota on—"

"No, *before.*" She cocked her head. "You don't know who I am, do you?"

"Besides Countess Dracula?" he retorted, and was immediately sorry. She jerked as if he'd hit her.

"I was a tennis player. I was here with my coach, Ivan Mazarek? We sought asylum."

Where had he been? Wrapped up in his Big Problem. He shrugged.

"Sorry. I don't know anything about that. But, ah, aren't we all one big happy New World Order now anyway?"

"So they would all have us think." She threw back her head and raised her fists to her chest. "I'm so sorry. I didn't mean to leave you alive."

Whoa. His hand slipped into his jacket and touched his revolver. Futile, Stan. Futile. He cracked his knuckles and made a fist in his trouser pocket.

The moonlight drained even her lips of color. Even then, she was exquisite. "If you're left alive, you become . . . what you are now."

"Oh?" he rasped. "I thought it was the other way around."

"No." The beautiful hair waved back and forth, back and forth, as she shook her head in misery. "No, and they knew it too."

She held out her hands. "Please, help me find the people that did this to me. To us!"

And then she ran to him and threw her arms around him. Her lips sought, found his, and she kissed him so hard he staggered backward. It was heaven, pure and simple, especially when you have lived in hell for a year. He felt as if he were floating; he couldn't believe the sensations coursing through him. It was like . . . it was the way he imagined he would feel if he actually bit someone.

"Oh! I haven't touched another person in five years," she moaned, clinging to him. "Well, except . . . you know. I've been so lonely, so very lonely. The people at the Zigeuner, they try. But they could never really accept me."

"Yeah," he breathed. They kissed again. And again. They ran their hands along each other, starved, filling up. He tasted her blood on his lips. "You're so lovely."

"Am I?" She beamed at him. "I kept a picture of myself so I could remember what I looked like."

"You look swell. You're even more gorgeous than when you were . . . the other way."

"Human," she said wistfully, then glanced up at him through her lashes. His knees went weak. Her mouth was swollen and dotted with red, where his teeth had done a little damage.

"But do you know, if we are . . . together, for that time we *are* human again." She nodded. "That much they told me. They laughed at me and said I should go make myself an 'Adam.' When they threw me out of the car. After they murdered Ivan."

"Threw you . . ." But his mind ran back to what she'd said before that. "You mean, if we, um, get intimate, we change back?"

"For a little time only." She saw something on his face, and actually smiled. Her long, sharp canines glittered in the light. "I understand, however, that you are married."

"What?"

"The desk sergeant told me. We had a chat. I had to make sure you were the right one."

"I am the right one. My wife . . ." And as sudden as a gunshot, he knew he was leaving all that behind. Wife, job, sunlight, the whole ball of wax, meant nothing while he was in her arms. With her, he could be what he was . . . and what he used to be.

As sure as he stood there, he finally, fully Changed.

"I'm a detective," he said. "I know how to find people." He held her tightly, so tightly.

"And when we find them, we'll rip their throats out."

"Oh, yes," she said breathlessly, her face buried against his neck. "Yes, my darling, yes, we will."

Nancy Holder won the Bram Stoker award for her short story "Lady Madonna." She is the author of the novels *Making Love* and *Witch-Light* (both with Melanie Tem) and *Dead in the Water*, among others. Her short stories have appeared in numerous anthologies and magazines, including *The Year's Best Fantasy and Horror, Vampire Detectives, Cemetery Dance,* and others.

There are some who are born to guard their homes from evil.

The Time of the Bleeding Pumpkins

BY A. R. MORLAN

When I saw my wife standing out on our front porch, shivering in just a sweater draped over her shoulders despite the relative warmth of that mid-October morning—something of a heat wave for southern North Dakota, with the temperature well above freezing even at a quarter to seven in the morning—I suspected something was wrong. And as my car moved forward a few more feet, past the now mottle-leafed shrubbery that surrounded the porch, and I could see all of her standing in front of the door, I *knew* something was wrong.

She was holding one of the pumpkins she'd bought for Halloween in her arms—not the biggest one, but one of the mid-sized ones destined to be hollowed out and placed luminaria-style along the concrete walkway leading to the porch come Halloween night. Not taking my eyes from her pale, worry-twisted face, I parked the car in front of the house, yanked the key out of the ignition while struggling to release the catch on my seat belt, then slid across the passenger seat so I could emerge from the car directly before her. As I ran down the walkway, I finally let my gaze drift down from her haunted eyes and quivering lips to her midsection, where she cradled the still-intact pumpkin with shaking hands.

The pumpkin was bleeding.

Convex droplets of deep, dark crimson welled close to the dried-out stem, jiggling slightly with the trembling motion of the orange sphere. Their shining surfaces caught the first pale gold of dawn in winking dots of brightness that blinked like tiny eyes against the flat ochre of the pumpkin. And having worked for the majority of my adult life in various meat-packing plants (as well as a couple of slaughterhouses), I knew real blood by sight.

And by smell; as I stepped up onto the slab-poured concrete porch, that mineral-rich, slightly fulsome odor tweaked my nostrils. Wordlessly I took the pumpkin from Anya's hands (she reflexively began wiping hers against the thighs of her jeans) and brought the thing up close to my face to better examine it. . . . After I'd held it for a couple of seconds, I realized that Anya hadn't been shaking the thing—it had been shaking *her*.

It shook from within, as if an ogre's hand stirred the seeds and yanked the attached stringy filaments; as it vibrated, beads of blood began to slide down the latitudinal indentations, leaving a viscid, semitransparent trail of pale carmine in their wake. Instinctively I held the pumpkin up to my ear; the noises coming from within were faint but unmistakable to the ear of a fourth-generation *dhampir:* This pumpkin had been tainted by a vampire. And having been tainted, was in the process of vampirification . . . which in turn meant that its mere presence in the house would not only cause trouble for my family, but for all that entered the house.

And as I held that quaking, bloody *thing* in my hands (the same hands that for the last eight hours had handled long still, but equally bloody, hunks of cow flesh), all of the stories my father and grandfather had told me about the duties of a *dhampir*—he who was the direct male descendant of a male vampire; he who was born with the ability to hunt down other vampires—came back to me in a whisper of low voices. Male voices that mixed our adopted English with our far older native languages: the Romany of our original Gypsy tongue and the subsequent flavoring of Russian dialect my family's clan picked up during their time there:

The uppyr *drains the blood of those it envies. . . . The dead cannot hope to live as the truly living do, so they seek to ruin anything associated with life. . . . Remember the tale of the soldier who brought an* uppyr *to a wedding, how the* uppyr *began feasting on the happy couple. . . . To kill an* uppyr, *one must disinter it, dismember it, drive an aspen stake through its heart. . . .*

To be vampire is a most unnatural state. The vampire, the mulo, *is the most unnatural being of all. It is an affront to the living. . . .* Mulé *arise from the bodies of those who die suddenly or those who choose to die before their time. . . . But to kill them, aspen stakes might not be necessary; catch the* mulo *outside its grave, and a simple pistol shot will do. . . .*

There are those of our people who believe the mulo *lives but forty days . . . just as there are fools within any family. . . .*

Teach you the ways of vampire hunting? No such lessons were ever given to me, nor to your grandfather or his before him. . . . Did your mother need to teach you to eat? Just as all humans hunger for food right from the womb, so does a dhampir *hunger for the rightness of humanity and thus knows by instinct the means of achieving that balance. Your senses are attuned from birth toward this goal, just as the baby seeks out the tit. You will know, Greg, when a* mulo *is about to strike. What you decide to do with that knowledge is then up to you. . . .*

My wife's low voice brought me back to the present, to the unending expanse of tract houses surrounding me and that bleeding pumpkin.

"Greg, does this mean what . . . I think it does? I remember your family talking about—" Here her voice became a near-soundless whisper, virtually a mere mouthing of the word, "—vampire animals, and even vampire *plants.* So when I saw that thing shaking on the floor while all the kids were watching TV and quiet for a change, I got it out of the house."

Holding the quivering mass of smooth orange slightly away from my body, I nodded, then whispered, "Did any of the children see it? Not so much ours, but any of the others?"

By "others" I was referring to that latest group of immigrant children my wife, her younger sister, and a couple of teenagers from the local Lutheran-Episcopal resettlement agency here in Jamestown took care of each weekday morning from six to noon. While neither of us was Lutheran *or* Episcopalian, the manager of the meat-packing plant where I worked was in on the community effort to integrate immigrants into the fabric of Jamestown's social and cultural life—an effort that included providing daycare for the children of the most recent arrivals (all of whom were expected to get jobs and just plain assimilate into the North Dakota way of life here).

Just as my family's and Anya's people had done, practically everyone we knew or lived near or worked with had immigrated to this state within the last century. But the more recent arrivals were from exotic locales like Somalia, Bosnia, the Sudan, and where-*ever* it was that Kurdish people came from. Not to mention the previous influx of Vietnamese in the '70s and '80s. But the majority of the children still inside my house were refugees from the aftermath of Desert Storm or the civil war in Bosnia and the rest of what used to be Yugoslavia. Which is what *really* worried me.

"I don't know. I mean, the children have been trying to play with the pumpkins, wanting to paint them and all, but Marina explained to them about how you wanted to have a line of jack o' lanterns along the walkway. And they're pretty good about listening to her, so lately they've sort of lost interest in the damned things. Those church girls found some really good kid shows on cable, and—"

"So you don't think they noticed?" The unseen ghoul that stirred the inside of the pumpkin was using both fists now, churning the orb from within as the blood began to plop down on the concrete at my feet.

Anya shook her head, setting her chin-length blonde hair to rippling like wheatfields in summer when the winds blow hard and fast over their endless, flat stretches. Her pale blue eyes watered as she said, "It's just that I wasn't expecting anything like this. Not that I disbelieved your family's stories, Greg, but . . . it just seemed such an Old World thing. Like things that might happen in *another* place—not here in North Dakota. Not in such a . . . wide, open place where everyone *does* for everyone else. I mean, this place is like the proverbial melting—" I thought she was going to go the cliché route and say "pot," but she surprised me. "—*griddle,* with everyone tossed on the pan to fry together. What place does a . . . vampire have here?"

"Are *mulé* ever wanted anywhere? Just as most of those kids' parents weren't wanted where *they* came from—or just as they wanted to get the hell out, period—so might the *mulé* seek refuge here. It was simply a matter of time, I suppose—" The pumpkin was beginning to quiet in my hands; less blood welled up from the spot where the stem met the main body of the thing, and even the unseen sorcerer had stopped the endless mixing of its guts. "—before some *mulo* was scooped up by Immigration and Refugee Services in New York and dumped here. Family and all. Hell, who knows? One of them in there might be—"

Anya crossed her arms over the "She Who Must Be Obeyed" T-shirt the kids and I had bought her last Christmas and began shaking her head of wheat-fine hair again.

"I don't care who or *what* your great-great-whatever-grandmother slept with and got impregnated by, even if that offspring *was* a *dhampir;* you're *not* going into that house and killing any of those little darlings. Most of them barely speak English, for Chrissake—"

"It doesn't matter what a *mulo* speaks—"

"They're *babies!*"

"Who said I *was* going to do anything to them?"

Anya's mouth puckered into a stubborn moue before she said, "But you had to have been *thinking* it. That's what your kind does. Find and . . . *kill* vampires. But those kids are my responsibility. And that includes making sure my fourth-fifth-what*ever*-generation-*dhampir* husband doesn't drive an aspen stake through their little backs! Or pop them with a Saturday night spec—"

"It is in my nature to *find mulé,* not necessarily *kill* them," I cut in as the pumpkin finally stilled in my arms and stopped seeping blood. Just as I figured, being in the house had been what started the thing off. After directing a fast prayer of thanks for being born allergic to small animals (because vampirism could strike house pets as well) heavenward I added, "We have to get the rest of the pumpkins outside, at least into the garage. Just away from the house itself."

"But won't they freeze?"

Sometimes I couldn't believe Anya's Norwegian practicality.

"We'll buy new ones, damn it! It won't stop with them bleeding and moving; they'll begin to cause trouble for us. And that trouble can extend to cattle—who knows what sort of havoc it could wreak at my work? Or at the slaughterhouses where most of those kids' fathers work? As it is, I'll have to break this one up and scatter the pieces far from where any damage might be done. Have Marina start moving the other pumpkins by the door. Maybe those church girls could help."

Without waiting for her reply I hurried off to the back yard, which was walled in on three sides by a weathered wood-slat fence. Once in that relative enclosure, I hurled the pumpkin to the ground, where it split open on the limp, dead grass . . . and began to steam—a misty plume that flickered above the tangle of seeds and filaments the way steam hovers over fresh cow entrails in the coolness of a slaughterhouse.

That invisible ogre may have removed its hand, but its heat signature remained. The *mulo* within my house was a powerful one.

Behind me, I heard the moist sound of someone walking across the lawn, followed by my sister-in-law Marina's exasperated, "Gregory, do you realize how much these things cost?"

Turning around to take the medium-sized orange globe from her hands, I said, "Do *you* realize how much damage a *mulo* can do? How much his or her rampage can wind up costing just in property alone?"

Pursing her lips (which were thinner than Anya's, just as the rest of her was inversely fatter), Marina blew a silent raspberry of contempt before muttering, "It's probably just something the kids did when none of us were looking. You know how little ones are. And you and Anya are constantly filling their heads with all that Gypsy lore."

The pumpkin she'd just handed to me was beginning to quiver. Not overtly, but just enough of a vibration that I could feel it through my open palms. And in the ever-brighter light, I could see the faint shine of blood droplets oozing up along the edges of the stem. So I held it before her, tilting the thing so she could see the first pearl-sized bead dribble down the groove under it, and said, *"This* isn't mere 'Gypsy lore'—unless you took a side trip to the old meat shed out back and scooped a few drops of blood off a dressed steer. Although I'm sure you'd have lost an ounce or two of your *own* blood if you'd actually *found* a meat shed, let alone visited one."

Soon the brightest parts of her flat, usually placid, face were her blue-painted eyelids and those thin, quivering lips of hers; the rest looked as if she'd been bled as slowly as a kosher steer.

"You—" she began. But mindful there was a houseful of small children seven yards away from her, she settled for sticking her tongue out at me before waddling back to the sliding back door, her hips and buttocks rolling under the tight confines of her jeans.

I'd dressed out sides of pork with less fat.

Once dashed to the ground, the second pumpkin steamed only slightly. Perhaps I could salvage the rest if I stored them in the garage, I told myself as the sliding door screeched open behind me and I heard the muffled thud of one-two-four-six more pumpkins being deposited on the pine decking. As I heard the door slide shut, I turned to see what sort of faces my sister-in-law was making at me now, but instead caught a brief moving glimpse of another young woman—this one dark-haired, much thinner than Marina, and somewhat taller. But as the insulated curtain slid back into place inside the kitchen, she was merely a blur of long, brownish black topping a body clad in the ubiquitous dark blue of an FFA corduroy jacket and jeans.

Thanks to my current late shift at the packing plant, I seldom took more than a brief glance into the TV room where Anya and her sister tried to keep the morning-care kids before heading to the bedroom, but I was sure the two girls working with my women were both shorter and lighter-haired (one reddish, the other dishwater light brown). And neither of them were in the Future Farmers of America. True, the helpers had come and gone during the two and a half years Anya had been utilizing her B.S. in Early Childhood Education from the University in Fargo—using high school or college girls meant a fairly regular turnover—but for a new one to come in the middle of a semester was odd.

By the time I'd walked over to the back deck to pick up the first of the pumpkins, they'd already begun to feel coolish to the touch. Save for the one closest to the door—the one the FFA girl had most recently touched.

That one still rocked in place as just the tiniest bead of welling blood dribbled down one furrow. . . .

Once I finished putting the pumpkins in the garage, I took my time before going back into the house—partly because it was close to morning snacktime, when the little ones would be swarming around the kitchen, and partly because I didn't want to talk to Anya or that pain-in-the-behind she called a sister. There was still the car to restart and park in the garage and the bits of pumpkin from the back lawn to gather up and place in the burn-barrel out near the north fence. And as I tossed some dried grass clippings over the chunks of eviscerated, dying fruit, I realized that burning these pumpkins and housing the rest in the garage was not going to make the problem of this *mulo* in my house go away.

Oh, perhaps this particular bloodsucker wasn't a true Gypsy *mulo* (maybe my wife's most energetic use of the Americanized *vampire* was a better fit), but my Great-Great-Grandfather Stanislav, upon his unfortunate demise as the result of a particularly bloody and violent farming accident, had become what my people dubbed a *mulo*—literally "one who is dead." Which is to say not *entirely* dead, as my great-great-grandmother found when she made the foolish, if sentimental, mistake of hanging onto his clothing and personal goods after his death in that field of rippling, indifferent wheat so many decades ago.

Destroying the belongings of the dead was Gypsy custom, even here in the relatively tame, almost mundane, social order of North Dakota. But life had been so terribly hard, so indescribably bare-bones, out in their soddie that I suppose Great-Great-Grandmother's temptation to hang onto an extra set of winter clothing, a warm coat and wool-lined mittens, was irresistible. And I'm sure that in the total whiteness of a Dakota winter, that utter *blankness* of snow spread like cake frosting over an unendingly flat landscape, my great-great-grandmother took comfort in gazing at the family icons her husband had smuggled out of the Old Country.

As I held my lighter to a few twisted strands of grass prior to tossing them into the burn-barrel, I could empathize with her about hanging onto the belongings of a dead man (especially a dead man who'd died an accidental death), but only to a point. I had had fun with the kids going to the farmer's market late last month to pick out a suitable group of pumpkins for the house; Gregory Junior and Marta were both young enough not to have to go to school and young enough to gain incredible pleasure from something as simple as inspecting row after row of fleshy orange globes. But that didn't stop me from burning those pumpkins now, regardless of whether or not my kids had helped to pick them out.

And my great-great-grandmother should've just plain *known* better: In her day the Dakotas weren't much of anything when it came to meeting new people or learning anything to speak of concerning *their* ways. To this day we don't even have 650,000 people living in the whole damned state. And back then, how many different cultures might one encounter? Not even counting the Native Americans who lived here? You could probably count them on one hand: Russian, Norwegian, German, French . . . and not much else. And Gypsies can be found in Germany, too—even France.

But I suppose the loneliness and the pain of losing her husband was just too, too much. Just as the terror she had to have felt when he came back to her—a few nonessential parts still missing, casting no shadow in the weak noon sun—just *had* to have been mixed with a bit of dark pleasure at having company again . . . of any sort.

And company she did have with him; my great-grandfather, born a full sixteen months after the death of his father, was proof of that. As was the nearly demolished soddie my *mulo* relative left in his wake before my great-great-grandmother finally came to her senses and dispatched him via an iron needle thrust into his stomach. *That* she did remember from the recitations of Gypsy lore heard back in Russia.

But only after she'd ignored one of the more common bits of family knowledge.

Soon the smoke coming from the burn-barrel was a stinging, choking billow that drove me to stand a few feet away, though still close enough to watch it carefully. Eyes watering, I knew instinctively I could not afford to make the same sort of selective mistake my long-ago relative had made. This *mulo* or *upyr* or whatever the North Dakota bloodsucker wanted to call itself (a *Five*-H-er, with the fifth H being Hemoglobin?)—I had no choice but to stop it.

And considering that an unchecked bloodsucker might very well work its way through a huge chunk of the state's population—including immigrants who'd already gone through enough torment and persecution to last a normal lifetime—I couldn't afford to take modern-day morality into account, even should the creature be a child. But as I listened to the flesh of the pumpkin sizzle and sputter in the flames as if protesting its final dissolution, I seriously doubted I'd have to wield my skills as a *dhampir* against a small fiend.

A youngish one, perhaps, but almost certainly not a child.

◊◊◊

Knowing I'd arouse too much suspicion if I didn't eventually go into the house and to bed, I still waited until the last embers died out in the barrel, poured a layer of rainwater over them from the bucket I kept near the downspout, then walked slowly across the dead grass, up onto the deck, and into the house. The relative quiet told me Anya had unrolled the sleeping bags we usually kept in the spare bedroom and hauled them into the TV room: post-snack naptime, when the entire carpet was covered with piles of dark-haired and swarthy-complexioned little children. The two girls the church people had sent knelt next to a couple of kids, rubbing their narrow backs and soothing them into sleep. I recognized the redhead as Tanya something or other, a relatively cute junior from the high school. But the other one, the blue-jacketed one, was a total stranger.

In one sense.

Back when I first was dating Anya, I told her everything about my past (better to find out before marriage and kids that a woman thinks you're a basket case, rather than after), including the *dhampir* part. To which, after a few beats of silence there in the back of my father's 4x4, she'd simply said, "I know I've lived my whole life in a state where nothing much *seems* to happen. But I also know things *do* happen, all over, and too many of those things can't be explained. My people, back in Norway, believed in the *mara*—this beautiful woman who was actually an evil troll that did horrible things to people. Who's to say she didn't really exist? Who's to say *anything* can't . . . *be?*"

But the one thing I could never quite explain to Anya was *how* I knew when I was in the presence of a *mulo*. According to Gypsy lore, they could look and even act quite normal; they were known to exist in the daytime and cast shadows. I can't even explain the exact mechanics of the detecting process to *myself*; it goes beyond gut feelings or vibrations or anything else that overt. I suppose it's a . . . combination of a hunch and inherently well-honed powers of deduction, of intuition.

Or maybe just common sense; after all, this bleeding-pumpkins episode had occurred at the same time a new girl entered my house. A young woman I couldn't remember seeing before this day . . . and who wore a jacket commonly seen on high school students who dabbled in animal husbandry of some sort.

And vampire lore of virtually any culture often includes the drinking of animal blood when no suitable human victim is nearby.

Knowing *this* bloodsucker wouldn't dare to try anything with the children in my wife's care—at least not after the pumpkins had given her away so graphically—I slipped out of my shoes in the kitchen (which looked out onto the TV room) lest I make too much noise clomping across the tiled floor and wake the kids, then sock-footed my way to the bedroom at the back of my one-story, steep-roofed house. I sat down on the edge of our bed and set my alarm clock for just a bit past noon.

Anya may have longed to talk to me, but she knew better than to bother her day-sleeping breadwinner—especially after what she'd shown me on the front porch. I heard her padding about outside our bedroom door, but she didn't open it; this may have been her first encounter with the *mulo*, but Anya was a good woman, and a smart one: She knew better than to question what both of us knew had to be done.

◊◊◊

The steady, humming drone of my alarm jarred me into wakefulness; vague wisps of my dream lingered long enough in my mind for a few images to register: a jack o' lantern with bleeding fangs . . . a running figure in a death mask and dark-blue corduroy jacket . . . the circular mass of flames within a huge, huge burn-barrel. . . .

But as I quit the bedroom, the actual images themselves faded from my consciousness, leaving only the knowledge within me that something had to be done. Without question; without hesitation.

The TV room was empty of small, limbs-askew bodies when I passed the doorway. The odors of peanut butter, saltines, and damp diapers hung in the air like a miasma, though, and the *feeling* of all those tiny people was still tangible.

Just as the subtle disturbance of the *mulo*'s presence was still a part of that room, like the warmth a body leaves in the squashed contours of a soft, yielding chair.

Yet this might not have been her first day here; for the last week or so I'd been working time and a half to accommodate some new stores in one of the large grocery-market chains my processing plant routinely shipped meat to. I was always so tired upon coming home I could barely feel my way to my bedroom. . . . And with my senses dulled the *mulo*'s fiendish magic might have been able to work unchecked.

As I poured myself a cup of black coffee, I could hear my wife singing some Norwegian lullaby to our little ones down in their bedroom. I also heard the heavy displacement of plodding footfalls on the hallway carpet—Marina.

"What are you doing up, Greg?" My sister-in-law turned herself sideways to squeeze past the central work island and the jutting handles of our two-door refrigerator on her way to the stove at the opposite end of the kitchen. She still managed to graze both the handles and the edges of the countertop.

"Couldn't sleep; I was too worried about the *mulo*."

"*Mulo-schmoolo,*" she snorted while bending over to peer through the glass insert in the oven door. "I still think you should spend more time with the kids; you'd be amazed what the little squirts can and will do when you're not looking. But it's not for me to say how you throw your money around—"

"No, it isn't," I agreed flatly between sips.

Having verified the casserole bubbling in the amber-glass covered dish was in no immediate danger of leaking hot mushroom soup onto the over floor, Marina turned around and said, "Well, I suppose the plant does give overtime pay. . . . But it's still a shame. About the pumpkins. Especially when Basha was going to show the kids how to paint faces on them."

"'Basha?'" I echoed before nonchalantly pouring myself another cup of coffee I didn't particularly want. "She a new one from the high school? Seems like they come and go so quickly. . . ."

"Not exactly new-new; been here about a week, week and a half. One of the other girls moved, and Basha volunteered. That girl's carrying a load, lemme tell you. FFA, 4-H—" I almost choked on my coffee when she said *that*. "—FTA, a whole bunch of organizations. And she's a transfer herself; told me her family moves around a lot on 'count of her father being some sort of medical supply salesman—or was it farm equipment salesman? But she's *really* good with the kids. Doesn't mind if they sit on her lap even if, y'know, they're a little soggy or anything like that. The kind of stuff that makes some of those other girls turn up their noses. She's a *real* good kid," Marina emphasized with a shake of her permed head of hair, "so I was really sorry to see how hurt she was after you and Anya pulled that little stunt. She was awfully disappointed."

"Well, you know how it is: Better safe than sorry. Maybe I could make it up to her; does she happen to have art class today? Maybe I could call her teacher, put in a good word for her . . . for working with the kids and all?"

Behind Marina, the casserole finally began to leak; while she opened the door and tried to slide a cookie sheet under the dish (why she hadn't done so in the first place was one of those imponderables—considering Anya's casseroles always leaked anyhow), she said over her shoulder, "I don't think she has *any* classes today. She's already got all her credits to graduate, but you know how the school is about kids getting early graduation. And she says for transfers, it's even worse. *They* have to stay until next June."

"Too bad. . . . Do you know where she hangs out? After working here? I just wanted to let her know it wasn't personal—"

"That's sweet of you, Greg. While you're at it, you should tell her you were just joking about all that *mulo* crap. Basha said you talking about that would just scare the kids."

While Marina fiddled with the sputtering stove and the heavy casserole, I took another sip of coffee and smiled inwardly; I knew my Anya wouldn't mention vampires in front of her small charges, and *I* hadn't said anything about *mulé*, so only Marina (maybe) had mentioned it. But it was quite interesting that this Basha girl would know what a *mulo* was—and realize the fearsome potential of such a being.

Still, I had to be totally certain.

"I suppose Basha asked you why I was doing what I was doing?"

"No. Anya's rule about scary-talk around here is quite strict. You know I wouldn't have mentioned it. No, Basha brought it up. She seemed to have heard of this bleeding pumpkin nonsense in her family or something. The girl *is* dark-haired, like you, and considering what a melting pot North Dakota is, why shouldn't there be more Gypsies landing here? Everything *else* manages to find this place—"

"What's her last name?" Having drained the cup, I held it in both hands, my fingers suddenly cold enough to need that residual warmth.

"Oh gawd, something Polish. . . . Dolisowna, or something like that. Lots of letters that don't sound too good together."

The phone book was only a few feet away from the coffee machine, but I didn't bother looking up the name or the number—the book was too old. And Marina had already said more than enough for me to begin my hunt. Placing the ceramic mug on the counter with a decisive thunk, I said, "I think I'll take a spin around the neighborhood. I'm still too jumpy to go back to sleep."

Marina glanced at the nearly empty coffee pot on the base of the machine as I let myself out the sliding door and snapped, "Lay off the coffee and you won't be so jumpy. The casserole'll be done in about half an hour; you think you'll be back by then?"

Sliding the door shut behind me, I said through the glass, "Nah, you can have my share, okay? Tell Anya I'll be back," before hurrying to the garage to collect my supplies.

As I slowly cruised the relatively unfamiliar post-noon hours along the streets of my neighborhood, glancing out the windows for my prey, my burlap-bag-covered *mulé*-hunting supplies close by my side, I found myself thinking of the various waves of immigrants that had subtly changed this place, this town, but not this landscape. The influx of Asians in the '70s created a subculture of Vietnamese mom-and-pop groceries, bookstores, and video-rental places, all catering to various Asian groups, while the newest new-people, the Gulf War refugees, had filled up many of the otherwise empty apartments above storefronts, changing the street scene below from mostly pale, European faces to swarthy, black-eyed ones.

But no matter who came to this always-verging-on-barren land, the surrounding countryside remained the same: endless vistas of highway, of fields either rippling and golden with wheat or mowed and stubbled, the occasional farm barn or silos protruding from the flat landscape like fingers of the dead working their way out of the soil. And always, no matter how many people those church folks flew here from Minneapolis, there was this sense of openness—of sheer *space*—around each building, each person.

I doubted even a cockroach would be able to find enough tight, enclosed spaces to hide in here. But as for a *mulo*—vampires had a *need* for others, something beyond mere hunger. Call it a *necessity*. To a *mulo,* humans were the very air (although if humans weren't available, animals might serve as prey). And Marina had said this Basha girl was in FFA *and* 4-H. Her father might even sell farm equipment . . . although I had a feeling her parents might not even be alive—at least in the *traditional* sense—with a *mulo* under their roof.

One of the things I happen to like about this state is the easy way the city segues into the country. Go along either of the highways, 94 or 281, and pretty soon you're in wheat and cow country, where the houses sit back a ways from the road and are marked by the name-embellished mailboxes along the highway. Usually Old World names—lots of Russian, German, some Norwegian . . . but also some Polish, too.

Like *Dolishowna,* which had been written on a strip of colored tape and slapped onto the silvery-new mail receptacle in front of me. Marina had been close on the name; the h was silent.

As was the house at the end of the uneven gravel road bridging the twenty yards between the road and the building itself; the place was small, two-storied, and covered with that awful-looking asphalt siding people back in the '50s slapped on just about every frame house to avoid having to repaint the damned things. This siding was splintering along the bottom of the house, revealing the original thin, once light-gray clapboards underneath. I couldn't tell if the place had any curtains; all the shades were pulled down to the inner sills.

The converted barn-garage next to the house was open-doored and empty. The old silo out back was buckled in the middle and sagging to the left. But there was a chicken coop out beyond the crooked finger of a silo, and I heard the faint sound of a chicken struggling, then the whistling *whoosh* of a descending ax and the whispery flutter of wings beating reflexively into dead silence. Leaving the door hanging open, I left the comfort of the car and walked softly toward the distant coop—an unexpectedly easy task given the fact that I'd forgotten to put my shoes on back in the kitchen. The scruffy grass was cold and clammy underfoot, and the gelid ground *gave* slightly, like soggy padding under a carpet that someone's spilled soda on. Soon my socks were adhering to my feet like a second skin.

Basha was still wearing her deep blue FFA jacket. Only now its pinwale corduroy was dotted with shimmering droplets of blood from the chicken body she held above her face to let the blood drain into her open mouth. Out of some innate, if somewhat inane, sense of politeness, I let her finish her meal; this place was, after all, *her* current stomping grounds. And despite the rightness of my mission I was still the intruder here.

Flinging aside the limp, feathered body with her right hand while wiping her mouth with the wrist of her left hand, Basha let out a short, barking belch and was beginning to turn back toward her house when she saw me.

"Hi, Basha. I'm really sorry about making you get rid of those pumpkins," I began as I took a step forward with an easy casualness that belied my thudding heart and pounding temples.

Taken aback by my nonchalant tone (and my seeming to not notice her noontime snack of fresh chicken), she finished wiping off her face, then wiped the rest of the blood against the bottom of her jacket before smiling warily in return and saying, "It's no biggie. I mean, they *were* yours. I was . . . just thinking of the kids, y'know?"

I wondered if she thought perhaps I hadn't clearly seen what she'd been doing; the fall light *was* quite bright in its intensity at this time of day. And she was half in the shadows. . . .

"Yeah, they get real scared of stuff that bleeds. But that tends to happen when a *mulo* is around," I said with that same casual tone as I walked slowly toward her, hands swinging by my side in a friendly, no-weapons-*here* motion.

"You know what a *mulo* is, too? Are you a Gypsy, too?" It was clear from her tone that Basha thought—or hoped—she could talk herself out of this.

"Yeah. My people came over in the early part of the century. When there was all that trouble in Russia. My great-great-grand-father, he got himself into a jam over there, more or less got himself kicked out of the country. Lucky devil."

"My people were from a ways over, near Poland. We—they came over during World War II. But I suppose Gypsy ways transcend national boundaries, no?" In a surprisingly short time Basha had made her way to a position only a foot or so away from me; I was close enough to smell the cloying, iron-copper reek of the blood coloring the tiny cracks in her lips and to see just how incredibly wise her pale blue eyes were—not the sluttish wisdom of a promiscuous teenager but the genuine, almost sad, sexual perception of a female *mulo*.

"All Gypsies came from one people," I began while tensing myself for the inevitable (while a part of me began to realize just who Basha might have intended all along to be her victim). Sure enough, the girl had managed to sate only a small part of her hunger while feasting on that chicken; with an almost serpentine swiftness she hooked one arm around my neck and the other around my waist and, lips slightly parted, breath bloodily fulsome yet subtly spicy, began to incline her face toward mine. But long years of working in the slaughterhouses had taught me, too, something about moving swiftly lest I be kicked or gouged by a flailing hoof or claw or beak. And years of lifting heavy sides of beef had given me almost superhuman strength.

The sound of her neck snapping under my encircling hands echoed clear and sharp in the crisp autumn air.

◊◊◊

Old farmhouses tend to have something else in common besides sagging barn-garages, leaning silos, and rust-skirted chicken coops. Something akin to a burn-barrel, but much better for the job at hand: garbage pits, usually out back and often lined with gravel.

The one at Basha's new "home" was out behind the chicken coop; there was little else around it save for a lot of trampled dirt on its edges and the charred remains of something someone had burned there who knew how long ago—whatever it was had mold on it, so it had to have been quite a while ago. I could also see the rusted remains of broken farm equipment, some pottery, other less easily identifiable stuff. No stakes, though. Not that I really needed them; I'd brought some things from the garage that would work just as well–better, even, considering how extreme Basha's infestation had been.

I'd found out by accident (a freak fire had ignited some janitorial supplies in a slaughterhouse I'd worked in) how nicely bleach made a fire burn. Ever since then I'd kept a bottle out in my garage . . . just in case. Near the gas can . . . just in case. So I was able to saturate the old rags I'd brought to cover the body with bleach and gasoline before flinging them down on top of her. I added the parts of the chicken she'd killed, and since I couldn't be sure what might happen to the live ones once I left, I dispatched them quickly and dispassionately and added them to the pile.

While I had matches, I'd forgotten a bottle for making the Molitov cocktail I planned to ignite the pit with; the back door of the farmhouse was open, and with only a quiver of trepidation I stepped inside. The place was as I imagined it: rain-runneled wallpaper peeling away from the grayish plaster beneath, window sills flaking, mold and dirt encrusting the linoleum flooring, and no real food anywhere. Just an open, lightless refrigerator, a grease-spattered stove, and a five-legged, old-fashioned wood table. The cupboards under the antiquated ceramic sink were askew. And one held an empty soft drink bottle (for a soda currently advertised by punks on skateboards and snowboards) embellished with hillbillies and comically askew country-style lettering. I knew it had to be a collector's item, but it was the only bottle in the kitchen. And I had no intention of looking through the rest of Basha's place.

But before I quit the room, thirty-plus-year-old bottle in hand, I noticed a pile of things on one of the kitchen counters. A flyer from a local high school football game. And under it old photos—of Basha. Judging from the scalloped edges around the white part of the photos, they'd been taken in the late '30s, early '40s. When she'd arrived here during the WWII wave of immigrants. The '40s-style dress looked a lot better on her than the FFA jacket had. . . .

Not knowing for sure if the fire might eventually whip out of the pit and move to the house, I took the pictures outside with me. They fluttered into the pit like large pieces of confetti and landed close to her rag-covered body. Even if the house didn't burn, I thought she might appreciate the gesture, from one Gypsy to another—burning her belongings like that. I suppose I should've gone for her clothes . . . whatever else of hers was in that house. But the wind was shifting to the northeast, toward the house proper, and there were no other houses within eyesight on either side of the place. Just fields of chopped wheat beyond the sagging barbed-wire fence where the property line ended fifty feet away.

Even though this was my first *mulo* kill as a *dhampir*, I knew my father and my father's father would be proud of me. I didn't think she'd suffered, and my hands were clean of her blood. Just as the land would be scoured of her influence, the very earth under her burned clean and pure again. And I'd done what was right: I'd given her back her pictures, to burn with her in the proper, ancient, Gypsy way.

Being Gypsy *was* important to her—sadly, fatally so. If she hadn't wasted time talking to me, sharing common lore, she just might have escaped. The penalty of not assimilating *enough*, I supposed as I finished filling the old soda bottle with a clear liquid similar to the bright yellow treat it had once contained, stuffed a rag into its neck, and stepped back to toss it into the pit. As I ran away, I mouthed a fitting good-bye to my first kill as a *dhampir:*

"Welcome to the melting pot, my dear Basha. . . ."

Then I drove back home to the city, to my family, to my own world of work, to Anya and the children. All of them part of the state I'd been born in—the state of being that was, I now realized, more wholly American than I'd ever suspected.

True, I realized as I watched the glowing pit of flame recede in my rearview mirror, I was still a *dhampir* in my blood—my heritage—but I'd been born a native of North Dakota, home of all peoples. And Basha had been a threat to *all* those people—not just the Gypsies and not just the old-time natives. She'd been out to get the whole melting pot of them.

But while she still thought of herself as a Gypsy, I was one step ahead of her:

I was an *American.*

Thanks to John S. Postouit for his help in researching this story.

A. R. Morlan is the editor, with Martin H. Greenberg, of the anthology *Zodiac Fantastic.* Her stories have appeared in hundreds of publications, including *Love in Vein, The Year's Best Fantasy and Horror, Women of the West, The Ultimate Zombie, Weird Tales,* and *The Twilight Zone.*

Sometimes a cliché is just a cliché. . . .

Masquerade

BY HENRY KUTTNER

*L*ook," I said to Rosamond bitterly. "If I started a story like this, any editor would shoot it back—"

"You're too modest, Charlie."

"—with the usual kindly crack about the rejection-doesn't-nec-essarily-imply-lack-of-merit-but-the-story-smells. So here we are. Honeymooning. Storm comes up. Forked lightning crackles across the sky. Rain comes down in torrents. And that house we're heading for is obviously a deserted lunatic asylum. When we bang the old-fashioned knocker, there'll be shuffling footsteps and a very nasty-looking old coot will let us in. He'll be *so* glad to see us, but there'll be a mocking gleam in his eye when he starts talking about a legend of vampires that hang out around here. Not that *he* believes in such things, but—"

"But what makes his teeth so sharp?" Rosamond gurgled, and then we were on the rickety porch and knocking on the oak panel that lightning showed us. We did it again.

Rosamond said, "Try the knocker. Mustn't use the wrong formula."

So I banged the old-fashioned knocker, and there were shuffling footsteps. Rosamond and I looked at each other incredulously and grinned. She's very pretty. We like the same things—preferably unconventional—and so we get along well together.

Anyhow, the door opened and a very nasty-looking old coot was standing there, with an oil-lamp in one gnarled hand.

He didn't seem too surprised. But his face was such a nest of wrinkles it was difficult to make out any changes of expression there. A beak of a nose shot out like a scimitar and his tiny eyes were greenish in the dim glow. Oddly, he had thick, coarse black hair. The sort that would look well on a corpse, I decided.

"Visitors," he creaked. "We have few visitors here."

"You must get plenty hungry between callers," I cracked, and edged Rosamond into the hall. It smelled of must. So did the old man. He shut the door against the fury of the wind and beckoned us into a parlor. We brushed against old-fashioned beaded curtains and found ourselves back in the Victorian era.

Grandpop had a sense of humor. "We don't eat visitors," he remarked. "We just kill them and steal their money. But pickings are poor nowadays." He laughed like a triumphant hen with embryonic quintuplets. "Me," he said, "I'm Jed Carta."

"Carter?"

"Carta. Sit down, dry off, and I'll build a fire."

We were drenched. I said, "Can we borrow some clothes? We've been married for years, if you're wondering. But we still feel sinful. The name's Denham, Rosamond and Charlie."

"Not honeymooners?" Carta seemed disappointed.

"It's our second honeymoon. More fun than our first. Romance, huh?" I said to Rosamond.

"Yeah. It gits yuh," she agreed. A card, my wife. The only woman smarter than me that I don't hate. She's quite pretty, even when she looks like a drowned kitten.

Carta was building a fire on the hearth. "A lot of people lived here once," he remarked. "Only they didn't want to. They were mad. But it isn't an asylum any more."

"That's your story," I said.

He finished with the fire and shuffled toward the door. "I'll get you some clothes, he said over his shoulder. "That is, if you don't mind being left alone here."

"Don't you believe we're married?" Rosamond inquired. "Honest, we don't need a chaperon."

Carta exhibited a few snags of teeth. "Oh, it ain't that. Folks around here have got some queer ideas. Like—" He chuckled. "Ever heard tell of vampires? People been saying that there's been a sight of deaths in the neighborhood lately."

"Rejection-doesn't-necessarily-imply-lack-of-merit," I said.

"Eh?"

"It—doesn't matter." I looked at Rosamond, and she looked back at me.

Carta said, "Not that I take any stock in such things." He grinned again, licked his lips, and went out, slamming the door after him. He locked it, too.

"Yes, darling," I said. "He had green eyes. I noticed."

"Did he have pointed teeth?"

"He only had one. And that was worn down to the bone. Maybe some vampires gum their victims to death. It doesn't sound conventional, though."

"Maybe vampires aren't always conventional." Rosamond was staring into the fire. Shadows were dancing around the room. Lightning flared outside. "Rejection-does-not-necessarily—"

I found some dusty afghans and shook them out. "Peel," I said briefly, and we hung our garments before the blaze, wrapping up in the afghans till we looked like indigent Indians. "Maybe it isn't a ghost story," I said. "Maybe it's a sex story."

"Not if we're married," Rosamond countered.

I just grinned. But I was wondering. About Carta. I don't believe in coincidences. It was easier, somehow, to believe in vampires.

The door was opened, and the man who came in wasn't Carta. It looked like the village idiot—a gross, obese mountain of a man with thick, slobbering lips and rolls of fat around his open collar. He hitched up his overalls, scratched himself, and smirked at us.

"He's got green eyes, too," Rosamond remarked.

The newcomer had a cleft palate. But we could understand what he said, all right.

"All our kin's got green eyes. Grandpaw's busy. He sent me back with these. I'm Lem Carta." Lem had a bundle across his arm, and he tossed it at me. Old clothes. Shirts, overalls, shoes—clean enough, but with the same musty smell.

Lem clomped over to the fire and let his monstrous body sink down in a crouch. He had the same beak of a nose as Grandpaw

Carta, but it was half-buried in pads of drooping fat. He giggled hoarsely.

"We like visitors," he announced. "Maw's coming down to say howdy. She's changing her clothes."

"Putting on a clean shroud, eh?" I hazarded. "Go away, Lem. And don't peek through the keyhole."

He grumbled, but shuffled out, and we got into those musty garments. Rosamond looked very pretty—the peasant type, I told her, which was a lie. She kicked me.

"Save your strength, darling," I said. "We may need it against the Cartas. One big horrid family. This is probably their ancestral mansion. Used to live here when it was a madhouse. Paying guests. Wish I had a drink."

She stared at me. "Charlie, are you beginning to believe—"

I said, "That the Cartas are vampires? Hell, no! They're just local yokels trying to throw a scare into us. I love you, honey."

And I nearly cracked her ribs as I hugged her. She was shivering.

"What is it?" I asked.

"I'm cold," she said. "That's all."

"Sure." I drew her toward the fire. "That's all. Of course. Naturally. Toss me that lamp and we'll go exploring."

"Maybe we should wait for Maw?"

A bat fluttered against the window. They seldom fly during a storm. Rosamond didn't see it. I said, "No, we won't wait. Come on."

At the door I stopped, because my wife had fallen on her knees. She wasn't praying, though. She was staring down at some dirt on the floor.

I hoisted her up with my free hand. "Sure. I know. It's grave-yard mould. Count Dracula out west with the Hardys. Let's go look over the asylum. There should be a few skeletons kicking around somewhere."

So we went out in the hall, and Rosamond went swiftly to the front door and tried to open it. She turned wise eyes to me.

"Locked. And the windows are barred."

I said, "Come *on*," and dragged her after me. We went back along the hall, stopping to peer into the dusty, silent rooms, brimming with darkness. No skeletons. No nothing. Just a mouldy, musty odor, like a house that hadn't been lived in for years. I thought madly: Rejection-does-not-necessarily-imply—

We went out in the kitchen and saw dim light filtering into it through a doorway. There was a curious swishing noise that puzzled me. A dark lump resolved itself into young Lem, the white hope of the Kallikaks.

The swishing stopped. Jed Carta's cracked voice said, "Seems sharp now." Something came sailing out and smacked into Lem's face. He grabbed it, and, as we circled him, we saw that he was gnawing a chunk of raw meat.

"Good," he slobbered, his green eyes glowing at us. "So good!"

"Builds strong, healthy teeth," I informed him, and we went into the woodshed. Jed Carta was sharpening a knife on a whetstone there. Maybe it was a sword. Anyhow, it was big enough to duel with. He looked a bit disconcerted. I said, "Getting ready for invasion?"

"Never do seem to get through with my chores," he mumbled. "Careful of that lamp, there. This place is dry as tinder. One spark and it'd go up like blazes."

"Fire is such a *clean* death," I murmured, and grunted as Rosamond jabbed me in the ribs with her elbow. She said sweetly, "Mr. Carta, we're awfully hungry. I wonder if—"

He said, in a curiously low, growling voice, "That's funny. I'm hungry too."

"Sure you're not thirsty?" I put in. "Me, I could do with some whiskey. Blood for a chaser," I added, and Rosamond punched me again.

"There are times," she said acidly, "when you just ask for trouble."

"It's camouflage," I told her. "I'm scared stiff, Mr. Carta. Honest. I keep taking you seriously."

He put down the knife and cracked his face into a smile. "You're not used to country ways, that's all."

"That's all," I said, listening to Lem gnawing and slobbering over his raw meat in the kitchen. "Must be great to live a clean, healthy life."

"Oh, yes, indeed," he chuckled. "Henshawe County's a nice place. We've all lived here a long time. Of course, our neighbors don't visit us much—"

"You surprise me," Rosamond murmured. She seemed to have got over her wariness.

"But we're a pretty old community. Pretty old. Got our customs, going 'way back to Revolutionary times—even got our legends." He glanced at a side of beef that hung from a hook nearby. "Got a legend about vampires—the Henshawe vampires. But I mentioned that, didn't I?"

"Yeah," I said, rocking on my heels. "You don't take stock in it, you said."

"Some folks do, though," he grinned. "But I don't hold with them yarns about white-faced devils in black cloaks flying through cracks and turning into bats. Seems to me a vampire might change with the times—you know? A Henshawe County vampire wouldn't be like a European one. He might even have a sense of humor." Carta cackled and beamed at us. "I figger, if he acted pretty much like other folk, nobody'd suspect what he was. And then he might keep on like he was before he—" Carta glanced at his work-gnarled hands. "Before he died."

I said, "If you're trying to frighten us—"

"I'm just joking," Carta said. He turned toward the side of meat that hung from its hook. "Fergit it. You said you was hungry. How'd you like a steak?"

Rosamond said hastily, "I've changed my mind. I'm a vegetarian." Which was a lie, but I seconded my wife's motion.

Carta giggled unpleasantly. "Maybe you'd like something hot to drink?"

"Maybe I—what about whiskey?"

"Oh, sure. Lem!" the oldster called. "Rustle up some likker 'fore I lay into you."

Presently I was holding two cracked cups and a cobwebbed bottle of cheap bourbon. "Make yourselves at home," Carta invited. "You'll run across my datter somewheres. She'll talk a blue streak." Some secret thought seemed to amuse him, for he giggled in that oily, unpleasant grate. "Keeps a diary, she does. I tell her it ain't exactly wise, but Ruthie's mighty set in her ways."

We went back to the front parlor, sat before the fire, and drank bourbon. The cups were filthy, so we hoisted the bottle. I said,

FIELDS OF BLOOD

"It's been a long time since we've done this. Remember how we used to go driving out to the park with a bottle—"

Rosamond shook her head, but her smile was curiously tender. "We were such kids, then, Charlie. It seems so long ago."

"Our second honeymoon. I love you, darling," I said quietly. "Don't ever forget that. Don't mind my wise-cracking sometimes." I passed her the bottle. "It isn't bad."

A bat fluttered against the window pane.

The storm wasn't letting up any. Thunder and lightning still made a conventional back-drop. The liquor warmed me. I said, "Let's explore. Dibs on the first skeleton."

Rosamond looked at me. "What was that carcass hanging up in the shed there?"

"It was a side of beef," I explained carefully. "Now come on or I'll bat your teeth in. Bring the bottle. I'll take the lamp. Watch out for trap-doors, secret panels, and clutching hands."

"And the Henshawe vampires?"

"Trap-doors," I said firmly. We went up rickety, creaking stairs into the second story. Some of the doors had barred gratings let into them. None was locked. The place had once been an asylum, all right.

"Just think," Rosamond said, drinking whiskey. "All the patients were kept here once. All insane."

"Yeah," I agreed. "Judging by the Cartas, the malady lingers on." We halted, staring through a grating at an occupied cell. A woman was sitting quietly in a corner, manacled to the wall, tastefully clad in a strait-jacket. A lamp stood near her. She had a flat dish-face, sallow and ugly; her eyes were wide and green, and a twisted half-smile was on her lips.

I pushed on the door; it swung open easily. The woman looked at us without curiosity.

"You a—a patient?" I asked weakly.

She shook off the strait-jacket, shrugged out of the chains, and stood up. "Oh, no," she said, with that same twisted, frozen smile. "I'm Ruth Carta. Jed told me you were here." Feeling, apparently, that some explanation was called for, she glanced at the strait-jacket. "I was confined in an asylum for a few years, quite awhile ago. They released me, cured. Only sometimes I get homesick."

"Yeah," I said nastily. "I can understand that. Like a vampire wanting to go back to the old sod every morning."

She froze, her shallow eyes like green glass. "What's Jed been saying to you?"

"Just local gossip, Mrs. Carta." I extended the bottle. "Have a drink?"

"Of that?" Her smile got vinegary. "No, thank you!"

It seemed to be a deadlock. Ruthie stared at us, with those green, unreadable eyes and that fixed smile, and the musty smell was choking in my nostrils. What next?

Rosamond broke the silence. *"Are* you Mrs. Carta?" she asked. "How is it you have the same name as—"

"Be still," I said softly. "Just because we're married doesn't mean everybody is."

But Ruth Carta didn't seem annoyed. "Jed's my father. Lem's my son," she explained. "I married Eddie Carta, my cousin. He's been dead years. They's why they put me in an asylum."

"Shock?" I suggested.

"No," she said. "I killed him. Everything went red, I remember." Her smile didn't change, but I saw sardonic mockery in it. "That was long before such a defense was laughed out of courts. Just the same, it was true in my case. People make a mistake when they think *clichés* aren't true."

"Seems to me you've a lot more education than Lem or Jed," I remarked.

"I was at a girl's school in the east, when I was young. I wanted to stay there, but Jed couldn't afford it. It made me pretty bitter— tied down to drudgery here. But I don't mind the dullness now."

I wished Ruthie would stop smiling. Rosamond reached for the bottle. She said, "I know how you must feel."

Mrs. Carta moved back against the wall, placing her palms flat against it. Her eyes were preternaturally bright. And her voice was a whining rasp.

"You can't know. A young thing like you—you can't know what it's like to have a glimpse of glamour and excitement and pretty clothes and men, and then have to come back here, shut up to scrub floors and cook cabbage, married to a stupid lout with the mind of an ape. I used to sit by the kitchen window and look out and hate everything and everybody. Eddie never understood. I used to ask him to take me to town, but he couldn't afford it, he said. And somehow I scrimped and saved enough for a trip to Chicago. I dreamed about that. Only when I got there I wasn't a kid any more. People on the streets stared at my clothes. I felt like screaming."

I drank bourbon. "Yeah," I said. "I know—I guess."

Her voice rose higher. There was saliva dribbling from her lips.

"So I came back and then one day I saw Eddie kissing the hired girl and I took up the axe and I chopped at his head. He fell down and jerked like a fish and I felt like I was a girl again. And everybody was looking at me and saying how wonderful and pretty I was."

Her voice was like a phonograph. It screamed monotonously. She slid down against the wall, till she was sitting, and froth foamed on her lips. She twitched all over. She began to scream hysterically, but it was even less pleasant when she started to laugh.

I took Rosamond's arm and propelled her out into the hall. "Let's find the boys," I said. "Before Ruthie finds an axe."

So we went downstairs, to the kitchen, and told Lem and Jed about it. Lem giggled, his fat face quivering, and headed for the hall. Jed drew a pitcher of water and followed. "Ruthie gets them spells," he said over his shoulder. "They don't last long, as a rule." He vanished.

Rosamond still had the lamp. I took it from her, set it down gently on the table, and gave her the bottle. We finished it. Then I went to the back door and tried the lock. It was, of course, fastened.

"Curiosity was always my weakness," Rosamond said. She pointed to a door in the wall. "What do you suppose—"

"We can find out." The liquor was having its effect. Armed with the lamp, I tugged at the panel, and we stared down into the darkness of a cellar. It was, like everything else in this house, musty-smelling.

I preceded Rosamond down the steps. We were in a dark chamber like a vault. It was completely empty. But a strong oaken trapdoor was at our feet. The open padlock lay near it, and the hasp had been clicked free.

Well, we continued on our merry way by means of a ladder. It went straight down for perhaps ten feet. The noise of the storm was shut out. On a shelf at our side was a tattered notebook, with a pencil attached to it by a bit of grimy string. Rosamond opened it, while I peered over her shoulder.

"The guest book," she remarked.

There was a list of names, and, under each one, were significant notations. Like this:

"Thomas Dardie $57.53. Gold watch. Ring."

Rosamond giggled, opened the book to the last item, and wrote: "Mr. and Mrs. Denham."

"Your sense of humor kills me, darling," I said coldly. "If I didn't love you, I'd wring your neck."

"It's safer to wisecrack, sometimes," she whispered.

We went on. At the end of the passage was a small cell, with a skeleton chained to the wall. On the floor was a wooden circular lid, with a ring in it. I lifted the disk, held the lamp low, and we looked into the black depths of a pit. The odor wasn't by Chanel.

"More skeletons?" Rosamond asked.

"Can't tell," I said. "Want to go down and find out?"

"I hate dark places," she said, quite breathlessly, and suddenly I let the lid slam back into place, set down the lamp, and was holding Rosamond very tightly. She clung to me like a child afraid of an unlit room.

"Don't darling," I muttered, my lips against her hair. "It's all right."

"It isn't. This awful—I wish I were dead. Oh, I love you, Charlie! I love you terribly!"

We broke apart then, for footsteps were sounding through the vault. Lem and Jed and Ruthie appeared. None of them seemed startled to find us here. Lem's eyes were fixed on the skeleton; he licked loose lips and tittered. Ruthie was staring blindly, with that same fixed, twisted smile. Jed Carta gave us one look, green and malicious, and put down the lamp he was carrying.

"Hello, folks," he said. "So you found your way down here, hey?"

"We were wondering if you had a bomb shelter," I told him. "One feels a bit safer, with world conditions as they are."

He cackled. "You don't scare easy. Here, Ruthie." He took a cattle-whip from where it hung on the wall and thrust it into the woman's hands. Instantly she was galvanized into activity. She walked toward that chained skeleton and began to lash it. Her face was a dreadful smiling mask.

"It's the only thing that'll quiet her when she gets these spells," Jed told us. "Been worse since Bess died." He looked at the skeleton.

"Bess?" Rosamond asked weakly.

"She—used to be a servant girl here. We figger this don't hurt her none now, and it keeps Ruthie quiet, mostly."

Mrs. Carta dropped the whip. Her face was still frozen, but, when she spoke, her voice was perfectly normal.

"Shall we go upstairs? It must be unpleasant here for our guests."

"Yeah," I said. "Let's do. Maybe you've got another bottle kicking around, Jed?"

He nodded toward the wooden disk on the floor. "Wanta look down there?"

"I already did."

"Lem's pretty strong," the old man said, apparently at random. "Show 'em, Lem. Use Bessie's chain. Won't matter if it's busted now, will it?" All the Cartas seemed vastly amused.

Lem lumbered over and snapped the chain easily. "Well," I said, "that's that. Small Fry here uses his hands. You've got a knife. What does Ruthie use? Axe, I suppose."

He grinned. "You don't think we really kill people who stop by here, now! Or, if they have cars, drive 'em into the big pool back of the house."

"Not if you're the Henshawe vampires, too," I said. "You'd be scared to death of running water."

"It ain't running," he said. "It's stagnant. You shouldn't take any stock in such things."

Rosamond said softly, "All the doors are locked, and the windows are barred. We found your guest book. We looked into your oubliette. It adds up, doesn't it?"

"You fergit such notions," Carta advised. "You'll sleep better if you do."

"I'm not sleepy," Rosamond said.

I picked up the lamp and took her arm. We preceded the others along the passage, up the ladder into the cellar, and thence to the kitchen. I noticed that a huge tub filled with water stood in a dim corner.

We could hear the storm now, in all its raging fury.

Carta said, "I aired out a bed for you two. Want to go now?"

I shook the lamp. "Put more kerosene in this, will you? It'd scare my wife frantic if it went out in the night."

Jed nodded to Lem, who shuffled off and came back with a sloshing can. He refilled the lamp.

We all went upstairs. Jed went first, a scarecrow figure with a coarse black wig. After us followed Lem, loutishly grinning, and in the rear Ruthie, with her fixed smile and wide, shallow green eyes.

"Hey," I said, "you're going to have to drag our bodies downstairs to the cellar, Jed. Why make more work for yourself?"

"Figgered you might be tired," he chuckled. "Anyway, I got a few chores to tend to—but I'll see you later."

It was a nightmare procession upstairs that screamed protest under our feet. I said so, flippantly.

Rosamond pursed her lips. "A bit too melodramatic."

"There should be thirteen steps," I remarked. "That'd be a subtle touch. Thirteen steps to the gallows," I explained to Jed, who was peering back at us with an inquiring scowl.

He cackled. "You're taking stock in things that ain't so. If you think we're murderers, why don't you leave?"

"The door's locked."

"You might ask me to unlock it."

I didn't answer that, for the mockery in his voice was unpleasant. Lem slobbered happily at our heels. We went along the hall to an end bedroom. It smelled musty. Branches tore at the barred window. A bat flung itself frantically against the pane.

In the room, we waited. I put the lamp on a dusty bedside table. Lem, Jed, and Ruthie stood by the door. They looked like three green-eyed wolves watching us.

"Did you ever stop to think," I asked, "that we might not be sheep? You haven't even asked us where we come from or how we got here."

Jed favoured us with a one-toothed grin. "Guess you ain't

familiar with Henshawe County, Mister. We haven't had no law here to speak of for a long time now. We been mighty careful—I don't reckon the federal gov'ment pays us any mind. And Henshawe County can't support a sheriff worth his salt. Don't try to bluff us, 'cause it won't work."

I shrugged. "Do we look worried?"

There was grudging admiration in Jed's tone. "You don't scare easy. Well, I got my chores to do before—bedtime. See you later."

He vanished into the dark.

Ruthie jerked her hand. Lem licked his lips and vanished.

The woman's smile was a frozen grimace. "I know what you're thinking. What you're afraid of," she said. "And you're right."

Then she stepped back and slammed the door. We heard the lock click.

"Jed forgot to give me another bottle," I observed. "I'll be sober pretty soon. And thirsty. Very thirsty." I heard my voice change a little. "It's all right, darling. Come here."

Rosamond's lips were cold; I could feel her shiver.

"This room's like an icebox," she murmured. "I can't get used to the cold, Charlie. I can't get used to the cold!"

There was nothing I could do but put my arms around her as tightly as I could.

"Try remembering," I said quietly. "It isn't night. It isn't storming. We're not here. We're back in the park, and it's afternoon. Remember, dear?"

She buried her face in my shoulder. "It's hard to remember, somehow. It seems like forever since we saw daylight. This horrible house—oh, I *wish* we were dead, darling!"

I shook her a little. "Rosamond!" She gulped.

"Sorry, dear. Only—why did this have to happen to us?"

I shrugged. "Call it luck. We're not the first in this spot, obviously. Keep your eyes closed and remember."

Do—do you think—they suspect?"

"How could they? They're too busy playing their own little murderous game."

I could feel the shudder of utter revulsion that went over her.

"We can't change what's coming," I had to remind her. "We can't change them—or us."

Slow tears stole from under her lashes. And we clung together like children afraid of the dark. I couldn't think of a wise-crack. It's hard, sometimes.

The lamp flickered and went out. I didn't have any matches. It didn't much matter now, of course. Not now.

"Wish Lem had remembered the other bottle," I murmured after awhile. "Whiskey helps. I'm glad we were allowed whiskey, anyhow."

The storm was passing swiftly. Already moonlight drifted in wanly through the windows. I remembered *Dracula,* and the shapes that had materialized in the moon-rays. They made even the window-bars look diaphanous.

But I told myself, the Cartas weren't vampires. They were just murderers. Mad, cold-blooded, remorseless. No, I reminded myself, if the Cartas had been vampires, they wouldn't have pretended to be. Real vampires don't—look at *Dracula!*

I held on to Rosamond and shut my eyes. Somewhere a clock struck midnight.

And then—

Well, it was about two o'clock when the key I had been expecting rattled in the lock. The door opened and Jed Carta stood on the threshold, shaking from head to foot, the lamp jerking in his hand. His voice cracked as he tried to speak.

He couldn't. He just beckoned for us to follow him. We did, even though we knew what to expect. I could hear Rosamond whimpering very softly, "I wish we were dead. Oh, I wish we were dead!"

Jed took us into a bedroom across the hall. Ruthie Carta was lying on the floor. She was dead. There were two tiny red punctures in her skinny throat, and indented channels marked the courses of drained blood-vessels.

Through an open door I could see into the next room, and the gross, motionless body that lay there. It was Lem, and he, too, was a corpse.

Jed Carta almost screamed, "Something came and—" His face was a shaking, knotted mask of fear. "The Henshawe vampires!" he forced out, scarcely able to articulate.

"Dog eat dog," I said. I glanced at Rosamond. She met my eyes with the shrinking revulsion I had come to know so well, and a shame-faced eagerness behind the revulsion. I knew it was time to wise-crack again—anything to get that look out of Rosamond's eyes.

"I've got a surprise for you, Jed," I said, and moved nearer to him—nearer. "I know you don't take any stock in such things, but believe it or not, we're the Henshawe vampires."

Henry Kuttner (1914-1958) was primarily known for his work in science fiction, but occasionally turned out a witty dark fantasy or horror story like "Masquerade." The best of his short fiction can be found in *A Gnome There Was, No Boundaries,* and *Return to Otherness.*

Haven't you ever wondered about those family butchers?

There Will Always Be Meat

BY JENNIFER STEVENSON

ob Duselschetner smelled trouble before he saw it. That's the way it is in hog farming. You come out to the feedlot at four-thirty in the morning and the smell of chewed-open hogbelly hits like a ton of bricks. Heart sinking, Bob rounded the fence, hoping it was just one feeder with a burst appendix.

But all was quiet at the feedlot. The boys and girls shouldered each other against the fence or wiggled their tails at the troughs. No dead feeder. No bust belly.

No mistaking that smell either. Bob took his morning's random urine samples from the drains around the pen, sniffing, while a knot formed in his middle. He dumped mash and water into the mixer, tested the pH, then poured, keeping his feet out of the way. A feeder is only two hundred pounds, but you don't want him stepping on you on his way to breakfast.

He couldn't put it off. Bob followed his nose, ever more nervous, into the breeding shed. Emmaline was in heat. Big Jake had been with her since Tuesday, not getting very far. Poor old guy was just about bacon. If Emmy wasn't such a good farrower she'd have been bacon herself two years ago, such a temper she had. Not that sows were made sweet.

"Now you've done it," Bob scolded as he entered her pen. The boar's corpse lay on its side, belly bloated up and crap and chitterlings oozing out the anus. That was the smell. Emmaline stood over it with her jaws still buried in its throat. Bob felt sad about the waste—Big Jake had been nine hundred pounds live weight last Fourth of July, but no use trying to salvage any of that, once she's had her dirty muzzle in him. "Get off now, Emmy. He's dead all right."

She looked up at him with red light in her eye. "Girl, you want it, you got to sit still for it," Bob said flatly, his fists on his hips. "G'wan. Git." The sow licked her jaws and backed reluctantly away from the corpse. Bob ran the one-ton winch over the breeding pen. It'd take him the better part of an hour to shift Big Jake, even with the winch. That would put a dent in his morning. He unhooked the sling. "C'mon, Jake."

When he put a hand on Big Jake's left fore, he did the doubletake of his life. The corpse looked peculiar. Its torn throat gleamed pale pink under the shed's florescents. Bob walked around the corpse's other end. The entrails were torn out, pretty normal for swine cannibalism, but they hadn't been eaten. They were licked clean. Bob backed away. The black boar looked gray. Bloodless. Emmaline let out a growl behind him: the unearthly half-human sound of an angry sow.

Bob caught on just two seconds before Emmaline rushed him. He'd been a hog farmer for nineteen years. Two seconds was plenty. He landed on his prat outside the pen with his feet in the air and an aching back, watching the sow slaver at him through the pen slats. Luckily she had enough sense to remember she couldn't break out of the pen—hogs are smart, but they still aren't smart enough to know that at twelve hundred pounds they're stronger than when they were sucklings. She skidded to a stop. There wasn't a speck of blood on her muzzle.

Bob locked the shed and limped around it to the utility sink outside. He scrubbed his hands, poured himself a glass of water, drank it, and, hands still shaking, pulled his cell phone off his belt.

At the Iowa State Department of Agriculture, Lute Wickerberg talked quietly with his officemate.

"I agree. The most important thing is keeping it quiet until we got it under control." Wickerberg spoke calmly and seriously. He would talk like that on Judgment Day, keeping folks orderly and suitably informed while the Civil Defense teams amped the last trump over the P.A.

"What's upsetting me is, how?" said the officemate, Steve Schuyler, as he ran a quick scan through uploaded county records. "This system has been in place since before statehood. We haven't had a problem yet." Steve had taken the call first. He would work with Wickerberg on this, it was foregone: minimum spread of sensitive information. Steve had come out from New Jersey, where half the farmers were ex-lawyers. He hadn't quite adjusted to Iowa ways yet, the incredible patience and long-headedness and tolerance that separated his current population from the whiners and summons-spewers of his home state. This bit of news would test that tolerance to its limit.

"Not since 1854," Wickerberg corrected. "Outbreak up near Ida Grove. That was the bad winter."

Steve's forehead wrinkled. "More than a hundred and fifty years."

"Won't matter to people, once they find out."

Together they shuddered.

Steve flipped through screens on his terminal. "The local inspector says everybody in his territory is squeaky clean. Never even had a warning."

"That's how it is with those old-timers—in Iowa," Wickerberg added. Steve gave him a suspicious look, but Wickerberg's stone face didn't crack.

"Maybe," Steve said hopefully, "it's isolated. Spontaneous. Just the one sow."

Wickerberg looked at him with understanding. They both knew how likely that was. "Maybe it is," he said kindly.

The phone rang.

They sat in the Duselschetner farmhouse kitchen, where the table was big enough to spread out all Wickerberg's reports. Steve had come up with cross-county inspection printouts for two years back—more than ten times the incubation period—and Wickerberg had summoned the other two farmers to meet at Duselschetner's. Sybil Duselschetner sat with her fists pressed down on her table while Bob went around with the coffeepot and the Spruills and Lou Chenakzy babbled. Abel Spruill was weeping. The racks of blood samples had come mostly from his place.

"Now, friends," Wickerberg said in his flattest voice. Steve didn't see how he got away with it. Wickerberg was the uncuddliest man he'd ever worked with at Ag, but he got across somehow. "I've asked you to talk with us together because I think we can answer a lot of questions fast that way. You all buy from the same grain elevator. Your kids all go to the same school. You all use the same vet, the same butcher—"

"We all know where it comes from," Lou said emphatically.

"Well, what are you going to do about it, Lou?" Sybil said in a hard voice. "Your own cousin—"

"Yeah, yeah. You're right," Lou waved a hand.

Abel spoke up. "It's the darned corporates. Like to see me gone out of business. Must know I wouldn't eat anything from one of—" he choked.

Bob Duselschetner said, "They've never done any harm. They're clean; they do beautiful work."

"So the hard part is settled, as Mr. Chenakzy says," Wickerberg cut in. "I want to pinpoint the first date of symptoms. From there we can backfigure the first date of infection. Mr. Chenakzy?"

Lou breathed deeply. "Tuesday. Day before yesterday. About two-thirty I went to swill the sow and her new litter. She's—she's never been an eater before. She's the most god-awful color." Lou didn't look so good himself. Sybil Duselschetner pushed his coffee cup into his hand. Lou drank.

"You didn't destroy the animal? Good. Mr. Spruill?"

Abel Spruill was speechless. His brother said, "Tuesday night. Our oldest feeders! Every one of 'em ready for market." He bit his lip.

"Did you destroy them?"

"Had to. Thirty-two feeders." He shook his head slowly.

"Wait a minute, Hopper. You've only got a dozen or more feeders ready for market," Bob objected. "You said so yourself last week. We were going to share a truck, remember?"

Spruill said nothing, and Duselschetner shook his elbow. "Hopper, you didn't kill 'em all?"

"Had to," Hopper Spruill squeaked, breaking down.

"That's way too many for one—one vector," Steve started to say, but Wickerberg cut him off.

"I think that you may have been a bit hasty, Mr. Spruill, although I understand and appreciate your eagerness to maintain proper sanitation. Do you happen to have the carcasses?"

Hopper nodded. "I was just going to incinerate 'em when I got your call. Came over here instead."

"Did you leave the boys to do it?" Duselschetner asked.

"Boys are at 4-H tonight." Hopper drew his sleeve over his face. "Better be."

Wickerberg glanced at Steve and Steve went out on the porch to make the call. Thirty-two feeders would be a big load. He asked for the twenty-four-footer and a decontam crew of four, and left his number for the crew to check in when they'd finished the pickup.

He was just snapping his phone shut when a car full of kids roared up and piled out into the yard. They seemed to be in high good humor, until they saw the state plate on Wickerberg's car. Then they huddled into a group.

"That's my Dad's truck too," said one to another and got shushed.

A stocky boy who looked a lot like Sybil Duselschetner came up to Steve.

"Sir? Any trouble?" His voice was changing. A row of 4-H pins was stuck in the lapel of his denim jacket.

Steve looked the kid up and down and then waved the others over. They came reluctantly. Iowa farm kids were the soul of courtesy. None of their business if Duselschetner had trouble with Ag. Besides, they'd hear it through the grapevine fast enough. If Duselschetner was talking.

When they were standing close around him like a young vigilante meeting, exuding protectiveness and worry, Steve explained. "So you can see why we've brought all three families together to talk about it. And you understand how important it is that nothing get out until we've—contained the vector." Steve was no good at using that kind of high-ag language. He hoped they'd forgive him for euphemizing. The kids stared solemnly back at him. He said earnestly, "We don't want a panic. We don't want anybody getting, getting blamed for," he trailed off, "for things."

There was an exchange of glances around the little group. Five kids. Not all of them Duselschetner's, obviously. One boy got a few sideways looks that made him go red to the roots of his black hair.

Duselschetner's boy looked around at his friends and threw his arm over the black-haired boy's shoulder defiantly. He said straight to Steve, "That's right, sir."

Steve looked at the black-haired boy. The boy took a deep breath and stepped out from under the Duselschetner kid's arm.

"Sir, could I speak to you alone?"

◊◊◊

Night was falling. Steve made another quick call to the decontam crew. Then he went back into the kitchen. Things were past the shouting stage. The farmers sat around looking glum, as well they might. A way of life was in danger, a pivot point of the whole Iowa small farm life cycle. Hell, there were lives in danger: Their friends could get mobbed. And if nothing was done, they'd all be ruined.

Steve cut in on Wickerberg making one of his flat, calming speeches about "community." "Found our vector."

Wickerberg got up. "Outside, Steve."

"No, sir, I think these folks deserve to know. Right in their own back yards as it is."

Wickerberg just looked at him. Three generations of Civil Defense volunteers glared out of his eyes and dared Steve to disturb the peace in an irresponsible manner.

"Sir, I've been out on the porch with the butcher's kid."

Bob Duselschetner buried his face in his hands. His wife raised her clenched fists off the table and put them down, very gently.

"He's in a special 4-H science class with the rest of the kids around here. Seems they got a new teacher."

"I don't believe it," Lou Chenakzy said loudly.

"Please, Mr. Chenakzy. She's one of these new genetics experts, trained out of the Davis labs—got her own analyzer rig and waldobox. Been teaching the kids about reconstructing DNA." Steve paused while comprehension formed in the face of his partner. Steve cleared his throat. He felt a little embarrassed, even after twenty years in-state. "She's from Manhattan."

Wickerberg nodded slowly. "What is it, a flea?"

"He thinks so. His lab partner is working with fleas." Steve coughed. "I warned the decontam crew to take precautions."

"Lab'll determine that," Wickerberg muttered. "Can I talk to the kid?"

"He's waiting to go home with us," Steve said. Steve was impressed with the kid. The boy knew he was in deep shit, had half-ruined the Spruills, destroyed his parents' business and probably every other small-town butcher in Iowa too. He stood his ground and waited to be driven home to his folks, to watch them get the bad news and take whatever pitiful medicine could be dished out to him. Solid stock. Damned shame to lose it, Steve thought.

He gathered up the files on the table while Wickerberg took fax numbers from the stricken farmers. The farmers were silenced. They looked as white as the butcher's boy.

In the car Wickerberg questioned him while Steve drove.

"I thought I had isolated it, sir. It's just a tag. A nanoseeker could clean it off every cell in the body in a couple of days. It shouldn't affect anything else. Just people. And swine," he added bleakly, as if realizing what cold comfort that was. "I hadn't realized how close the match is." He fell silent.

"You understand the importance of federal regulations against working with human DNA," Wickerberg said. Steve was sure the kid would get a Wickerberg tongue-lashing, once the old man had worked up a head of steam.

"I do now, sir."

The county blacktop was dark as pitch. Inside, the Ag car was lit only by the glow of the dash. The kid sat between Steve and Wickerberg, his hands on his knees and his seatbelt cinched around his skinny waist. Steve felt a prickle on the back of his neck. The kid pointed to a road heading off into deeper country darkness. "That way."

Steve and Wickerberg waited outside while the kid went into the butchery to fetch his folks. His mother came out and went into the house with two pasteurizing bottles full of blood. She was followed by her husband, wiping his hands on his apron. Like all the old-timey Iowa butchers, he was normally pale. His face glowed white as a mushroom under the porch light. "I guess you'd better come inside."

Steve inspected the place while Wickerberg talked. The killing room smelled of chlorine and steam. The stainless steel tanks gleamed. Not a speck of old blood on the enameled basins, the big choppers, the circular saw on its sliding table. He stuck his head into the locker and sniffed: sweet and fresh. Like all old-timey Iowa butcheries, it was as clean as kasreth. One more reason the small farmers continued to use these little family operations instead of the yards in Dubuque or the corporate farms' rolling plants: They wouldn't accept diseased animals. Never even let 'em off the truck.

The kid's mother tenderly put her hand on her son's hair. "Darling, maybe we don't want to be cured. Did you ever think of that?"

He covered his face. "I thought I was so close. I'm sorry, Mom."

"I don't understand," the butcher was saying in a painful voice. "The animals that come here stay here. The hides are sold, or burned, but—well, we'd know if they weren't clean." His voice cracked on the last word. "How did this flea get to the pens at the farms?"

"Not through you, sir, but your son. Through his friends. They're in the same 4-H group. Probably got infected right there in the lab," Wickerberg said. "I can't tell you how sorry I am."

Inadequate word, all around, Steve thought. They were looking at the arrest and, at best, deportation of some hundred and twenty Iowa butchers and their families. If the deportations could be done before the lynchings started. The butcher stood a little straighter. His wife put her arms around her boy.

"Then why—" the butcher stopped, and said more slowly, "why don't the kids have it?"

The boy raised his head.

Steve thought a minute. "That's a good question." He asked the boy, "How far did you get with your—your tag cleaner?" As if he knew the first thing about DNA waldoing.

But Wickerberg seemed to know. He stood still, then turned. "Son, I think we'll drop by your 4-H lab and pick up your project. And then if you don't mind, we'll drive straight to Ames. There's proper containment at the lab there."

The kid's face shone with awful hope. "Yes, sir, right away. Dad, can I—?"

Wickerberg said to his father, "We need to know just how it was done. Have him home tomorrow, probably."

His father nodded. Steve went outside and flipped his phone again.

◊◊◊

Three weeks passed. There was a protest outside Ag in Ames. Not animal rights this time, Steve noted with relief while getting out of his car, but Greens complaining about the amount of grain cattle eat. Greens didn't throw blood anyway. Slowly and politely, he shouldered his way up the long steps in front of Ag and made his way to the conference room on the second floor.

The stricken farmers had driven up with the butcher's family. They sat drinking coffee and watching the kid show off slides of his project. His father stood by, grinning nervously, his face unusually red. Wickerberg, of course, was following it all. He talked rod-and-helix talk with the kid.

"This defect here makes a handle where the tag attaches," the kid tapped the screen. "It appears in about one thousandth of a percent of the population in the old country. The virus tags on and then replicates throughout over a period of maybe forty or fifty years. So maybe more people have it but they die before anybody realizes."

"Will the nanoseeker take just the tag?"

"First pass, yes. Then you send around another one and it

repairs the handle. I wanted the first one I designed to do both, but I guess I got too ambitious."

Lou Chenakzy nodded. "So what about the fleas?"

"The fleas carried it from him," Wickerberg said. "Spread it through the class. Then they rode the 4-H kids home and gave it to the swine. If young Dr. Schweitzer here hadn't tinkered with the tag, it wouldn't have been able to find a handle on normal swine."

"And the kids never got it?" Bob Duselschetner said.

"Nope." Wickerberg passed a benevolent glance to the kid. "You did something right, son."

The kid blushed and looked at the floor.

Steve set his briefcase on the table and opened it.

"Ahem. I got receipts for the electronic funds transfers, Mrs. Duselschetner, Mr. Spruill, Mr. Chenakzy. The Livestock Epidemics Act covers you like a rug. Check if those are the amounts you put in for, please."

Steve said awkwardly, "Mr. Tomescu, the inoculation worked. You and your wife are free of infection." He swallowed. "You don't have to be butchers anymore. Nor, of course, your son. I take it he has a great future in Ag, once he finishes school."

The butcher spread his hands. "Do we have to?" He looked at the ruddy fleshiness of his fingers wonderingly. "It wouldn't be so easy to do a good job. Even if we stayed in the trade."

The other farmers got up one by one and went to the window, keeping out of it. Later they'd gossip the question to rags, of course. But it was Tomescu's business. They let them have their privacy.

Wickerberg cleared his throat. "The governor has agreed to a program of reinfection on a case-by-case basis. You know how big she is on saving small farms and traditional businesses."

Lou Chenakzy put his hand on his cousin's shoulder. "Do what you want, Radu. You and Doris can come and stay with me if you want. As for the business—well, I don't want to take my stock to Dubuque. Never have. But don't feel you've got to do something on my account."

The butcher looked at his son. "Things are changing so fast. How can we keep going this way? Who's going to take over the business when—if we retire?"

The kid said, "Well, to be honest, Dad—" and trailed off.

Tomescu bit his lip. He said to Wickerberg, "Can we think it over?"

They drifted over to the window and looked out on the protesters.

"Lot of energy down there," Chenakzy said.

Sybil Duselschetner said comfortably, "There's always been meat, and there always will be."

"There certainly has," Tomescu said. He seemed lost in thought.

Hopper Spruill glanced at the butcher standing beside him. He said delicately, "Ain't you ever been tempted, Radu?"

The butcher squinted at him for a long moment. "I get you," he said finally. "You got to think ahead, Hopper." He snorted. "We start eatin' people, we got to be responsible about it. We got to breed 'em. Inoculate 'em. Control blood lines, keep 'em clean, watch what they eat." He shook his head, looking down on the protesters. "You know how smart the goddamned hogs are— would you want to have to deal with people?"

"Huh." Hopper pulled down the corners of his mouth. "I reckon that's so."

Meanwhile Steve was at the butcher's other elbow. "Sir?" he said in an undervoice. His carefully prepared speech came out in stutters. "Seems to me you may find—small family business and everything." He waved his hands. "Sudden labor shortage—I mean I sort of wanted to take some time off, pursue research. Just a couple of years. I don't know as I want to be a vampire for life," he added with an awkward grin.

Tomescu glanced with sorrow at his son and back at Steve. He smiled tremulously. "Well. I guess we could give you a try."

Jennifer Stevenson's short stories have appeared in *Horns of Elfland*, *Women at War*, and other anthologies. Educated in Iowa, she now lives in Evanston, Illinois, with her husband and their two cats.

Demon drink comes in many forms. . . .

Plague

BY JOHN LUTZ

1901, Fredricksburg, Kansas

ount Alronza Matraque Mearitoir, alias Billy the Idiot, pounded his gavel on the table and called the meeting to order.

"We have," he said, "a situation that has reached the proportions of an emergency."

"Surely not," said Wallace Beard from the nearby town of River Bend, where he owned and managed a dry goods emporium.

"I have the statistics," the count said. "Nationwide, during the past year, ten of us have perished."

Around the large table sounded a collective intake of breath, or something like that.

"Perished how?" asked Leonard Clinger, the mayor of Fredricksburg, where the secret meeting was taking place in the basement of City Hall. He talked softly. His fear was that Sheriff Adamson, a hotheaded and formidable lawman, would discover something irregular was going on and arrive to investigate.

"Simple lack of nourishment, nothing else," said the count. He was—when not using the persona of Billy the Idiot, the Fredricksburg village buffoon—a tall and commanding figure, pale of complexion and fierce of eye, and with long, wiry limbs that looked, and were, capable of squeezing the life from the strongest enemy within seconds. "They sought the elixir and found it, yet it was insufficient. They weakened, they fell, and lost the struggle to return to their native-soil lair before dawn. The sun destroyed them where they lay."

The twenty other members of the American Board of the Worldwide Life Everlasting Society looked concerned. They had all flown into Fredricksburg earlier that evening for the annual meeting. Secretly, of course. No one outside the inner circle suspected that the worldwide society existed, much less how large it was, and the members were pledged to keep it that way.

"We are seeing," Baron von Gundelfinger said in his imperious manner, "more and more of the horseless carriages. Could it be that their odorous fumes are tainting the air and causing us to need more sustenance?"

"It's a problem never before encountered," said Davy McElroy from Boston. He was still dressed for the docks, where he worked loading and unloading cargo ships.

The count thought Davy should have cleaned up for the annual meeting, used some other form once he'd arrived in Fredricksburg. And that gold loop earring. If someone did happen upon the secret meeting, what would they think of a man dressed like a pirate in the midst of others dressed as fine gentlemen—with the exception of Adam Dark, who was a huge bat.

The meeting was always a risk, especially at the beginning, when members were arriving. So far the townspeople's suspicions hadn't been aroused. Billy the Idiot moved freely and unnoticed among them, watching, eavesdropping, and he was sure the influx of members from around the country hadn't been noticed. Of course, had it been noticed, the people would have known something was wrong. Flying in for the meeting was the only practical thing to do, but it was chancy considering that the airplane had only recently been invented.

"It isn't the exhaust of the internal combustion engine," Wallace Beard said. "In fact, I find that quite invigorating if not nourishing." There was a murmur of agreement around the table.

Von Gundelfinger screwed his monocle in place over his right eye and squinted at the count. "I am not convinced there is a problem, my dear Gaelic friend." He sneered as he spoke. "I doubt the accuracy of your statistics."

"National Headquarters in Erie, Pennsylvania, supplied the statistics. They know what's going on around the country. They have their finger on the— Well, they know what's going on."

"That I doubt," said von Gundelfinger, who thought he'd been slighted and cheated by the count in the national election and lost a post at Headquarters. He'd demanded a recount, which, of course, the count wouldn't agree to.

"I don't think," said Vernon Walters, who had a corner on the blacksmith business in River Bend (where horses weakened then disappeared regularly without explanation), "that we have quite the emergency the count describes. Though it is, of course, a matter to watch carefully."

Victor Hurt, who with his pale, gaunt wife Amelda owned and managed an inn (where guests weakened then disappeared regularly without explanation), said, "I agree. The count hasn't really made the case that the situation demands extreme action."

"Why wait until it does?" the count asked in exasperation. "Wouldn't it be wiser to take action now?"

"Only if there's no doubt action needs to be taken," Walter Beard said. "The ten who perished might have been the victims of—"

"They were the victims of diluted and ineffective elixir," the count said.

"But you said the sun—"

"Of course! It was the sun that actually destroyed them. The debilitating effects of the elixir were transferred from the source; then they became incapable of reaching shelter in time."

"A matter to watch," Vernon Walters repeated.

"Unless there is any other business," Baron von Gundelfinger said, "I make a motion that we adjourn."

"I second—"

"No, no!" Viscount Duval interrupted. "I propose further business."

Von Gundelfinger observed him coldly through his monocle. "Such as?"

"Leeches! What are we going to do about leeches? They are being used more and more often at medical facilities and are now posing the threat of competition, or at the very least lessening the quality of the elixir."

The count rolled his eyes. Leeches again. The little creatures were a fixation for Duval, had been for centuries. A crisis had arrived, and still they must discuss leeches.

"I have *been* a leech!" Baron Smatwack said indignantly. "We— they pose no threat whatsoever."

The count sat back and listened while the annual argument about the leech threat thundered around the table. He wasn't worried about leeches. How much elixir could the tiny creatures consume, even in great numbers? And of course they kept people alive, so that the stock of elixir was propagated. It wasn't leeches. It wasn't the fumes of the noisy internal combustion engines in the horseless carriages. The count was sure about what was causing the problem, but he knew that the board would disagree with him, then among themselves, and nothing would be done until it was too late. They were all in immortal danger, and he was the only one aware of it.

As he listened to the familiar and futile bickering about leeches, he realized what he had to do. He decided to act independently, outside the circle of the organization.

Well, almost independently. He knew the perfect man to help him in his task.

◊◊◊

Everyone else had left town, the lucky ones heading east catching a high, warm wind to hasten the nighttime passage home.

On a bench outside City Hall the next night, Billy the Idiot sat next to a darkly handsome young man wearing a well pressed suit and vest with a starched white collar, polished boots, and a gold watch chain. No one was close enough to hear what the two men were saying. Horse-drawn commercial wagons, surreys, and now and then one of the clattering horseless carriages passed on the gas-lighted street beyond the elm trees, and pedestrians strolled the wooden walkways. Occasionally someone would venture close and glance over at Billy and the handsome man, probably wondering who the man was and what nonsense Billy was telling him, but Fredricksburg was a large enough town that a stranger was not that uncommon a sight.

The handsome man was Adam Dark, no longer a bat. At the count's request, he had remained behind in Fredricksburg so they could talk. He said, "So you really see this as a dire threat."

"I do," Billy told him earnestly. "It's increasing every year, getting out of hand. And you can help to stop it."

"I?" Adam raised a dark, arched eyebrow in surprise.

"It requires your expertise. You have a reputation with women, Adam."

"And not unfounded," Dark said proudly.

"You can seduce and control them easily."

"We can all do that," Dark said.

"Not so easily initially. You perfected your techniques in France before the revolution."

"A good time to be alive," Dark said, somewhat wistfully. "If one had position, as had I. Ah, how the courtesans schemed to meet the English trade envoy."

"And I understand you have no difficulty in the here and now. Even initially."

Dark smiled. "I could boast, but that would be . . . unlike me."

Billy thought, if only those people passing by could hear us, they'd wonder who was the idiot. But he said, "There's no need to boast. I have confidence that you can help."

"Explain exactly what you want," Dark said, gazing up at the starlit sky. "Time's fleeting, and we both have needs tonight."

"There is a woman who might help us. . . ." Billy the Idiot began.

When he was finished talking, Adam Dark was not only convinced of the threat to the elixir, he was sure he was the logical choice of his kind, the only one who could stop the threat before it became a catastrophe.

Adam Dark was disappointed to learn that she was not an attractive woman. She stood six feet tall and weighed 180 pounds, and her demeanor was that of the bear. Yet he knew that Billy the Idiot was right. The elixir that was the very stuff of existence for the society was plentiful, but what good did that do if it was thinned and lacked its sustaining quality? Its deplorable state made more infusions necessary, increasing the risk of exposure. Risk was also increased by the debilitating effects of the worst of the elixir, and under the usual circumstances of infusion it was almost impossible if not impractical to know the exact physical condition of the source.

So Adam worked his charm on the woman, who despite her ferocious appearance was no stranger to the ways of men. She'd divorced her first husband. Her second was a man she seldom paid attention to and who was about to divorce her. All of which made her susceptible to Adam's solicitous presence and disarming smile.

He feigned interest in her all-consuming cause, agreed with her that her "mystic seizures" were an intervention and guidance of the Lord. Her mother, she told him, had suffered delusions and believed herself to be Queen Victoria. Adam, who had known English Queens, had to smile when the woman told him that. He supported her sense of mission and encouraged her to dress starkly in black and white. "A bit too severe?" she had once asked him in a moment of infatuation. He favored black himself, he assured her.

In the restaurant of the hotel in Wichita, Kansas, he waited until the other diners had left and they were alone by candlelight in their semiprivate booth. He'd let her rail about the 1890 Supreme Court decision, agreeing with her every impassioned word.

"Only *you* seem to understand me," she said fervently, gazing at him over the glowing hurricane lamp. Blackness pressed at the windows, giving him confidence. Tonight would be the night.

"That is because you speak with common sense and divine guidance," he said, "a rare and valuable combination."

"If only we could stop what's happening . . . mark the evil for what it is and stamp it out."

"Oh, you and I think exactly alike on that.' He moved closer to her on the smooth leather bench seat. Beyond a scrolled wooden screen, a white-coated waiter stood near the door. He was the only other person in the dim restaurant.

"As we do on so many matters," she said, and sipped the water the waiter had left.

Adam caught the woman's gaze and held it with the hypnotic

FIELDS OF BLOOD

power of his eyes. "You alone have the strength to lead the way," he told her, even as he watched her strength wane. "If you need moral support, I will be there for you. You and I and the good and the just. It was ordained to be so in heaven."

"Yes, yes," she said breathlessly, "heaven."

He leaned toward her. She parted her lips to return his kiss, but he cupped her chin and turned her head gently to the side, smiling in a way she'd never dreamed possible.

That was the first infusion.

The rest was a matter of time.

◊◊◊

On a moonless night three months later, Adam Dark sat alone at a table near the back of a saloon in Wichita and waited. He appeared to be drinking a glass of red wine, but of course it wasn't wine at all. A piano player was entertaining the many patrons with the latest popular song of 1901, something that Adam found completely tuneless, and the place was noisy with laughter and music and the clinking of mugs and glasses.

The good times, Adam knew, were about to end.

The door burst open and she stepped inside. The look in her eye—powerful and eerie and determined—caused those who glanced at her to be trapped in the mesmerizing effect of her gaze.

The music stopped, then the laughter and conversation, and everyone was staring at the tall, starkly dressed woman.

There was a hush as she raised a hatchet from the black folds of her skirt.

The bartender, a husky man in a white shirt and red vest, hurried around from behind the long mahogany bar. "Whoa! Just a minute now, lady. If you—"

She advanced on him, brandishing the hatchet. He froze, then backed away from her.

"The scriptures forbid the corruption of the holy temple of the body!" she screamed.

Adam Dark couldn't have agreed more.

"Scriptures?" the bartender said, confused as well as afraid.

"Woe to those of you who flaunt their hedonistic ways and

defy the Word. Who imbibe not in the spirit of the Lord but in the spirits of alcohol that rob the children of God of their senses and morality."

A few of the men seated at the bar laughed, partly at what she was saying, partly at the rare sight of such a woman in a saloon. The only women they'd seen in the place were dressed quite differently. Talked differently, too.

Her eyes flashed dark fire in her pale features. "I smite the work of Satan!"

So saying she swept her hatchet sideways across the bar, knocking mugs and glasses onto the floor.

"Whoa! Hey!" the amazed bartender said.

She strode past him and around behind the bar, where she began smashing the hatchet into the wooden kegs. Spirits flowed liberally onto the floor. "Death to the demon! Clean the land of the alcohol abomination! Family first, not John Barleycorn!"

"Praise the Lord!" Adam Dark yelled, leaping to his feet.

"Tell 'em, sister!" an obviously drunk man wearing a fedora shouted from the end of the bar.

The hatchet arced and smashed. Geysers of beer and whiskey erupted. Now half the men were sitting in stunned silence, while the other half were yelling and cheering encouragement. A good bit of destruction was always popular in most Wichita saloons.

The bartender took a few steps toward the bar, then stopped and shrugged. His job didn't include having his head laid open by a six-foot-tall woman with a hatchet. He crossed his arms over his barrel chest and stood watching, his brows knitted in a frown more of puzzlement than anger. He wasn't the owner, after all.

"Praise her courage!" Adam Dark yelled. "Embrace her cause!" He hurled his half-full wineglass to the floor smashing it.

"Praise her!" the drunk yelled even louder.

A small man in a wrinkled suit halfway down the bar stood up and said, "Whiskey's been my ruin! I lost my family and friends to the bottle. My children—" He began to sob uncontrollably.

"Siddown and shuddup!" a huge bearded man at a table shouted. He hoisted his beer mug and drank deeply.

Then the noise of the gushing kegs, the yelling, the relentless crash of the hatchet, created a din that was like a Beethoven symphony to the ears of Adam Dark. As he remembered Beethoven's performances, anyway.

When every keg was ruptured and empty, the woman strode out from behind the bar. Her eyes, yearning and mad, met Adam's in a cold instant of calm, and he smiled at her.

Returning his brief smile, she walked toward the door, hatchet raised high and expression fierce, and disappeared into the night minutes before the police arrived.

◊◊◊

1911, Fredricksburg, Kansas

Billy the Idiot dropped the newspaper on the table at the annual board meeting.

"Carry Nation is dead," he said. "It had to be arranged because of her celebrity. If she'd gone on indefinitely, not looking any older, people would have noticed. But her work, along with that of the various temperance organizations to which we've contributed generously, has significantly reduced the risk that whoever we choose as the source of the elixir will be inebriated, causing insufficient nourishment and in some cases a drunken state that can lead to loss of reason, then exposure to the sun. Our membership is no longer being depleted by the taint of alcohol in the blood of the country, and there's no doubt that someday prohibition will become the law of the land and the stock of elixir will be undiluted and rich in nutrients."

"The woman was stark raving mad," Baron von Gundelfinger said, "which is worse than being drunk."

Adam Dark, who had feasted on her blood for years, said, "I'm not at all sure she was mad."

They all stared at him.

"Our use of Carry Nation and our involvement in the temperance movement has purified the stock of the elixir," he said, "but hasn't it occurred to you that our motives are an abomination to the Lord? Isn't our very existence an affront to providence? Ours is a plague on the land more deadly than the demon rum!"

Billy the Idiot cleared his throat. "Er, Adam—"

But Adam had stood up, very tall in human form, and from beneath his long black cloak had withdrawn a wooden mallet. His eyes were glowing madly with a fierce self-righteousness no one had before observed in him. "Ageless though our curse," he proclaimed, "immortal though we seem, we are the minions of Satan!"

With his free hand he drew from beneath his flowing black cloak a wickedly sharp wooden stake.

There was a loud, collective gasp.

"Seize him!" Billy the Idiot shouted.

At that moment the doors flew open and the sheriff and his deputies, all armed with mallets and wooden stakes, rushed into the room. Their eyes were terrified, but their jaws were set.

The struggle lasted until shortly after sunrise.

There was only one survivor. Whatever explanation might have been left for the people of Fredricksburg, it was never accepted as fact.

It was, after all, only the word of the village idiot.

John Lutz won an Edgar award for his short story "Ride the Lightning" and has written several novels and dozens of short stories in the mystery, horror, and suspense fields. His novels include *Bonegrinder, The Flame,* and *The Ex.*

Eternal life can be hard thing to give up, even when you want to.

Too Short a Death

BY PETER CROWTHER

ey . . . *hey!*" The man on the stage was trying to make himself heard, laughing while he was doing it and waving his hands conspiratorially, as though he were Billy Crystal in the *Mr. Saturday Night* movie. But the sound that he was trying to drown out was not the sound of people enjoying *him* but rather of them enjoying each other or their food or their drinks.

"Yeah, Hillary Clinton." The man frowned and shook his hand as though he had picked up something that was too hot to hold. "You heard . . . you heard Bill wants six more secret service agents assigned to her, yeah? Well," he reasoned with a shrug, "after all, if anything happened to her, he'd have to become President."

In humor terms, it was one step—a small one—up from *Take my wife . . . please!* But somebody let out a loud guffaw and David MacDonald turned around on his seat to see who it had been. At one of the tables over by the coatracks two men were laughing, but it was clearly not at Jack Rilla.

"Thanks, Don," Jack Rilla shouted into his microphone. "My brother Don," he added for the audience's benefit. "Nice boy."

The man at the table—who was clearly no relation to the comedian—turned to face the stage and gave Jack Rilla the bird, receiving a warm burst of applause.

MacDonald had never enjoyed seeing somebody die on stage, so he turned back to his food.

He was enjoying the anonymity. All the effete photographers and the snot-nosed journos had gone, taken up their cameras and their tape recorders and walked. Gone back to the city.

He was no longer news. "The most innovative poet of his generation," the *New York Times* had trilled, mentioning—in the 18-paragraph, front page lead devoted to his quest—the names of early pioneers such as William Carlos Williams, Edwin Arlington Robinson, and Ezra Pound; Kenneth Fearing, to whom they attached the appellation "The Ring Lardner of American verse'" the so-called war poets, including Richard Eberhart, Randall Jarrell, and Karl Shapiro—the Pulitzer winner whose "Auto Wreck" had been widely (and wrongly!) cited as the inspiration behind MacDonald's own "The Downer"' and even some of the Black Mountain College graduates, in particular Robert Creely and the college's head honcho, Charles Olson. This latter "revelation" enabled the hack responsible for the piece to tie it all back again to Williams and Pound, who, with their respective paeons "Paterson" and "Cantos," were commonly regarded as being among the North Carolina college's—and particularly Olson's—chief inspirations.

A neat job, but, in the main, entirely wrong.

MacDonald loved e. e. cummings, born a generation after Williams but infinitely more eloquent in his embrace of nature and naturalness and, to the end, delightfully whimsical. Similarly, he preferred Carl Sandburg—whose "limited" he had used in its entirety (all six lines!) as the frontispiece to *Walton Flats,* a surreal and fabulous (in the true sense of the word) novel-length tale of godhood and redemption which he had written in collaboration with Jimmy Lovegrove—to the Runyonesque Kenneth Fearing. And as for the "war poets," MacDonald rated Randall Jarrell above all others—Shapiro and his "V-Letter" included—even to the point of learning Jarrell's "The Death of the Ball Turret Gunner" when he was only twelve years old.

When it came to open verse, MacDonald settled for the Beats—Ginsberg and Ferlinghetti in particular—over the inferi-

or Black Mountain scribes, a fact which seemingly never ceased to amaze the self-styled poetry pundits. But it was *their* amazement that so astonished MacDonald, just as it astonished him how nobody seemed to give credit to the "Harlem Renaissance" and the fine work produced in the field of poetry by the likes of Etheridge Knight (of course), plus forerunners of the stature of Langston Hughes and Countee Cullen, and contemporaries such as Nikki Giovanni and Sonia Sanchez. As much as anyone— if not more than, in many cases—these writers, in MacDonald's opinion, were fundamental in recording the consciousness of a country at odds with itself, as he had gone to great pains to explain to a surprised David Letterman on live television a little over three years ago. Quoting the final few lines from Giovanni's "Nikki-Rosa"—in which the poet comments on the patronizing attitude of the whites—MacDonald took great relish in Letterman's damp forehead.

Sitting at the bar, MacDonald recalled the piece.

> *. . . . I really hope that no white person ever has cause to write about me because they never understand Black love is Black wealth and they'll probably talk about my hard childhood and never understand that all the while I was quite happy*

But the attention he had received in the press the following day was nothing to the coverage afforded his bold announcement that he was to forgo the novel on which he was working and, instead, go in search of Weldon Kees.

That was almost a year ago now.

The newspapers and the magazines had all followed: followed him to dry Californian towns, tracked him into the wastes of New Mexico, dogged his footsteps into the inhospitable Texas plains and now, back in the sleepy Nebraskan township of Beatrice, they had grown bored. After all, a fanatic is only of interest so long as he either looks like succeeding or looks like dying. Simple failure just isn't news.

Now no flashbulbs flashed as he walked still another dust-blown, night-time Main Street in some godforsaken town, in its own way

Too Short a Death

just one more boil on the fat backside of indulgence, a lazy, going-nowhere/seen-nothing grouping of weatherworn buildings and choked-up autos clustered around an obligatory general store and wooden-floored bar . . . with maybe a railroad track where no trains stopped any more thrown in for good measure.

Now no microphones were jammed between his mouth and some under- or overcooked indigenous delicacy as he continued his quest even through physical replenishment. Sometimes the questions had been more rewarding than the food. But the answers he gave were always the same, and the novelty had plain worn off.

Beatrice, Nebraska. A small, slow, company town lacerated by railroad tracks and gripped for eleven months of the year by permafrost or heatwave.

This was where he had started and, now, this was where it all ended. It was the latest—and, MacDonald now believed, the last—stop on this particular tour. Eleven months in the wilderness was enough for any man: Even Moses only spent forty days, for Crissakes.

Whitman's America had come to a dead end on the shores of the Pacific and, like the land itself, rolling lazily down to the waterline seeking only oblivion, MacDonald was tired. Tired of honky-tonk bars where he would search through a maze of good ol' boys and raunchy women, rubbing against tattoos and beer bellies, straining to see and hear through cigarette smoke and jukebox rhythms, carrying home with him the secondhand, hybrid musk of sweat and cheap perfume; tired of the revivalist espresso houses in the Village, where he would search through intense poets and poetesses, all wearing only dark colors and frowns, the *de rigueur* uniform. They, like him, searching, always searching.

He pushed the plate forward on the table, the meal unfinished. It had been a bean-bedecked and fat-congealed mush that maybe could have passed for gumbo if he'd been about 1,500 miles to the southwest. He wiped his mouth across a napkin from a pile on the corner of the bar, their edges yellowed with age, and noted the faded photograph of a town square with picket fences that wouldn't have been out of place in an *Archie* comic book or a Rockwell painting. He'd walked through that town square—in reality, little more than a pause for breath between developments in what was merely a typical Nebraskan suburb—to get to the bar in which he was now sitting. There had been no sign of the picket fence.

Just like Rockwell himself, it was long gone. But he had seen from the swinging racks in the drugstore that Archie was still around, though his hair was longer now. Nothing stays the same forever. Maybe this town had been Rockwell once, but now it was Hopper, filled up with aimless people like Jack Rilla, the unfunny comedian, all living aimless lives, staring unsmiling out of seedy rooming house windows at the telegraph poles and their promise of distance.

Weldon Kees, where are you? he said to himself.

The bartender slouched over to him and lifted up the plate quizzically. "No good?" he said, his jowls shaking to the movement of his mouth.

MacDonald frowned and shook his head, rubbing his stomach with both hands. "Au contraire," he said, effecting an English accent, "merely that you are too generous with your portions."

The bartender narrowed his eyes. "Aw *what?*"

"He said you gave him too much."

MacDonald turned in the direction of the voice to see a man in his early forties chasing an olive around a highball glass with a tiny yellow, plastic sword. The man looked like a movie star from the late fifties/early sixties, like maybe Tony Curtis or someone like that. He wore a plaid sportscoat, oxford button-down with a red-and-green striped necktie, and black pants rucked up at the knees to preserve two of the sharpest creases MacDonald had ever seen. Covering his feet, which rested lazily on the rail of his stool, were a pair of heavily polished Scotch grain shoes and, within them, a pair of gaudy argyle socks. MacDonald's eyes took it all in and then drifted back to the glass. There was no liquid in it. He hadn't noticed the man before, but then he wouldn't have. The bar was crowded to capacity, a good turnout for the amateur talent night promised on a rash of handbills pasted around the town.

The bartender nodded and, with another puzzled glance at

MacDonald, he turned around and slid the plate across the serving hatch. "Empties!" he shouted.

MacDonald swizzled the plastic palm tree in his club soda, twisted around on his seat and smiled. "Thanks. You want that freshened?"

The man turned to him and gave him a long, studied look, taking in MacDonald's plain gray jacket and pants, green, soft-collared sport shirt buttoned all the way to the neck, and nodded. "Yeah, why not, thanks. Vodka martini. On the rocks. Thanks again."

MacDonald raised his hand a few inches off the bar, and the bartender acknowledged with a short nod that looked more like a physical affliction.

"You here for the competition?"

MacDonald took a long drink and put his own glass back onto the bar. "That's right. You?"

"In a way," he said. "But really only to enjoy the efforts of others. I'm not actually a performer myself." The strange and self-knowing smile suggested hidden complexities in the statement.

MacDonald nodded and glanced at the stage, ignoring the opportunity to probe. At this stage of the journey he had had it with barroom confessions. Jack Rilla was telling a story about three men from different countries being sentenced to die . . . but being given a choice of the method of their execution. It was horrible.

"How about you?" the man said. "Are you a performer?"

"There's some that might say so," MacDonald replied, grateful to be able to turn away from what Jack Rilla was doing to stand-up comedy.

"What do you do?"

"I write poetry."

"That so?" The interest seemed genuine.

MacDonald nodded again and drained his glass as a crackly fanfare of trumpets sounded across the PA system to signal the end of the comedian. Nobody seemed to be clapping.

Turning around so they could watch the small stage at the end of the adjoining room, they saw a fat man with a Stetson starting to announce the next act. By his side were two younger men holding guitars and shuffling nervously from one foot to the other. The fat man led the halfhearted applause and backed away to the edge of the stage. The duo took a minute or so to tune their instruments and then lurched uneasily into a nasal rendition of "Blowing In the Wind."

MacDonald shook his head and held up the empty glass to the bartender, who had apparently forgotten them and had now taken to slouching against the back counter. "Refills over here," he shouted. The bartender lumbered over and refilled the glasses, all the while mouthing the words to the song. MacDonald took a sip of the soda.

"Not too good, huh?" the stranger said.

"The service or the entertainment?"

The man jerked his head at the stage.

"I've heard better," MacDonald said. "It's probably safe to say that Dylan'll sleep easy."

The man smiled and nodded. "I knew a poet once," he said.

"Yeah?"

"Uh-huh." He lifted the glass and drained it in one perfectly fluid motion. MacDonald recognized the art of serious drinking . . . drinking purely to forget or to remember. He had watched somebody he used to know quite well doing just the same thing over a couple of years . . . watched him in a thousand bar mirrors. He called those his wilderness years. The man set the glass down again and cleared his throat. "What kind of poetry you write?"

"Kind? It's just poetry."

"The rhyming kind?"

MacDonald gave a half-nod. "Sometimes," he said. "Depends on how I feel."

The pair of troubadours finished up their first song, receiving a smattering of applause, and launched immediately into another. This one was their own. It showed.

MacDonald reached into his pocket and pulled out the plastic button. The number on it was 23. He looked at the board at the side of the stage: beneath the number 22 was a piece of wipe-off card bearing the legend *Willis and Dobbs.*

While Willis and Dobbs crooned about some truck driver

whose wife had left him for another woman—modern times!—a small group of four men and two women chatted animatedly at the table right down in front of the stage. A tall spindle of metal stood proud in the table center and boasted the word JUDGES. They didn't seem to be talking about Willis and Dobbs. Maybe it was just they didn't like country music.

Willis and Dobbs finished their song almost in unison and bowed while the audience applauded and whistled in relief. As the duo shuffled off the stage, the fat man with the Stetson shuffled on the other side, also applauding. As the fat man reached the microphone, MacDonald took another swig of the club soda and slid off his stool. "Wish me luck," he said to the stranger.

The man looked around. "You on now? Hey, break a leg," he said, slapping MacDonald on the arm as he walked past him.

The usual nervousness was there. It was always there. He made his way through the people standing up in the bar section and then walked down the two steps to the adjoining room where he threaded his way among the tables to the stage. All the time he walked he was memorizing the lines, though he knew them by heart. He reached the stage as the fat man told the audience to give a big hand to Davis MacDonald. The timing was impeccable.

He walked over to the microphone and nodded to the room, raising his hand in greeting. "Hi there," he said.

A smattering of nods and waves and mumbled returns acknowledged him. The man at the bar had turned full around on his stool to watch him. He raised the glass—which MacDonald saw had been replenished—and nodded. MacDonald nodded back. Then he faced the audience and lifted one finger to his mouth.

As always, the silence was almost immediate. It flowed over and around the people sitting at the tables, flowed through and into them, touching their insides and calming their heads. The only way you could recite poetry and feel it—whether reading it yourself or listening to it being read by others—was to do it in silence. After all, who ever heard of a painter painting onto a canvas that already had something on it?

There were a few nervous shuffles as MacDonald paced from

one side of the stage to the other, his hands thrust deep into his pants pockets. At last, satisfied that this was as good as it was going to get, he removed the microphone, pointed over the heads of the onlookers to some impossible distance, and began.

She's down!
Like a wounded mammoth her body sags and,
across the sidewalk,
in a shower of fabled jewels,
she spills the contents of her bags.

The empty street becomes alive
with do-gooders, tourists and passersby,
all holding breath.
Transfixed, and with mouths agape,
they see her features lighten under death
while, alongside,
the treasures once so richly cherished—
a loaf, some toothpaste, matches, relish—
lie discarded on the paving slabs.

And ooohs *and* aaahs, *the silence stab.*

It takes some time but, action done,
the audience turns away its eye and,
with a thought as though of one,
thinks there one day goes I.

On the final line, MacDonald turned his back on the audience, walked slowly back to the microphone stand and replaced the microphone. A smattering of applause broke out around the tables. MacDonald nodded and raised his hand, mouthing the words *thank you, thank you.* He caught sight of the man at the bar. He looked as though he had seen a ghost.

After "The Downer," MacDonald recited his "Ode To the City."

Beneath the legends of the stars
the drunks cry out in a thousand bars

while pushers prowl in speeding cars . . .
civilization is never far in the city.

Bronchitic winos cough up more phlegm
to mouth the glassy teat again,
and venereal ladies stalk the concrete glens . . .
though love has long since left the city.
The neons wink cold, thoughtless lies,
to flood the dark and strain the eyes,
while the flasher opens wide his flies . . .
because nothing hides inside the city.

MacDonald lifted the microphone from the stand again and walked across to the left of the stage.

Smoke-bred cancers maim the flesh,
the addict chokes his vein to strike the next
while the abortionist clears away the mess . . .
as all life dies within the city.

The dropouts pass around the joint
and the rapist hammers home his point,
but the suicide doth himself anoint
in the fetid, stagnant waters of the city.

The kidnapper pastes together a note
and then binds his charge with silken rope
while frantic parents give up hope . . .
which died long ago in the city.

And now, as ever, the audience was his.

"In Mendaala When It Rains" came next, followed by "Dear Diary" and "Conversation." Then MacDonald paused and, unfastening the top button of his sport shirt, sat down on the front edge of the stage. "I want to finish up now with a couple of poems written by a man I never met," he said, the words coming softly, "but who I feel I've known all of my life.

"This man stole from us. He stole something which we possessed without even realizing . . . something which we could never replace. The thing he took from us . . . was himself." He shrugged out of his jacket and dropped it in a pile at his side. "On July twentieth, nineteen fifty-five, Harry Weldon Kees, one of *your* . . ." he pointed, sweeping his outstretched arm across the audience. ". . . your town's . . . most famous sons—disappeared from the north end of the Golden Gate Bridge.

"He left . . . he left many things behind him—not least a fifty-five Plymouth with the keys still in the ignition—but the worst things that he left were holes."

The faces in the audience looked puzzled.

"Those holes, ladies and gentlemen," MacDonald went on, "were the spaces that he would have filled with his poetry. Yes, he was a poet, Weldon Kees, and I'm here . . . here tonight, in Beatrice, Nebraska . . . his hometown . . . at the tail end of what has been almost a year-long search for him. Because, back in nineteen fifty-five, Weldon's body was never found. And because there have been some stories that he is still alive . . . somewhere out there. And if that's true, then I felt I had to find him." He stood up, shrugged, and said, "Well, I tried."

"Weldon . . . wherever you are . . . these are for you."

Reciting from heart, as he did with all of his "readings," Davis MacDonald recounted Kees' "Aspects Of Robinson" and, to finish, "Late Evening Song."

> *For a while*
> *Let it be enough:*
> *The responsive smile,*
> *Though effort goes into it.*
> *Across the warm room*
> *Shared in candlelight,*
> *This look beyond shame,*
> *Possible now, at night,*
> *Goes out to yours.*
> *Hidden by day*
> *And shaped by fires*
> *Grown dead, gone gray,*
> *That burned in other rooms I knew*

Too long ago to mark,
It forms again. I look at you
Across those fires and the dark.

"Thank you, ladies and gentlemen . . . thank you for listening to me." MacDonald replaced the microphone and ran from the stage, leaving tumultuous applause behind and around him.

When he got back to the bar and slumped onto his stool, he saw that the man next to him was nursing his drink in his hands and, his head tilted back, staring into the long but narrow angled mirror above the bar. MacDonald followed his stare and saw it all then: the bar, the back of the bartender's head as he moved by, the man's highball glass, and himself staring. But there was no reflection of the man himself.

He turned around quickly, mouth open, to stare right into the man's face and saw immediately that he had been crying.

"I'm Robinson," he said. "A friend of Weldon Kees."

MacDonald looked back at the mirror and shook his head. Then he looked back at the man and said, "How do you *do* that?"

"You tell a good story in your poems," he said. "I have a story, also, though I'm no weaver of words like you and Harry."

MacDonald slumped his elbows on the bar. "I think I need a drink."

The man stood up and straightened his jacket. "Come on, you can have one back at my place."

"Is . . . is Weldon Kees still alive?"

"No."

"Did he die that night? *Did* he jump off the bridge?"

The man shook his head. "Let's go. I'll explain on the way."

When they left the bar, the sidewalks were wet and shiny, reflecting shimmering neon signs and window displays. As he walked, MacDonald could also see his own malformed shape in the puddles but not that of the man who walked beside him. "I think I'm going mad," he said.

The man gave out a short, sharp laugh. "No, you're not."

MacDonald turned to him and grabbed hold of the arm in the plaid jacket—

Robinson in Glen plaid jacket, Scotch grain shoes,
Black four-in-hand and oxford button-down

The words of the poem he had just recited hit him suddenly and he pulled his hand back as though he had been burned. "How *can* you be Robinson? Robinson would have to be—" He thought for a moment. "He'd have to be around eighty or ninety years old."

"I'm actually much older even than that," the man said.

MacDonald looked down at the sidewalk, saw his reflection . . . alone. He pointed at the puddle. "And what about that?"

"The mirror from Mexico, stuck to the wall,
"Reflects nothing at all. The glass is black."

He smiled and shrugged.

"Robinson alone provides the image Robinsonian."

"What are you?" MacDonald asked.

The man stared into MacDonald's eyes for what seemed to be an eternity, so long

His own head turned with mine
And fixed me with dilated, terrifying eyes
That stopped by blood. His voice
Came at me like an echo in the dark.

that MacDonald thought he was not ever going to answer his question. The worst part of that was that, while he stared, he simply did not care. "I think you can guess," he said, suddenly, releasing MacDonald from his gaze.

"Oh, come on!" MacDonald laughed. "A vampire? You're telling me you're a vampire?"

The man started to walk again. Over his shoulder, he said, "My kind go by many names. And, yes, vampire is one of them." MacDonald started after him, his mind ablaze with stanzas from Weldon Kees' poetry.

The dog stops barking after Robinson has gone.
His act is over.

And

These are the rooms of Robinson.
Bleached, wan, and colorless this light, as though
All the blurred daybreaks of the spring
Found an asylum here, perhaps for Robinson alone.

And even

This sleep is from exhaustion, but his old desire
To die like this has known a lessening.
Now there is only this coldness that he has to wear.
But not in sleep.—Observant scholar, traveler,
Or uncouth bearded figure squatting in a cave,
A keen-eyed sniper on the barricades,
A heretic in catacombs, a famed roue,
A beggar on the streets, the confidant of Popes—

All these are Robinsons in sleep, who mumbles as he turns,
"There is something in this madhouse that I symbolize—
This city-nightmare-black—"

He wakes in sweat
To the terrible moonlight and what might be
Silence. It drones like wires far beyond the roofs,
And the long curtains blow into the room.

MacDonald suddenly realized that he was running . . . running to catch up with the man. But, while the man was only walking, MacDonald was getting no nearer to him. *Good God,* he thought, *it's true. All of it.*

The man turned up some steps and stopped at the door of a house. As MacDonald reached the man, he stepped inside and waved for MacDonald to enter.

Inside, the house smelled of age and dirt. A narrow hallway gave onto some stairs and continued past two doors to a third door which was partly open. "I'll get you that drink," the man said and he walked along the hall to the end door. MacDonald followed without saying a word.

The room was a kitchen. Dirty dishes that looked as though they had been that way for weeks were piled up in and beside the sink. In the center of the room, a wooden table with a worn Formica top was strewn with packets and opened cans. MacDonald saw several cockroaches scurrying in the spilled food.

The man opened a cupboard and pulled out a bottle of Jim Beam and two glasses. He poured bourbon into the glasses and handed one to MacDonald. "I first met Harry back in 1943. He was writing for *Time* magazine and *The Nation* where he did an arts column." He pointed to a chair littered with newspapers. "Sit down." MacDonald sat and sipped his drink. The man continued with the story.

"He was also doing some newsreel scripts for Paramount—he'd just done the one about the first atomic bomb tests—and he had recently taken up painting. He was as good at that as he was at anything, exhibiting with Willem de Kooning, Rothko—" He paused and shook his head. "I'm sorry . . . are you acquainted with these names at all?"

MacDonald nodded.

"Ah, good. Yes, with Rothko and Pollock–and he was holding a few one-man shows. So, I guess it's fair to say that life for him was good.

"I met him one night in Washington Square. I say one night when, actually, it was well into the early hours of the morning." He paused and took a drink. "I was hunting."

"Hunting?"

"Yes. I was out looking for food."

"Are we back to the vampire shtick now?"

The man ignored the tone and continued. "I usually arise in the early evening. If it's too light outside, I stay indoors until the sun is about to set. Contrary to fable, we can exist in the sunlight although it hurts our eyes and causes headaches like your migraines. So we don't do it. Not usually.

"This particular evening, I had already fed upon a young woman down near Port Authority. She had just arrived in town from Cedar Rapids, Iowa, and she offered me herself for twenty dollars. That was a steep price for a prostitute back in 1943, I can tell you. But she was an attractive girl and she knew it. How could I refuse?

"I killed her in an alley, and drank my fill." He drained his glass and waved it at MacDonald. "More?"

"Huh? Oh, no. No more, thanks. I'm fine with this."

The man turned around and poured himself another three fingers. "Always the truth is simpler than the fiction, don't you find?" he said as he turned back to face MacDonald. "The truth is that we do not have to hunt every night. A complete feed will sustain us for many days—sometimes a couple of weeks—before we start to grow hungry again. Vampires, as you call us, are not naturally aggressive . . . any more than humans, we hunt and kill merely to feed.

"Anyway . . . where was I? Ah, yes. When I met Harry—he was calling himself Harry back then, and I guess I just never lost the habit—when I met Harry, he was working on notes for his second book. He was walking through the Square where I was sitting. I was completely sated at this time, having—" He waved his hand. "The girl and so on."

MacDonald nodded and took a drink, eyeing the open door at his side.

"Anyway, he sat down beside me and we started to talk. We talked about the city and the night—both of which I know well—and then he mentioned that he was a writer. I think that's what Harry regarded himself as more than anything else: a writer.

"And he asked me if I enjoyed reading. I told him not very much at all. Then he mentioned his poetry: Did I like poetry? I told him I really wasn't qualified to comment on it. I did have some books, I told him, but, I said, frankly they might as well be filled with blank pages for all the good they are to me.

"Some time later, of course," he said, leaning forward from his place against the kitchen counter, "he wrote—in the first of what I came to regard as my poems—

> *The pages in the books are blank*
> *the books that Robinson has read."*

MacDonald took another drink and hiccuped. "Did he know . . . did he know that you were a, you know . . .?"

"Not immediately. But, eventually, of course, yes." He took a drink and rubbed his hand against the glass. "We were . . . we were alike, you know. Alike in so many ways."

"Alike? How?"

"Well, alienated. I suppose you could say that we were both outcasts from society. In those days I lived in New York.

"I have, of course, lived in many places—I won't bore you with the details: Harry covered some of them in his 'Robinson At Home' . . . uncouth bearded figure; keen-eyed sniper; a beggar on the streets; confidant of popes—but when I lived in New York, it grew too hot for me in the summertime. I used to go up to Maine, to a little coastal village called Wells. Do you know it?"

MacDonald shook his head. Holding out his empty glass, he said, "I think I *will* have that refill now."

The man took the glass. "Of course." He filled it to the brim and handed it back. "Harry didn't like me going off in the summer. He said it made him feel lonely."

"Lonely? Were you both . . . were you living together at that time?"

"Oh, gracious no. Harry was married—Ann was her name: nice girl, but entirely unable to cope with living with someone like Harry. And, of course, as he became more and more taken with my . . . shall we say, *company,* he became even less livable with." He sniggered. "Is there such a phrase as 'livable with'?"

MacDonald shrugged *why not?* And took another drink. The man smiled in agreement. "So, Ann took more and more to drinking. In 1954 she went into the hospital and—oh, of course, by this time we were in San Francisco. Did I mention that? We moved across to the West Coast in 1950. Harry took up with some new friends—Phyllis Diller, the comedienne? And Kenneth Rexroth?"

MacDonald nodded to both names.

"Wonderful poet, Ken Rexroth. Wonderful." He took a drink.

"We moved out West because, as I say, Harry hated the summers in New York when I was away. You remember 'Relating To Robinson?'

(But Robinson,
I knew, was out of town: he summers at a place in Maine,
Sometimes on Fire Island, sometimes on the Cape,
Leaves town in June and comes back after Labor Day.)

He laughed suddenly. "I tell you, I never—*never*—went to Fire Island. Or the Cape. That was Harry. He was just so pissed off with me for leaving him." He shook his head and stared down into the swirling brown liquid in his glass. "So pissed off," he said again, but quieter.

"So—San Francisco. It was fine for a while, but Ann grew more and more restless. Harry had taken up playing jazz. He was good, too. Incredible man. So versatile. But our relationship—and the constraints placed upon it by his being married—was starting to take its toll. You see, Harry was growing older . . . and I was not.

"In 1953, he wrote 'The lacerating effects of middle age are dreadful, God knows . . . what the routes along this particular terrain are, I wish I knew. The trick of repeating *It can't get any worse* is certainly no good, when all the evidence points to quite the opposite.'" He shuffled around and lifted the bottle of Jim Beam. "You see," he said, flicking off the screwcap with his thumb, "I wanted Harry to let me taint him."

"Taint him? How do you mean?" MacDonald watched the cap roll to a stop on the dirty floor. Its sides were flattened.

"I mean . . . to make him like me."

"A vampire?"

"A vampire. He would have had eternal life, you see. It doesn't happen every time. Not every time we feed. That's another thing the legends have got wrong. We only taint our victims if we allow our own saliva to enter the wound. Most times, we do not.

"But, no, Harry wouldn't hear of it. He said that life was too precious—which was a paradox of a thing for him to say—and he couldn't face the prospect of hunting for his food. I told him that I would do all of that for him . . . but it was no use."

MacDonald took a deep breath and asked the question he had wanted to ask for several minutes. "Were you lovers?"

The man's eyes narrowed as he considered the question, and then he said, "Of a sort, yes. But not in the physical sense. We were soul mates, he and I. I had the information and the experiences of the millennia and Harry . . . Harry had the means to put them into words. Such beautiful words." He fell silent and, lifting the bottle to his mouth, took a long drink.

"By the time 1955 was upon us, we both knew that we couldn't carry on this way. In his poem 'January,' Harry wrote:

> *This wakening, this breath*
> *No longer real, this deep*
> *Darkness where we toss,*
> *Cover a life at the last."*

And MacDonald added: *"Sleep is too short a death."*

"You know it?" the man said, clearly amazed and apparently quite delighted.

"I know them all."

"Of course, you would.

"Well, that year, we decided that Harry would have to disappear. I suppose we had known it for some time. Harry had often toyed with the idea of his suicide—even before he met me. He kept a scrapbook of cuttings and notes, and a chronological list of writers who had killed themselves or simply disappeared. One of his favorites, you know, was Hart Crane. He threw himself off a ship."

"Yes, I know. His poem 'Voyages' is one of my own favorites."

"Harry's, too," said the man. He sighed and continued. "And so we decided that he would jump—or appear to jump—from the Golden Gate Bridge. The day he did it was one year to the day since his official separation from Ann."

"Where did he go?"

"Mexico. Mexico City. He lived in Mexico—we lived in Mexico, I should say—very happily. We led as close to a normal life as we could . . . which was very close indeed.

"Harry wrote poetry and short stories—many of them published under *noms de plume*—and we spent the nights together, talking. I would tell him of all the things that I had seen and experienced and Harry would put them into poems and stories.

"Then, in 1987 a journalist for the *San Francisco Examiner* wrote that he had met Harry in a bar in Mexico City back in 1957."

"That was true, then, that story?"

The man nodded enthusiastically. "Every word. Absolutely true. The journalist was Peter Hamill.

"Harry was pretty zilched-out that night, I remember," the man said wistfully. "He'd been drinking Jack Daniel's and then, because it was my night to hunt, he went off by himself—something he did very rarely—and polished off several bowls of marinated shrimp and most of a bottle of mescal. We thought nothing more about it until, like three decades later, for crissakes, the story appeared in the *Examiner*. Needless to say, we left Mexico City within a few days."

"Where did you go then?"

"Oh, different places. Central America at first, but then Harry got to hankering for the States so we moved up to Texas." He took another drink from the bottle. "Then, when Harry's health got really bad, we moved back to Beatrice."

"What was it? What was wrong with him?"

"Cancer. He was riddled in the end. He died three weeks ago. I don't think I'm ever going to be able to cope."

MacDonald didn't know what to say.

"Even in the final days, I begged him to reconsider. If he'd let me taint him, he could have conquered the cancer. Then we could have lived forever. But he wouldn't." The man dropped the bottle and slid down the side of the counter to the floor. MacDonald jumped unsteadily from his chair and went to help him. He found a cloth by the side of the sink and ran cold water over it, flicking pieces of food and a couple of dead bugs into the sink. Then he rubbed the cloth over the man's face.

"I want . . . I want you to see him," he said. His voice was shaky and slurred.

"See him? I thought you said he was dead?"

The man nodded. "He is."

"He's dead and he's still here? Here in the house?"

Another nod.

"Where?"

"Upstairs. In his room."

MacDonald turned around and glanced back down the corridor towards the front door. Suddenly the smell of decay which permeated the house made sense. Kees had died three weeks ago. The weather was warm.

The man shuffled himself back up to a crouched position. "I . . . I want you to see him *now.*"

MacDonald took his arm and helped him up. "Okay, okay."

"C'mon, then, let's go." The liquor was clearly having an effect. On MacDonald, it seemed to be having no effect at all. He felt as though he had never had a drink of alcohol in his entire life.

They staggered down the dark corridor to the foot of the stairs. "You sure you want to do this?" MacDonald asked.

"Sh—" he belched loudly and hiccuped. "Sure. Harry'd want to meet you."

They started up the stairs, swaying from side to side, MacDonald against the handrail and the man called Robinson buffeting against the wall.

At the top of the stairs, the smell was deeper and thicker. It was now pure decay.

"Thish way." Robinson said, and he took off by himself along the narrow corridor toward the end room. He reached it with a thud and took two steps backward, stretching his right hand out toward the handle.

MacDonald ran forward. "Here, let me," he said, against his better judgment. Robinson stepped aside.

MacDonald took hold of the handle and turned it. His first impression was that the air that escaped from the ancient pyramids must have smelled like this, only milder. It stank. He lifted his hand to his mouth and swallowed the bile that was even then shooting up his throat. He pushed the door open and stepped into the room.

It was almost pitch-black. The curtains were drawn across the narrow window, but a small night-light glowed beside a wide bed that ran from the side wall into the room. In front of the bed and along to the side beneath the window, stretched a long desk strewn with huge piles of manuscripts and sheets of paper. On the table was a typewriter, a confusion of pens and pencils and erasers, a half-full—or half-empty—bottle of Jack Daniel's, and an array of empty glasses, some upright and some on their sides.

On the bed itself was a body, though its resemblance to anything that might once have lived was tenuous. It was dark and wizened, and seemed to move and writhe where it lay. MacDonald realized that Harry Weldon Kees now provided a home for a multitude of insects and larvae.

The door clicked shut behind him.

MacDonald spun around and faced Robinson. "You . . . you're not drunk," he said.

The man smiled. "Sorry. I've had what you might say was a lot of practice in holding my liquor." Then he opened a cupboard by his side. "I have a job for you."

"A . . . a job? What kind of job?"

"I want you to kill me."

MacDonald laughed and made a move toward the door. "What the hell is this . . .? I'm getting out—"

Robinson pushed him back and MacDonald stumbled against the bed, throwing his arm out to steady himself. MacDonald's hand sank into something which seemed damp and clammy. He felt things pop under its weight. "Oh, Jesus!" He jumped away from the bed and looked at his hand. It was covered in what looked like leafmold. He shook it frantically. "Oh, God," he said. "Oh, Jesus . . ."

"Here." Robinson reached into the open cupboard. He pulled out a flat-headed wooden hammer and handed it to MacDonald.

MacDonald took it and said, "Oh, Jesus!"

Then Robinson reached in again and pulled out a wooden pole, its end sharpened to a fine point.

MacDonald started to whimper.

"Here. You'll need this, too."

"No, I won't."

"You—"

"I'm not doing it. I'm not doing anything else. I'm getting out of this—"

Robinson took hold of MacDonald's jacket, crumpled it in his fist, and pulled the man toward him. "You'll do what I say you'll do . . . if you *do* want to get out of here."

MacDonald started shaking and stepped back away from Robinson. The man had spoken right into his face, breathed right over him . . . but the smell had not been of Jim Beam's, it had been of blood. Heavy and metallic. "Why? Why do you want me to do this? Why *me?*"

"Because I want to sleep the long sleep. Because . . . because I'm lonely. And because you are here."

"Is . . . is there no other way?"

Robinson shook his head. "At least one of the legends is true. A stake through the heart. It's the only way."

MacDonald looked at Robinson and fought off looking around at the thing on the bed. "What if I don't?"

"I'll kill you."

◊◊◊

It didn't take long for them to get things organized. Robinson stretched out on the bed next to Weldon Kees and held the stake's point above his chest with his left hand. With his right hand, he held the hand of the body by his side.

While he thought about trying to make a break for it, MacDonald heard Robinson sigh a long, deep sigh. "It feels funny," he said. "Funny to be lying here at last, lying here waiting to die.

"I've come close a couple of times—well, more than a couple, I'd guess—but I've always managed to turn things to my advantage." He turned his head to Weldon Kees and smiled. "Old friend," he said softly. "You and me, forever now." He looked up at MacDonald, smiled at the man's shaking hands around the shaft of the hammer. "You've no idea, have you?" he said.

"About what?" MacDonald lowered the hammer, grateful for the pause.

"Loneliness. The ache of ages spent completely alone. I thought that loneliness was all behind me. I thought that Harry would eventually relent and let me taint him. But it was not to be. He even begged me not to bite him if he should slip into some kind of coma before the end. He said if I did, then he would never speak to me again." He shook his head. "I couldn't live without Harry's words. I *cannot* live without his words. Death can only be a release." He closed his eyes and shook the stake gently. "Do it. Do it now."

MacDonald lifted the hammer high. As he started to bring it

down, Robinson's eyes opened and fixed upon him. "Burn us when you're through."

The hammer hit the stake squarely, as though MacDonald's hand had been guided right to the very end. The pole went into the body hard and lodged in the mattress beneath it. Robinson's body arched once, high in the air, and then slipped back.

MacDonald watched in fascination as the skin shriveled and pulled back, exposing teeth that looked nothing like what he expected a vampire's teeth to look like. The eyeballs jellied in their sockets and sank back out of sight. The flesh and muscle atrophied, the bones powdered, and within seconds Robinson's clothes sank back onto the dust. There was no blood.

As if in a daze, MacDonald put down the hammer and walked across to the desk. He lifted a pile of papers and scattered them about the desktop. He could not help himself. As he threw the sheets around, he tried to read some of the lines . . . some of the title pages. He started to cry.

He threw sheets onto the floor . . . high into the air and watched them flutter onto the lone body on the bed. "Please . . . please, God let me take just one sheet. . . ."

In his head, amidst the confusion, he heard a voice he did not recognize. It was an old voice, but it sounded gentle and wise. It said, *Take one sheet, then . . . but only one.*

MacDonald grabbed a sheet and jammed it into his sportscoat pocket. Then he picked up a book of matches, struck one, and ignited the whole book. He tossed it onto the scattered sheets, turned calmly around, and left the room.

The fire took longer to get going than he expected.

In the movies, the conflagration is always immediate. But here in reality, it took almost an hour. MacDonald watched it from across the street, watched the first flames reach up to the waiting curtains, watched the first glow in one of the downstairs rooms, smelled the first smoke-filled breeze blowing across the sidewalk.

Then it was done. And only then did MacDonald feel released from the power of Robinson's eyes.

As he started back to the heart of Beatrice, a gentle rain began to fall. MacDonald pulled the crumpled sheet from his pocket and, in the occasional glow of the streetlights, started to read. It was a poem. A complete work captured on a single sheet of paper. It was called "Robinson At Rest." It began:

> *Robinson watching a movie, safe*
> *In the darkness. The world outside spills by*
> *Along sidewalks freshened by rain.*
> *He says to the man by his side, "Is that clock correct?"*
> *"No," the answer comes. "It's stopped*
> *At last."*

And seventeen lines later it ended:

—Weldon Kees (1914-1993)

Peter Crowther is the author, with James Lovegrove, of the novel *Escardy Gap* and the editor of numerous anthologies, including *Narrow Houses, Heaven Sent,* and *Dante's Disciples.* His stories have been included in *The Year's Best Fantasy and Horror, The Year's Finest Crime and Mystery, The Fortune Teller,* and other anthologies.

The artist is like a vampire, stealing a bit of life and keeping it young and beautiful forever. . . .

Purr of a Cat

BY HUGH B. CAVE

She was a forlorn-looking thing, and it was raining, and I had driven so long over that lonely Minnesota road, without a soul to talk to, that I'd have welcomed the devil himself for company. So I stopped.

"All right, sister," I said. "Jump in."

"Thank you," she said. "I—I'm so cold."

I snapped the heater on. Ordinarily I don't use it when driving alone at night, because it makes me drowsy and I might fall asleep at the wheel. But she was shivering, so I leaned across her and thumbed the switch—and suddenly got a good look at the girl.

My breath stuck in my throat. Suddenly I forgot all about my assignment to paint pretty pictures of brooks and woodlands. One look at this girl was like a shot in the arm, jolting to life the *artist* in me. To hell with the Nu-Way Calendar Company and its paltry few bucks a week. The most beautiful girl in the world was sitting beside me!

I stared at her without apology. A man has a right to stare at such dazzling loveliness. I put my hands on her shoulders and turned her toward me, and soaked up the wonder of her flawless skin, the deep dark glow if her eyes, the warm red invitation of her mouth. "Lord!" I whispered wonderingly. "Oh, Lord!"

She wasn't scared. Those deep eyes returned my stare without blinking, and she actually smiled a little. Or was that my imagination?

"What's your name?" I asked hoarsely. "Who are you?"

"Roseen," she said. "That's my name: Roseen."

"Where do you live?"

"A little way from here, near Endonville. With my father."

"You're going to pose for me!" I cried. "You understand, Roseen? I'm going to paint a picture of you!" In my eagerness I almost told her *how* she was going to pose for me, but yanked the words back just in time. That would come later, when I'd had a chance to win her confidence.

With an effort I stopped staring at her and got the car rolling again. But my gaze kept jerking back to her, to her face, her wet black hair, the ivory smoothness of her slender throat. And when, presently, she shrugged out of the wet raincoat she'd been wearing, I stared so hard I nearly ran the car into a highway fence.

She wasn't wearing much under that coat. Just a cotton dress, sort of old-fashioned. It was damp and it clung to her body, revealing the perfect thrust of her full young bosom, the flat line of her belly, the inviting flow of her legs. Every little nerve in me began to pound.

"Are you going far?" she asked.

"To Endonville," I muttered after a moment. "I'm supposed to stay there a week or so, painting the beauties of this backwoods region."

"You will not like it there." She moved closer to me, and I could feel the warmth of her. A strangely intoxicating kind of warmth, like too much raw liquor running in my blood. It put wild ideas into my head.

"Why won't I like it there?" I said.

"The hotel is small and dirty. Perhaps my father will let you stay with us."

I don't know what it was—maybe just a germ of common sense fighting to crawl through my eagerness and warn me—but for a second I felt a bright, sharp premonition of danger. I wanted to say, "Oh, no, you don't!" and tell her I was wise to what happened to careless guys who accepted her kind of invitation. But I didn't say it.

Instead, I whispered, "Swell! That would be swell!"

She slid closer. "I think it would be very nice, too," she said softly—oh, so softly! And then I stopped the car. What the hell—it was so easy, so natural. I just took her into my arms and shaped my lips to hers. I felt her slim little body throbbing under my hands, and her breasts pushing hard against me. And the low, purring sound that filled the car was not what I thought it was. It wasn't the heater. It came from deep within her—the sound a kitten makes when it is very warm and contented.

It was after midnight when we got to Roseen's house. There hadn't been another house along the road for five miles or more—nothing but deep black woods, with the rain pounding down in a wild fury. We stopped now, and I gave the house a leery look. It wasn't too inviting, what I could see of it in the dark. It looked old as the hills. The rain had flooded the yard, and the ancient building appeared to rise out of a boundless swamp.

But there was a light burning in one of the downstairs windows, and that looked good to me after so many miles of forsaken road. And Roseen's hand was warm in mine as she said, "Come! We'll ask my father if you may stay!"

Her father—she introduced him as Felcher Davis—got up off a shabby old divan and stood scowling at me. He was a big man, heavy-bones with an abundance of flesh, though not remarkably tall. His eyes were small and black and set deep in fat, and he had thick gray hair that grew almost as long as a woman's.

"You name's what?" he said. His voice had the breathlessness of a whisper, but it was a whisper you could have heard a long way off.

"Blake," I told him. "Frank Blake."

"He's an artist, father, and wants to paint my picture," Roseen said, smiling.

The old man looked at me a while, then shrugged and sat down again. "He can stay if you want him to," was all he said.

The girl's hand touched mine, and she led me to the door. When I looked back, Felcher Davis was still sitting there like a bloated gnome in the yellow light of an oil-lamp that needed cleaning.

"You must be tired," Roseen whispered. "Come!"

That was an old house! What little furniture it contained was about ready to disintegrate. The carpets were so threadbare you could see the floor through them. But I wasn't interested in the house. Not with Roseen beside me, showing me my room, telling me softly that her room was right next to it along the hall—with a connecting door.

"The door is locked on my side, Mr. Blake. You see?" Smiling, she steered my hand to the knob and, and, yes, it was locked. "But maybe it will not always be locked," she whispered. "Especially if I am sure my father is not listening. . . ." Melting into my arms, she tipped her lovely head back, with her eyes shut and her red lips parted for a kiss. When she slipped out of my room a little while later, I didn't think the connecting door would be locked for long.

I pulled my pajamas out of my suitcase and got into them, wishing the room were a little less gloomy. It smelled of dust, age, and disuse. There was no curtain at the window, and the glass rattled every time a gust of rain struck it. The wall-paper was damp and stained, the bed a prodigious old four-poster that could have accommodated three of me without any crowding.

Anyhow, I went to bed and tried to sleep, but couldn't. The rain beat against the house. The wind howled. I heard a door slam shut downstairs.

Curiosity pulled me out of bed, to the window, and I saw Roseen's father prowling out to the road. Where, I wondered, was he going at this time of night?

Just for the hell of it I tried the connecting door, but it was still locked. So I crawled back into bed.

I was over-tired, I guess. Or else very emotionally worked up. Anyway, I was a long time getting to sleep, and then did some dreaming. In fact, I rode a galloping nightmare!

In this nightmare I was stark naked and wandering down a long, dark hall. Not just an ordinary hall, but a black tunnel that had no ending and was filled with a strange assortment of sounds and shapes. Some of the shapes were cats. White cats. They walked along with me, rubbing against my legs. One of them leaped to my shoulders and purred softly against the curve of my neck—a pleasant sensation, warm and thrilling, that did something to the temperature of my blood.

I heard a lot of whispering, a lot of feline sounds that seemed disturbingly human. There was no end to the tunnel. I just kept on walking, on and on, until the eeriness of the place took hold of me and I was terrified. Then I ran. I ran away from the cats. I kicked and screamed at them, got hold of the one on my neck and flung it against the tunnel wall.

I ran until I woke up, and when that happened I wasn't in bed any more but in the middle of the room, throwing my arms around like a madman. I was naked and drenched with sweat, and the echoes of my screams still lived in the darkness around me.

I was afraid of the dark. I fished a match out of my trousers and lit the lamp on the old-fashioned bureau, then sat on the bed until my body stopped shaking. There was a queer, throbbing sensation in my neck, where I carry a strawberry birth-mark the size of a quarter. I got out my shaving mirror and looked at the mark. It seemed redder.

But then common sense won out. Calling myself a fool, I went back to bed and slept like a babe. When I woke up, my watch read nine-thirty and the room was full of sunlight.

I got dressed and went downstairs and found everything laid out for my breakfast—scrambled eggs, toast, coffee, a pot of marmalade. The food was only lukewarm, and there was a note propped against the salt-shaker.

"Father and I must go to work," it said. "Please make yourself at home. I look forward with great longing to your company this evening." It was sighed, "Roseen."

Queer people, I thought, but generous!

Well, I hung around. If she had to work days, I'd paint her picture in the evenings. I thought about it a lot—how I'd paint her. If I could get her to pose for me against the drab, musty background of my room, her white young body glowing with life against those deathlike shadows . . . what a picture! I thought about it a lot. Would she consent to bare her body to a stranger?

I went up to my room, set up an easel, and went to work on the background. Then I got restless. That old house was too still, too empty. I was jittery again, and went prowling around to reassure myself there was nothing to be afraid of.

It had no right to be still standing, that house. Its timbers were rotten. There were gaps in the walls and floors through which rats and other crawly things probably roamed at will. I tried to open some of the windows, and couldn't. When I looked closer to find out *why* I couldn't, I found they were nailed shut.

About eight o'clock it got dark.

I was sprawled out on a couch in the kitchen, tired and half asleep—though why I should have been tired after doing nothing all day I don't know—when all at once I sensed something beside me. I hadn't heard anything come in, but something was there. I opened my eyes, and at that moment a low voice whispered my name and a pair of eager red lips closed over my own. Roseen!

What a greeting! What a way to come home! There she was on her knees beside the couch, with her arms curled around my neck and those hot red lips of hers scalding my mouth with a kiss that sent fever-flashes through me.

She must have come home from work *and* changed, because she wasn't wearing any ordinary house-dress or work-dress. The gown she wore belonged on some midwest belle of a century ago, when on special occasions they bravely showed the world forty-nine percent of their beautiful bosoms and you wondered how in the world they kept the dress from slipping down to reveal the rest.

Have I said Roseen was beautiful? In that gown she almost wasn't real!

I held her off at arm's length for a moment and studied her, then bent closer and touched my lips to her skin in a gesture as old-fashioned as the gown she wore. And I knew then that I was going to get that gown off her and paint her in the nude. Nothing was going to stop me.

"Where's your father?" I asked, trying to be casual.

"He won't be home until late," she declared, smiling. And added, with her mouth close to mine, "Very late, my beloved."

Well, it was easy. She knew she was beautiful. She was proud of her beauty. She *wanted* me to paint her.

We went upstairs and I showed her what I'd already done—the dark, shadowy background, the faint suggestion of an old oil-lamp burning off-stage in a corner. I explained where and how I wanted her to stand. She said softly, "Oh, it will be lovely. I know it will!" Then the old-fashioned gown rustled to the floor and there she stood, and for a few seconds I had to shut my eyes.

104   F I E L D S   O F   B L O O D

I'm no amateur, you understand. I've really studied, and have done some nudes that were highly praised by the critics. I know what the human body looks like, both male and female. I know the names of the bones and muscles in it, the textbook names for breasts and shoulders and hips and legs. But, looking at Roseen, I forgot all that. She was just—she was just Woman.

All woman, and so stunningly beautiful she stopped the beating of my heart and caused my breath to lump up, strangling me. God, what perfection! Pale shoulders curving into arms that were made for an eternal caress. Full, flawless breasts with a hint of arrogance to them, as though they too were proud of their exquisite loveliness and recklessly willing to accept any challenge. Long, glowing legs that flowed like milk from the most feminine of hips.

I stepped forward to pose her, and knew I was going to have trouble. Because she was made for love and I wanted to paint her—I really wanted to *paint* her, to get that wondrous beauty down on canvas for others to marvel at. It was a fever in me. But when I touched her, I almost lost my head. She was so warm, so alive, so—so eager.

But, by God, I posed her and went back to my brushes.

I worked perhaps an hour, and it was torture. Every time I lifted my eyes to look at her, my control threatened to explode. But I stuck to it. The painting began to take shape. I'm a fast worker once the mood is on me, and I got things done.

Then she sighed a little and came toward me, put her head against my shoulder and closed her eyes. "I am so tired, so sleepy, my beloved," she whispered. "We will rest a while now? Please?"

I remember very little after that. But I do recall turning to pick up her gown, which lay where she had dropped it an hour before. I recall the light, languid touch of her fingers as she caught my arm and drew me back. I recall standing there, staring down at her, at the red smile on her parted lips, the trembling of her upraised hands, the pale, smooth wonder of her body.

The lamp sputtered then and went out, but hell, I'd have blown it out anyway.

◊◊◊

I was a sick man when I awoke. Weak. It was broad daylight and there was a sound of rain at the window. I swung my feet out of bed and sat up, and the room began swimming. It was like a nasty hangover, only worse. My head ached. There was no strength in me. And that burning sensation was in my neck again, only worse.

I groped for my watch and couldn't believe my eyes. Eleven o'clock! I'd slept fourteen hours. Or *had* I slept? Where was Roseen?

I got up and knocked on the connecting door, opened it and walked into her room. I hadn't been in her room before, and it surprised me. The curtain was drawn at the window. The place smelled musty and dead, as though it hadn't been touched by a breath of fresh air in years. I went slowly over to the bed and saw that it hadn't been slept in. Worse, it didn't look as though it had *ever* been slept in. I pulled the covers back and they were so old, so yellow, so brittle, they fell apart in my hands.

I replaced them and hid the damage. Something told me it would be safer that way. Roseen had lovingly whispered a promise to pay me a visit in *my* room, but I hadn't been invited to cross that threshold into *hers*. There might be a difference.

I went downstairs and, as before, my breakfast was laid out in the kitchen. The note this time was shorter. "Darling," it read, "I shall not live until I am with you again tonight." I wondered whether the old man had read it and, if so, what he thought about it.

After eating I felt better and went upstairs to work on the painting again. I worked until mid-afternoon, fighting off a weakness that was at times almost overpowering. I finished the background.

It occurred to me then that I ought to build a crate for the picture. Otherwise, when I left here, it might be banged up in the car on those bad backwoods roads. I went through the kitchen and down a flight of decayed steps into the cellar, in search of tools and some wood. Right away I began to feel uneasy.

There was an odor in that cellar. I tried to tell myself it came from the damp dirt floor, but it was not that kind of odor. I poked around, getting uneasier by the minute. The cellar was a gloomy hole filled with refuse and the remains of discarded furniture. There were two small windows, high up against the ceiling, covered with cobwebs.

Something *lived* down here. The odor was a dead giveaway. An animal of some sort, or several of them. I suddenly remembered the cats that had pursued me in my nightmare. Maybe that hadn't been a dream, after all. But if there were cats in the house, why hadn't I seen them upstairs?

I searched the cellar thoroughly, but if there were cats in it—or any other breed of animals—I couldn't find a trace of them. Just that stifling smell. When my jitters began to get the best of me I went back upstairs. An hour or so later it began to rain, and I had to light some lamps.

I was in the parlor when Roseen came, and as before I didn't hear a sound until she was suddenly there before me. She wore her party dress again. Getting up off the divan, I put my hands on her shoulders, stared at her, and said softly, "You make less noise than anyone I've ever known. How do you get around? Do you float?"

Her red lips laughed at me, and she put an end to my questioning by kissing me. That was answer enough! With her gorgeous body pressed against mine and my arms around her, I lost all interest in quiz programs. After a while I drew her to the divan.

"Tonight," I said, "we'll finish the painting." The mere thought of having her pose for me again put a blow-torch in my blood-stream. Her slim, white body against the musty shadows of that upstairs room . . . her mouth smiling at me . . . her warm eyes mocking me as I posed her . . . Tonight, with the rain beating against the windows, I would get something more than art into my picture. I'd get mood. It would be a picture to drive men crazy. It would make me famous.

And yet, even though the artist in me was wild with eagerness, something else in me whispered an eerie warning. This house, the odor in the cellar, the decayed bedroom next to mine . . . it all added up to a mystery that grew more sinister every moment. Who was this girl Roseen? Why did she and her father live in such a place? Where did they go in the daytime?

I could get an answer to that last question, at least, by asking her. "Look," I said. "Did you just get home from work?"

She nodded, smiling.

"But surely you don't work in that dress!"

"I came in quietly," she whispered, "and changed into this just for you. Am I not beautiful in it, my beloved?"

"But," I protested. "I didn't hear you come in. I—"

Snuggling closer, she took my arms and wrapped them around her. What could I do? With the lamplight glowing so wonderfully on the pale satin of her shoulders, and her parted lips silently pleading to be kissed . . . hell, the questions could wait.

Suddenly, from the adjoining room, I heard the voice of her father urgently calling her name. "Roseen! Come here! Quickly!"

The girl squirmed from my embrace and sprang to her feet. Evidently her father's tone of voice was significant. Without even a glance at me, she sped across the parlor and disappeared.

I stood there scowling. The eerie silence of this old house was such that any sudden outcry bred tension. *I* felt tense. Cat-footing across to the doorway, I looked into the room beyond. Roseen and Felcher Davis stood together at a window that faced the road, peering out in silence as though afraid of something.

I strode to a parlor window and looked out, too. It was dark as sin out there and raining harder than ever. The road was invisible. I could hear trees tossing in the wind but couldn't see them. Then I saw a light.

It appeared to be a flashlight approached through the stormy dark. Another one blinked on behind it, then a third. Closer they came. I saw the shapes of men behind them. We were evidently about to entertain callers!

Suddenly I was aware of a movement behind me, and swung around. Nothing was there, yet I had an uncanny feeling that something had rushed past me with incredible speed. Yes, by God! A strand of spider-web in the doorway to the adjoining room was fluttering like a pennant in a gale!

Striding for the second time to that doorway I saw with amazement that the adjoining room was now empty. Roseen and her father were gone. But in order to leave that room they must have passed within a yard of me, and I had heard nothing. True, I had sensed a sudden swift movement, but . . .

Someone was thumping noisily on the front door. That was a sound I could understand. Almost with relief I strode to the door and opened it.

They were men and there were five of them, grizzled, earthy-looking fellows apparently from the village, as solid and real as the rugged midwest countryside that had spawned them. They filed in silently, and the last one slammed the door shut to blot out the wind and rain. Ringing me, they looked me over before their leader, a barrel-chested, black-bearded fellow as tall as I and a good fifty pounds heavier, came a step closer and said, "Who are you? What you doin' here?"

I hadn't the slightest idea what they might want, but it seemed wise to humor them. "My name is Frank Blake," I said. "I'm an artist. I came here to paint some pictures."

They exchanged looks. Then a man at the rear, near the door, pushed forward and dumped something at my feet.

Wide-eyed, I took a sudden backward step. The thing was a dog, and it was dead.

"You know anythin' about this?" the fellow demanded, scowling at me.

"What—do you mean?"

"Dog's been kilt. Third one this week, mister. Not shot nor run over, but *sucked*. Look at it."

Sucked. It was an ugly word but descriptive. And accurate. I looked closer and shuddered. There was a small gash in the animal's throat; no other mark on its body anywhere. Why did my hand go suddenly, involuntarily, to the mark on my own throat?

"Dog was kilt near here," the fellow snarled. "Got yellow mud on its feet and under its belly. Only yellow mud in miles is right close to this place." He suddenly thrust his face close to mine. *"What you doin' in this house, mister?"*

"I told you! Painting!"

"Painting' what?"

"Now look here," I said. "If you think I'm killing your dogs, you—"

"No decent man would live in this house."

"I tell you—"

"Used to be mighty queer things go on around here when old man Davis and his daughter was alive," the leader of the group said darkly. "More than dogs was kilt then. The year before they died—the worst year—babies took to dyin' all too frequent. No one's lived in this house since that time, mister. We think you better not stir things up. You better git."

I stared at him. "They—died?" I muttered. "Davis and his daughter *died?* What are you talking about? Who said they were dead?"

"Been dead seven years, mister." He glanced at his companions. "They died hard, but they're dead."

"You're crazy. Why, they were here in this room just minutes ago!"

They looked at me. Just looked. Not a word was uttered, and the rattle of wind-driven rain against the windows was strangely loud in that tense stillness. Suddenly I couldn't stand their stares any longer.

"By God, I'll show you!" I shouted. "I've been painting the girl's picture. You wait here. I'll get it!"

I barged upstairs to my bedroom and got the picture and took it down to them. I propped it on the divan. "There!" I said. "Is that Roseen Davis or isn't it?"

They stared at the painting. It was almost finished and was so beautiful it took your breath away. There she stood, white as an alabaster statue, every gorgeous, flowing line of her accented by the background of shadows against which she stood. Her lips curved in that inviting smile, her arrogant young bosom glowingly lovely, her hips and legs so smooth, so soft, so warmly alive that it made my blood pound just to look at her.

But these men didn't see what I saw. The picture didn't warm *their* blood. They suddenly backed away from it and began muttering. They gave me quick, wide-eyed stares that said they were afraid of me, afraid of *it*.

One of them croaked, "Let's get out of here, fellers!"

They fled, and I was alone.

They must be crazy, I thought. Closing the door, I carried the painting back upstairs, set it on the easel, and stood there admiring it.

I'd been there about five minutes, I guess, when the door creaked behind me. Startled, I turned—and there stood Roseen.

"Is it that beautiful?" she whispered, smiling.

I grinned at her. "Yes, it's that beautiful," I said. "But it's not alive. I'll take the original." Putting my hands on her white shoulders, I said then with a frown, "Where the devil did you get to? I had visitors."

"Visitors?"

"Some men from the village."

"Oh," she said, nodding. "The queer ones, no doubt. You must not be afraid of them."

"They told me—"

But she wasn't having any more of my questions. Her arms went around my neck, warm and soft as kittens, and she put her mouth against mine to silence me. After that I didn't care what the villagers had told me. To hell with them.

"You said," she whispered, "we would finish the picture tonight."

I nodded. After moving the easel into position I stared at her while the fancy gown rustled to the floor and she took her place in the shadows. Then I went to work. As before, it was the hardest work I'd ever done. The nearness of her set my blood to boiling. Every trembling nerve in my body ached to be loving her, not painting her, and I grudged every moment I had to stand there smearing paint on the canvas. Yet I had to have that picture!

Except for the wind and rain, there wasn't a sound in the old house as I worked. That helped; it enabled me to concentrate. By midnight I was finished.

"Come and look at it," I said.

Gliding to my side, she studied my work and voiced a little sigh of happiness. "It is so like me I am almost jealous of it," she murmured. "Perhaps you will love it more than you love me."

I laughed a little and reached for her. She stepped back. Her white body was etched against the glow of the lamp for a moment, then suddenly the room was in darkness. I waited with my heart pounding and my arms outstretched. In the dark her lips found mind and she slipped into my embrace.

I don't remember much of what happened after that. I don't recall going to sleep. I don't know how much of what I dreamed was really a dream.

Anyway, I was in that long tunnel again, only it was a bigger tunnel this time, a longer one, and there was only one cat. The cat was white and beautiful, the most gorgeous creature of its kind I had ever seen. Walking along beside me into the endless dark, it rubbed against my legs, looked up at me, and purred. After a while it leaped gently to my shoulder and put its mouth against my throat.

Its mouth was warm and moist, and as the sound of its purring grew louder I began to feel drowsy. I stumbled. There was a strange weakness in me, a lassitude that blurred my vision and made it hard for me to walk. Leaning against the wall of the tunnel, to rest, I became aware of an odor, a familiar odor, that reminded me of a cellar somewhere.

The weakness overwhelmed me and I lost consciousness.

◊◊◊

When I awoke I was in bed, alone, and the room was murky. It must be almost morning, I thought. My watch read six-thirty. I felt weak, almost too weak to move. There was a queer burning sensation in my neck.

I lay there trying to recall what had happened after I finished the painting, but it wouldn't come back. It was all a deep, vast blur in which nothing would take shape. I seemed to remember warm lips against mine, and a soft, sweet body in my arms . . . whispers in the dark, and a pleasant purring sound of contentment, and a hot mouth pressed against my throat . . . but it was all a pattern of shadows, half forgotten already, and I was too weak not to bring it back.

The room grew darker. I didn't understand that. I looked at my watch again and struggled out of bed and dragged myself to the window. The moon was up! In God's name what had I done?— slept through a whole night and day, and into the beginning of another night? There could be no other explanation!

Suddenly, from the deeper darkness of the woods at the edge of the yard, a shape emerged. A flashlight winked, went out again. The shape prowled forward, followed by others. Remembering the villagers who had come last night to question me, I sensed trouble.

The prowlers separated as they approached the house. For a while I tried to follow them with my eyes, but it was like striving to follow dim ghosts through a dream. I reached for my clothes.

That frightening weakness took hold of me again, and getting dressed required every ounce of my strength. Opening the door, I went along the hall to the stairs.

I smelled smoke. I heard a voice outside yelling triumphantly, "There, by God, that will do it!" Then I heard a noise like paper rattling, only it wasn't paper; it was the old, dry timbers of the house being consumed by flames? A cloud of strangling smoke poured up the narrow stair-well.

"They've set fire to the house!" I muttered. And I hated them. God, how I hated them! This house had become a part of me, or I of it. It meant hours of supreme bliss with a beautiful girl. It meant strange journeys through that long, dark tunnel into a land of dreams. And they'd set a torch to it! Damn them! Damn their rotten souls to hell!

I raged along the hall, cursing the smoke, the flames that leaped up to engulf me. The flames beat me back to the door of my room and I knew suddenly that I'd be trapped if I didn't get out of there. This house was old. It would go up like old paper. I snatched my painting and went stumbling through the smoke to the stairs.

As I groped down them, a sound poured up from below, knifing through the noise of the fire. A shrill, keening sound, a scream like that of a wounded animal. The kind of scream you hear at night, sometimes, in a zoo or a circus—where the big cats are. It shrilled around me as I stumbled across the parlor to the front door.

I got the door open and fell across the porch, picked myself and my painting up and crawled to the steps, crawled down them and across the yard. Behind me the house was an inferno, hurling out heat. When at last I was safely out of the heat, I turned and looked back . . . just in time to see a white blur, a lean white shape that looked like a giant cat, leap out through a cellar window.

For an instant the shape seemed to hang suspended in air, so tremendous was its leap. Then it flashed along the ground and vanished into the woods.

I don't remember anything else. I passed out.

When I came to, there was no house. It was daylight, and raining, and the cellar of the old place was just a grim hole in the earth, filled with black, smoldering debris. I walked around it.

After a while I walked over to my car to see if it was damaged. The paint was blistered and the tires looked queer, full of lumps, but it would run. I got into it—with my painting of Roseen—and drove away. I drove all day and half the night before stopping.

My doctor can't figure me out. "The weakness," he says, "is due to loss of blood. You've lost an awful lot of blood somehow, yet I can't find a break in the skin anywhere. Can you explain it?"

Sure I can, but not to him. Not to anyone. No one's going to call me crazy and insist on a battery of mental tests. I'll get over the weakness, Doc says. It will take time and rest, but after a while I'll be myself again. "Provided," he warns, "what caused this condition is not repeated."

I wonder about that, especially at night. She didn't die in the fire. I saw her escape—I'm sure of it. And maybe she'll find me. Maybe I'll even go back there, so she can find me without too much trouble.

Nights I sit and stare at the picture, then shut my eyes and see her standing there in the shadowy bedroom of that old house, white and warm and beautiful . . . with a smile of invitation and promise on her red lips, and her arms outstretched. I can hear her whispering, "Come with me, my beloved. Come with me . . ."

And maybe I will.

Yes.

If I look at the painting long enough, maybe I will.

Hugh B. Cave, a prolific writer for the fantasy, suspense, detective, and adventure pulps, is the author of many novels, including *Death Stalks the Night, Lucifer's Eye, Legion of the Dead,* and the collection *Murgunstrumm and Others,* which won a World Fantasy Award for best collection.

Once bitten, twice shy. . . .

Death on the Mississippi

BY WENDI LEE AND TERRY BEATTY

Sam Clemens stood at the window of his tiny stateroom and took a deep breath of Mississippi river air. From his vantage point, he could see the small town of Muscatine, Iowa. People were crowded on the banks of the dock, pointing to the river steamboat *Minneapolis* and murmuring excitedly.

A sharp rap at his door startled him.

"Mr. Clemens?" someone, probably the first mate, called out. "Would you like to go ashore?" Close to half an hour ago, the *Minneapolis,* bound for the Twin Cities from New Orleans, had shored up for the night.

"No," Clemens replied a bit too quickly. He could hear voices through the thin door of his cabin, as if the first mate were conferring with someone else. Through the open window, a gentle spring breeze came in off the river and circulated through his room. Clemens could see only part of the river town, but it looked none the worse for wear, in fact, it seemed to have grown a great deal since he, as a lad of eighteen, had worked as a printer for his brother's newspaper, *The Muscatine Journal.*

"Sam?" a gruff voice demanded. "You in there, Sam? Come on out, you old goat."

He wondered if his ears were working correctly. "Coop? You're still living here?" He took the length of the cabin in two large strides but, upon clutching the door handle, froze. Suspicion quickly replaced the pleasure he had found in hearing Jim Cooperman's gravely voice. It probably was his old friend, then again, it could be a trick. Thirty years ago, Clemens had met a man, if he could be called such, who induced such fear in the now legendary writer that even now he could not bring himself to leave his cabin and visit the town of his youth.

Coop pounded on his door again, his gravely voice calling out for Clemens to open up. "Are you ill, Sam? Should I send for a doctor?"

"No."

"Then why won't you come out and meet your public? The good people of Muscatine are gathered on the riverside, waiting to catch a glimpse of the famous Mark Twain. Don't disappoint them."

Clemens went back to the porthole and peered through it. Old and young alike milled around the banks, men and women and children, talking to each other as they waited patiently to cheer the arrival of the beloved writer.

He thought quickly. "Coop, what I need is a bottle of whiskey."

Despite the warm day, Sam felt a sudden chill working its way slowly from the middle of his back to the base of his neck. He slumped against the door, undecided.

◊◊◊

Young Sam Clemens sat on his front steps, looking down at the dark-stained rough-hewn wood of which his current home was made. The place was more a cabin than a house, and in comparison to the grand brick home that sat directly across the road, it seemed more a shack. The Mississippi rolled by, only a few hundred feet away, and the smell of it made him long to get back on a riverboat and leave this one-horse town behind him. Dawn was breaking, but Sam had no enthusiasm for this new day.

It had been almost a year since he had been summoned to

Muscatine to assist his older brother Orion in running the news-paper. He had thought he had come here to be a reporter, but so far he had spent most of his time in the print shop, setting type and running the presses. This was not the sort of journalism career he had in mind for himself. And it might not have been so bad if only Orion had any money to pay him, but the newspaper had yet to make a profit. Working like a dog for no pay, and still living with his mother and brothers, when what he really wanted to do was travel and see the world—this was not the life Sam Clemens wanted to lead. In fact, if it hadn't been for Gabrielle, he probably would have packed up and left months ago. Still, how was a penniless would-be reporter supposed to impress the daughter of one of the wealthiest men in town? Sam could not imagine himself in a more hopeless situation.

The sound of wood being cleanly split had been coming from around the back of the house for the last half an hour, but now it had stopped. Henry Clemens, his shirt sleeves rolled up, his unruly hair hanging down over his sweaty brow, came out from around the corner and sat on the step next to his older brother. "You look as if you've been thinkin' too much, Sam." His shirt was wet with the sweat of handling an ax. "Maybe you could do a little work around here for a change," he said with a sly wink. "Maybe bring in the wood I just finished splitting. That is, if you have the time 'fore you go off to be Orion's galley slave for another day."

Sam didn't reply for a minute, taking in the sounds of the crick-ets and frogs on the banks of the river. The sun shone bright on the morning dew. "I've been thinking about moving on, Henry."

Henry leaned forward quickly, a startled look on his face. "You can't do that to Orion. He needs you. Heck, nobody else would work for him for free." He paused for a moment, raised his eye-brows and said, "And what about Gabrielle Krueger?"

Sam allowed himself a rueful laugh. "She has Albert to comfort her." Gabrielle was the eighteen-year-old daughter of Hermann Krueger, a wealthy businessman, and despite her Germanic back-ground and the bulky build of her father, she looked for all the world like a china doll. Her fine dark hair, her porcelain skin and sky-blue eyes were enough in themselves to make Sam's heart skip a beat, but add in the most angelic voice he had ever heard, and you had the reason why Sam stayed here, even though he had every other reason in the world to be moving on.

Although both Sam and a young man named Albert Kessler had been wooing her for almost a year, Gaby hadn't expressed a preference for either suitor. Sam couldn't imagine why she would ever choose him over Albert. It broke his heart to even think it, but he had nothing to offer her, and perhaps it would be for the best to step aside and let her be happy with Albert. Sam ran a hand through his thick, unruly hair. "Henry, I sometimes think I'm meant for something more than this . . . this town. Orion promised to let me write for the paper, but I've been here a year and he still hasn't given me much of a chance."

Henry laughed. "He published those letters you sent here about your travels out East, didn't he?"

"Of course he did, Henry, but that was before he asked me to come here to work."

"I guess there's just been nothing here to write about, Sam. Orion'll give you a chance when something worthwhile comes up."

Sam had to admit that Henry had a point. "The most exciting thing that's happened this year was when I happened upon that lunatic with the knife."

Henry frowned. "You still insist that really happened?'

"Of course it happened," Sam replied. "It was on a Sunday, as I was out for a walk in the fields just up river. From out of nowhere, this lunatic appeared before me, extracted a butcher knife from his boot and proposed to carve me up with it unless I acknowledged him to be the only son of the Devil."

"Sounds mighty like one of your made-up stories, Samuel," Henry said, a half smile and raised eyebrows underscoring his skepticism.

"I did not make this up, Henry. The man held a butcher knife on me! I tried to compromise on an acknowledgment that he was the only member of the family I had met; but that did not satisfy him; he wouldn't have any half measures; I must say he was the sole and only son of the Devil—and he whetted his knife on his boot. It didn't seem worthwhile to make trouble about a little thing like that; so I swung round to his view of the matter and saved my skin whole."

"I still say it sounds like one of your stories." Henry's tone made it clear that he wasn't going to let his older brother pull his leg *this* time.

But Sam hadn't invented this tale, and what he hadn't mentioned to Henry was that he had followed the madman at a distance, curious to discover from where he had come. The stranger led him up onto the bluffs that overlooked the river, then crawled like an animal into a hole in the ground on the side of the bluff. Sam's natural curiosity had prompted him to return to the bluff the next day, but the whole incident had put such a fright into him, that he could not bring himself to investigate this strange happening any further.

A hoarse shout from Jim Cooperman caused the Clemens brothers to look up the road in the direction of town. Coop was the *Journal* reporter who wrote most of the social news—births, engagements, marriages, and deaths were his territory. His face told Sam that he was not bringing good news.

"Sam!" Coop said breathlessly, stopping in front of the porch and resting his hands on bent knees. "Orion wants you at the newspaper immediately. There's been a murder."

"Deaths are your department, Coop," Sam replied soberly as he stood to face his friend.

Coop shook his head. "Sam, it's Gabrielle."

Sam stood there, staring at Coop, not wanting to accept this as the truth, feeling his heart pound so in his chest it seemed like it would explode. Fighting back tears, he heard his own voice in a clipped monotone say, "Tell me what happened."

"They found her body about an hour ago, up on the bluffs, just up river. Don't know how she was killed, but the undertaker says he's never seen anything like it."

Without a word, Sam began an easy run toward the newspaper office, a winded Coop following at a slower pace. Henry stayed behind on the porch of their house.

Orion Clemens was seated at his oak rolltop desk, his elbows resting on its beaded leather top, his head in his hands, when Sam burst into his office. There was just a moment of silence, then Orion looked up at his younger brother. "I'm sorry you had to hear it this way, Samuel. They've taken the murderer into custody. He's over at the jail."

It was hard for Sam to talk with the lump that had formed in his throat, but he forced himself. "Why do you need me?"

"The killer won't talk to any of our reporters. Only to you." Orion took his pipe from a compartment in the rolltop. He leaned back in his chair, tamping loose tobacco into the bowl of the pipe.

Sam shook his head. Everything was happening so fast, it was hard for him to comprehend. "Why would the killer want to talk to me? If you put me in the same room with him, I may kill him myself."

Coop and Orion exchanged glances over Sam's head. Some silent signal had been given and Coop took over. "The man being held is Albert Kessler."

"Kessler." Sam frowned. "But he wouldn't have killed her. He loved her."

Coop and Orion avoided Sam's direct gaze. "Sometimes there is little difference between love and hate," Orion intoned. "Gaby hadn't yet chosen between you two, but her mother told the sheriff that she was close to a decision. Albert was the last one to see her. He claims that they had a picnic on that bluff. They argued, and she chose not to accompany him back to town."

Sam rubbed the back of his neck. He was still reeling from the news that Gaby was dead.

"Will you go see him?" Coop asked.

"No one could blame you if you turned down the offer," Orion added. "I can get someone else to do the story."

Sam looked up. Here was his golden opportunity, handed to him with a vicious twist, making the triumph taste bitter. Sam wanted nothing more than to grieve for his beloved, and was tempted to reject the offer. Still, doing *something* about the murder would be better than sitting by the river and grieving uselessly for Gabrielle, even if it was only writing the story.

"Sam?" Orion looked at his brother, worry lines etching his brow.

Sam picked up a tablet of paper and a pencil from Orion's desk. "I've got to get to the jail." He left his brother and friend behind.

Muscatine was not a place where crime ran rampant. The jail was small, with only four cells. Usually empty, each cell had an occupant this day, but Sam paid not a whit of attention to three of them, drunkards or drifters, no doubt. It was only Albert Kessler that Sam wanted to see. The sheriff was not in, but the jailer, a short, squat man, knew Sam and let him in to visit with Albert.

The first thing people noticed when they met Albert were his startlingly blue eyes; then they took in the dark blond mustache, muttonchops, and his pomaded blond hair parted on one side. Sam had overheard many a young woman whisper to her companion about Albert Kessler's good looks. Sam had gotten to know his rival slightly over the last six months and found him to be pleasant enough, if a little short on imagination. He was the bookkeeper at the general store and hoped to open his own mill one day.

In the cell, Albert sat on the edge of his cot, his shoulders hunched, his hands clasped together as if in prayer, his head down.

"Albert?" Sam stood just inside the closed and locked door. "I heard you wanted to see me."

The man looked up, a tortured expression on his face. "I didn't do it, Sam. I loved her. Why would I want to kill her?"

"Why did you ask for me?"

Albert stood up and shrugged. Despite his sedentary job, he was muscular. He leaned against the wall, the small, high window above throwing a halo of light on his crown. "If I can convince you of my innocence, maybe I can convince the court."

"That's all?" Sam asked, a steel edge to his voice.

Albert gestured impatiently. "Let me ask you something. Why would I kill her? What would I gain by killing the girl I love?"

"Maybe you were jealous," Sam suggested. "Maybe she had made up her mind to marry me, and she spurned you."

Albert cocked his head to the side. "Had she?"

Sam shook his head. "If so, I had not been informed."

Albert took a step toward him. "I want you to find the killer. I want whoever did this to Gaby to pay for it."

Sam raised his eyebrows, but said nothing.

"Oh, I know what you are thinking. What if I did it? Fine. If you discover that I am guilty, then so be it. But I think you know in your heart that I didn't kill her. You felt the same way about her that I did. If I could have killed her, so could you." Albert slumped to the floor, his elbows resting on his knees. He looked up at Sam one more time. "You want to find out what really happened to her more than anyone, including her parents."

Sam could see Albert's point of view. Gaby's parents were good people, but if someone came forward to say that Albert was the last one seen with Gaby, and the sheriff had Albert locked up on that charge, Hermann Krueger was complacent enough not to ask any questions about guilt or innocence.

"All right," Sam conceded, sitting on the cot, his tablet and pencil at the ready. "I'll look into Gaby's murder. I want the real killer. I've been asked to write an article for the *Journal* on the murder. So since I'm here, I'll start with you. Why did you leave her there alone on the bluff?"

"We went for a picnic supper and to watch the sun set over the river. I'd saved enough money to buy the mill, and I was ready to propose to her." Albert snuck a sheepish look at Sam. "When I asked if she would give her hand to me in marriage, Gaby didn't answer. I cajoled, pleaded, and pressed her to accept, but she just grew quiet. 'It's Sam, isn't it?' I asked. 'You're in love with him, not me.'"

"You were angry, then?" Sam asked.

Albert shook his head. "I was puzzled. Why was she being so evasive? I knew about you, of course. Then she said something unusual. 'It's not Sam. I've met someone else. In fact, it's funny that you brought me up here, because I met him right on this spot.'"

"She didn't mention a name?"

Albert shook his head. "I was too distraught that my plans were for nothing. I didn't ask. She helped me gather up the picnic items and pack them away. Then she gave me a peck on the cheek and declined to accompany me back to town."

"So you left her behind?"

Albert turned his face toward Sam. It was difficult to look at the accused man's eyes. "She insisted. I didn't feel right about it, but she told me she was meeting her new suitor there in a few minutes. If only I had been more firm, if I had stayed until he arrived. Maybe—"

"Don't dwell on what ifs," Sam said sharply. "You had no idea what would happen." Something eluded Sam, some bit of information, maybe something that would tie into Gaby's murder. After promising Albert that he would do all he could, he called for the jailer.

Before he could leave the jailhouse, Hermann and Gerta Krueger entered. Gaby had resembled her mother a great deal: slender and graceful, with high cheekbones and sleek dark hair. It was hard to imagine that Hermann Krueger had had anything to do with Gaby's existence. He was a large, rotund man. His nose was a shapeless mass in the middle of his red face, surrounded by two small eyes and thick lips. At the moment, his small eyes were fixed on Sam and his face was almost purple.

"What are you doing here?" Krueger asked in a cold voice, thick with a German accent.

"I'm writing an article for the *Journal*." Sam was having a hard time looking at the Kruegers. Mrs. Krueger seemed to have aged twenty years over the last few hours. Mr. Krueger apparently wanted someone, anyone, to blame for his daughter's death.

Krueger turned to his wife. "I told you, Gerta, that she would come to no good with two suitors such as this. One responsible for her death and the other making a circus out of it for his place of work."

Sam spoke up. "Mr. Krueger, I was just talking to Albert. He told me that Gabrielle had another suitor. Do you know anything about him, perhaps his name?"

All the color drained from Krueger's face for a moment. Then he reached over and grabbed Sam by his shirtfront, pulling him within an inch of his face. "He is lying. My daughter would never have been alone with a man who had not paid proper court." Tossing Sam aside, Krueger turned to the jailer. "I am here at the sheriff's request."

"Have a seat, Mr. Krueger," the jailer said, indicating a bench for the grieving couple to rest on. "He's out at the, uh, morgue."

Sam straightened his collar as Krueger brushed by him. He was about to leave when Gerta Krueger plucked his sleeve. "For what it's worth," the mother of the murdered girl whispered, "I don't think Albert has done such a thing. And about the man you say she was waiting for—"

"Gerta!" the strong voice ordered.

Mrs. Krueger's breath caught in her throat. She was so bird-like, Sam had the urge to protect her from her husband. She blinked rapidly, perhaps in an effort to hold back tears, and went back to what she was trying to tell him. "She told me there was someone else, but she didn't give me a name." With that, she fluttered over to her husband's side and Sam made a hasty exit before the sheriff returned.

The sun had just cleared the treetops by the time Sam left the jail. The morgue was located at the back of the undertaker's building. Sam knocked and was immediately let in by Ned, Dr. Whitacre's assistant.

"What are you doing here?" Ned asked. He was only sixteen, but was already learning the trade of undertaker.

Sam explained his reason for coming. Ned scratched his head, then led the way back to the lab. The body of a young woman was covered with a white sheet up to her neck. Sam held his breath at the sight. It was Gaby, or what was left of her. Dr. Whitacre looked up from his examination.

"Sam, you really shouldn't be here." He came around the slab and gently took Sam by his shoulders, propelling him out the door and into a chair.

Sam didn't realize until he was seated how weak his knees had been. He took a couple of deep breaths. "I had heard, but it didn't sink in until . . ."

Dr. Whitacre nodded sympathetically. "Yes, I don't think the Kruegers believed it until they came here to identify the body. I am sorry, Sam. I know you were courting. And so was that fellow Albert. I understand he's in jail for the murder." Dr. Whitacre walked over to a sink and rinsed his hands, then dried them. Shaking his head, he added, "But I don't understand how he could have killed her with—" Here, the doctor trailed off.

Sam prompted him. "With what, doctor? How was she killed?"

"It seems that all her blood was drained from her body. I can't understand how it happened, what kind of animal or human would do a thing like that." The doctor stared off into space for a moment, then turned back to Sam and Ned. "You see, her neck was slashed open as if by some wild animal."

The sun had set when Sam returned to his home and crawled

FIELDS OF BLOOD

into bed. He felt tired, but thoughts kept running through his head, keeping him from falling asleep. After interviewing Albert and seeing Dr. Whitacre, he had worked a full day at the paper, setting type and working the presses, trying not to let Gaby's death seem real. Sam could hear his younger brother Henry softly snoring on the other side of the room. Moonlight streamed, unbidden, through the window. Resigned to his insomnia, Sam finally got up and pulled on a pair of trousers. Stepping outside for a short walk, he heard the frogs croaking by the riverbanks and the crickets orchestrating their night music in the tall grasses.

Sam sank into deep thought, and kept walking in what he thought were aimless circles. His thoughts remained on Gaby and her untimely death. She hadn't deserved to die at such a young age or in such a violent way. The lack of blood in and around her body suggested that the creature that had killed her might have had a use for her blood. Sam shivered at the thought, recalling a childhood encounter with an old gypsy lady who had told him stories of creatures who lived only at night. They could assume, so she said, the shape of a human, wolf, or bat and they fed off the blood of the living. "You can only kill them with a stake through the heart, or by cutting off the head," she had said, her wandering eye not quite focusing on him.

Sam shook his head, half-smiling at the fanciful thought. He soon found himself standing in front of the darkened jail. He heard a bloodcurdling scream. Stumbling up the steps, he opened the outer door. He heard other men shouting inside, pleading for their lives. He tried the inner door to the office, but it was locked. Breaking the glass in the door, Sam was able to open it from the inside.

Sam was two steps inside when the door to the jail burst open. A great invisible force roared through the office, tearing chairs in half and overturning desks. The feeling of having encountered something evil kept Sam rooted to the spot.

Then it was gone as quickly as it had come. His heart in his throat, Sam made his feet move, and he found keys to the cells. Inside the jail, it was quiet, with the exception of one or two whimpers. The doors were ripped off their hinges and he knew there was no need for the keys. According to the roster by the inside door, there were still three other prisoners besides Albert Kessler. He checked the first cell, and found a man trying to claw his way out—through the far wall. When Sam put his hand on the man's shoulder, the prisoner yelped and cowered away.

"What happened, man?" Sam asked.

The man began to gibber incoherently and wrapped his arms around himself. It was the lunatic who had threatened Sam with the butcher's knife, no longer arrogant and menacing, but pathetic and helpless. "My father was here. He came to pay me a visit. Do you see what he did? Do you see?" With that, the man crumpled into a ball, whimpering.

Sam moved on to the next occupied cell. A man was sprawled half across his cot and half on the floor, his throat torn out, blood sprayed around the walls of the cell. Sam stumbled back as much from the scent of the fresh blood as from the scene. The next cell was much the same. In the final cell, Albert Kessler was slumped against a wall, his throat torn out like the others, a look of horror mingled with resignation frozen on his face. Bending over the corpse, Sam closed Albert's eyes, then thought about notifying the sheriff. He realized that the night jailer had probably gone home for a midnight supper with the missus, a tradition in a small town like this. Since the prisoners were locked up and sleeping for the night, an hour of abandonment would not be noticed.

He stood up and turned around—to face a man—if he could be called a man—dressed all in black, his hairless head covered with skin so pale and transparent that it seemed more like a living skull. The creature's eyes glowed red as fire. Trails of blood dripped down his chin.

The devil grinned at him, showing razor sharp teeth, "I see you have met my unfortunate servant. He seems to be under the delusion that he is my son. I suppose I should be flattered, but frankly I find his overzealous devotion something of an annoyance." The creature looked down and Sam followed his gaze. The lunatic servant had crawled from his cell and had wrapped his arms around his master's ankles. Looking back at Sam, the monster stroked his bloody chin with a clawlike hand, and said with a chilling laugh, "Perhaps I'll kill him, too. I haven't decided yet."

Sam fought the monster's hypnotic gaze. "You killed Gabrielle."

The lunatic looked solemn. "Killed? No. Not quite. She still lives. She'll pay you a visit some night."

Sam began to back away from the creature who stood there, laughing maniacally, as he seemed to turn into a cloud of mist. When Sam reached the door of the jailhouse, he turned and ran, praying that the thing would not come after him.

Upon reaching his front porch, Sam collapsed into a heap, breathing hard. He lay there, curled into a ball, feeling the warmth of his own tears streaming down his face. He felt a gentle hand touch his shoulder.

"Dear Samuel, there's no need to cry." It was Gabrielle's angelic voice.

Sam looked up to see her smiling down at him, whole, alive. He didn't know how this could be, but he didn't question whatever miracle it was that had brought his Gaby back to him.

"Gaby, oh, dear God, Gaby!" Sam threw his arms around her, holding her close, stroking her raven hair. It was then that he realized something was wrong. He touched her face, and her skin was cold.

"What's wrong, Samuel, don't you like me this way?" She smiled at him as he pushed away from her, a cold chill running through him. "Perhaps you'd prefer me like this." Suddenly she was no longer Gaby, but a monstrous feral creature, with leathery skin, gnarled fingers ending in hooked claws, eyes glowing red, and a mouth that opened to reveal deadly sharp fangs. She hissed and laughed all in the same breath. It was the most terrifying sound Sam had ever heard.

Sam backed away, and she came after him slowly, like an animal stalking its helpless prey. He kept walking backward, keeping the creature in his sight, and it kept after him, matching him step for step until he was behind the house.

"You can't run from me, Samuel," the monster said, a twisted smile on its hideous face, its voice a cruel parody of Gabrielle's

"I'm not running," Sam said, "just getting this." He had reached behind him and grabbed the ax Henry had used to cut wood. He lifted it in front of him, his hands shaking as he threatened the monster with it.

And suddenly it was Gaby again, young and vulnerable. "Oh,

Samuel, you don't wish to harm me." Her eyes burned into his. "I love you, Samuel. I want you to join me." She reached her hands out to him.

"You're not Gaby," Sam said through clenched teeth.

He swung the ax with all his strength he could muster, striking the creature across the neck as it surged forward, claws ready to strike, fangs bared and ready to drink deep of his blood. A high-pitched shriek came from the creature as Sam swung the ax once more, severing its head from its twisted animal body.

Sam sank to his knees, still holding the ax tight in his hands.

"Such a pity. I had hoped to enjoy her company for at least the next century." It was the skull-faced creature from the jailhouse. He stood over Gabrielle's decapitated corpse, holding her head in his clawlike hands.

Sam reared back, trying to get to his feet, holding the ax protectively in front of him. "Say away from me, or I'll kill you, too!" He shouted at the creature.

It laughed at him, "I think not, dear boy." And then there was the sound of church bells. The demon looked sharply away from Sam to see that the first rays of dawn were breaking. He looked back. "Tomorrow night, boy. Enjoy your last day of life." With that he scooped up Gabrielle's body and, sprouting great leathery wings, flew away toward the bluff.

Sam fell once more to his knees, and felt the blackness of sleep overtake him.

He was a boy again, back in Hannibal, exploring McDowell's cave with pretty little Laura Hawkins. Carrying candles, they wandered through the convoluted passageways. A cold breeze blew out the flame of Laura's candle. Sam used the flame of his own candle to relight it. Then she wasn't Laura anymore—she was Gaby, smiling, laughing and full of life, her face exquisite in the soft candlelight. And then the bats came, dozens of them, and then hundreds. They flew in a whirlwind around her as Sam tried in vain to brush them away. As quickly as they came, they disappeared, leaving no trace of Gaby.

"The demons hide in the dark," it was the old gypsy woman. She came toward him, and put a withered hand on his shoulder, "Sleeping in the day, to live only at night. In their coffins, they sleep."

A breeze made Sam's candle flicker, and for just a moment it was pitch-black in the cave. When the flame grew back, it was no longer the gypsy woman's hand on his shoulder, but the claw of the skull-faced monster. He tried to pull away, but the claw would not let go.

"Sam! Samuel."

Sam opened his eyes. His mother was bent over him, her hand on his shoulder. Henry sat nearby on his bed. Sam sat up, shaking, and ran his hand over his face. "What time is it?"

"Half past seven. Henry and I found you asleep out back. It was all we could do to get you inside and in your own bed."

Sam tried to shake the grogginess he felt from his less-than-restful sleep. "If it's seven-thirty, I'd better get down to the newspaper."

"Sam," his mother said sternly, "you will do no such thing. I don't know what your brother was thinking, asking you to look into that terrible business with poor Miss Krueger. It's clear it was too much for you. And now this awful occurrence at the jailhouse! No, I want you and Henry to stay home until things settle down. Besides, it's almost nightfall now. I have to go see about the bread I left to rise." She turned and left.

Sam turned to his younger brother, "Henry, please don't tell me it's half past seven in the evening. It can't be. I can't have slept all day."

Henry shrugged. "If you can call it sleeping. You tossed and turned and hollered so that Ma finally thought it best to wake you. You sure missed some strange goings on down at the jail. One of the prisoners got loose, killed everybody in their cells, and then ran off. They say he must've been the same fella that killed Miss Krueger."

Sam jumped out of bed and looked out the window. The sun hung low in the sky, barely touching the tip of the trees downriver. Broad strokes of the sunset's orange and pink and red were reflected in the calm Mississippi. Any other night, he'd have considered it a beautiful scene, but this night it sent a cold chill through him.

"Henry," he took his brother by the shoulders to show he meant business, "I want you to run down to the newspaper and get Coop. Tell him I want him to bring a pickax or a shovel and meet me at the bluff."

A worried frown creased Henry's brow. "Are you all right? What's this talk about getting Coop and bringing a pickax?" He shook his head. "If you want someone to go with you to the bluff, I'll volunteer."

"No, Henry. What I have to do is dangerous. If I don't come back, I don't want to be responsible for your life as well. Run as fast as you can and tell Coop to meet me."

"Can I tell him why?" Henry said.

Sam ran his fingers through his hair and glanced at the sinking sunset. "Just go. Hurry, climb out the window, so Mother won't see," he said tersely.

Henry did his bidding and Sam followed him out the window. He strode over to the woodpile. He chose a thick piece of wood and brought it over to the chopping stump. With ax in hand, he fashioned a crude but effective stake. He took both items and headed up the hill toward the bluff, racing the inevitable sunset.

There was a winding path that led to the top of the bluff, but Sam had no time for such formalities. He plowed his way through the heavy growth that covered the side of the hill, using the ax to clear the heavier growth that blocked his path, all the while resisting the urge to look over his shoulder to see how far down in the sky the sun had gone. He forced his way through a small patch of trees and bushes and came face-to-face with the lunatic.

"Go back! Leave us alone. Don't hurt my father." He threw himself at Sam, and together they tumbled to the ground. The lunatic's fists pounded at Sam's face and chest. With the blunt end of the stake, Sam struck the man a hard blow to the chin, it stunned the madman just enough to give Sam the chance to squirm out from underneath him. Sam got to his feet and kept a tight grip on the stake and the ax.

"I won't let you hurt him!" The madman shouted as he leaped at Sam. Sam quickly stepped to the side, sticking the ax handle directly in the lunatic's path. The man tripped and tumbled, his own momentum carrying him forward over the steep edge of the bluff. He twisted and turned all the way down to the muddy river water below. Sam stood at the top of the bluff, looking down, but the man's body could not be seen. Sam was sure, though, that the fellow was dead. No one could have lived through that fall.

Whatever relief Sam may have felt over dispatching the lunatic was quickly cut off, when he looked up to see the sun had nearly disappeared. Sam stumbled on through the trees to the small cave opening. Just as he reached it, dozens of bats exploded out of the hole, winging their way into the early night air. A startled Sam steeled himself, and began to wriggle into the opening, bringing the ax and the stake with him.

The cave smelled of death. There was not much light, but a candle and matches had been left near the opening of the cave and Sam used them. In the dimness, he could see that the cave was not very big, but it was large enough to hold a coffin. Next to the rectangular box was Gaby's decapitated body and Sam almost dropped his weapons when he saw it. His heart crept up to his throat as he gazed at what was left of her. He heard a creak. The lid of the coffin was opening. He began to shake, wondering how he was going to fight the dreadful thing inside.

The demon from the night before sat up and turned his head to greet Sam with a terrible smile. "I see that I do not have to go searching for you tonight. You have found me quite nicely—though I don't recall inviting you. And I see that you came alone. That is probably just as well," he said conversationally as he rose to his full height, "It is such a difficulty when an intended victim convinces the entire village that they should accompany him." He casually brushed cemetery dirt off of his clothing. Sam found that his feet were rooted to the spot where he stood. He wondered if it was his own fear, or some invisible power that this creature had over him.

Sam found the strength to move. He put the candle down and brandished the ax, cleaving the air where the creature had been a moment ago. A chilling laugh filled the cave. "That toy of yours will do you no good, young sir. You are mine now."

The creature lunged for him, fangs bared, claws going for his throat, and he made a terrible unearthly sound that almost paralyzed Sam. The monster's cold and bony claws sank into Sam's shoulder, causing him to drop the stake and ax as he struggled for his life. The unearthly creature emitted a feral growl, his deadly fangs too close for comfort. Sam could smell the monster's fetid breath.

Suddenly, the creature stiffened and howled, backing away from Sam. The monster began clawing at his back. As he turned around, Sam could see a pickax buried between the creature's shoulder blades.

"Sam!" Coop's voice came as a welcome relief. He could see Coop's figure outlined in the cave entrance.

Keeping the image of Gaby in the forefront of his mind, Sam retrieved the weapons he'd dropped, brought the stake up and, using the blunt side of the ax as a hammer, drove it into the demon's chest. The screech ended in a gurgling, but still the creature struggled to free itself. The demon's claws lashed out, barely missing Sam's throat and scraping his cheek. Sam held on, forcing the stake deeper and deeper into its chest cavity until the creature could struggle no more.

Once they had clambered back outside, Sam asked, "How did you find me?"

Coop smiled, but he was as white and shaky as Sam himself. "I saw the bats flying out from the side of the bluff, and thought maybe that's where you were. And then I heard that unearthly thing laugh. I suppose he's the one who killed Gaby, Albert, and the other prisoners." Sam nodded confirmation. "How in the world could something like this happen?"

Shaking his head slowly, looking back at the cave opening, Sam replied, "It's a long story, Coop. Let's put an end to it, and I'll tell you."

They took turns with the pickax and closed up the cave until there was not even a coin-sized hole to be found. Now anyone who came across the place would never guess that a cave was hidden there.

The disappearance of Gabrielle Krueger's body had always been a mystery to Muscatine, but it had been a minor mystery compared to what had really happened in the jail that night. Only Sam had lived to know the truth, and he kept his mouth shut, leaving town not long after. He knew that people would not believe what he himself had not believed until it was almost too late for him.

Sam had buried his memories of Gaby, the lunatic, and the skull-faced demon. It was only recently, after reading a book by a British author named Bram Stoker, that Sam Clemens had been able to put a name to the horror that had befallen Muscatine that spring. The old gypsy woman had called the creatures "Wampiri." Stoker's word was *vampire*.

◊◊◊

Coop continued to pound on the door. "Come on, Sam, open the damn door. Stop being a prima donna."

Sam allowed himself a small smile. That was Coop, all right. He opened the door.

Wendi Lee is a novelist whose books include the mystery novels *The Good Daughter* and *Missing Eden,* as well as numerous westerns. Her husband, Terry Beatty, is a cartoonist, best known for his work on the title *Ms. Tree* with Max Allan Collins. They live in Muscatine, Iowa.

"Hello. My name is Vlad, and I'm a vampire. . . ."

A 12–Step Program
(for the Corporeally Challenged)

BY TINA L. JENS

elcome to the first meeting of the Midwest Chapter of Vampires Anonymous. I know a lot of you cadavers have traveled a long way to be with us tonight, so take a few minutes to stretch your legs, wings, or whatever, hang your capes in the cloak room, then join us here in the circle. You'll find some refreshments on the back table, compliments of a Red Cross blood drive held this afternoon. A big flash of the fangs to Duchess Katie Longtooth for coordinating that project."

A polite round of applause followed the announcement. The group leader, Baron Brad Mooreland, shut the mike off. He watched with satisfaction as nearly thirty vampires from all across Illinois, Iowa, Ohio, Wisconsin, and Missouri flocked around the refreshment table in the basement meeting hall of the Temple Sholom on the far north side of Cincinnati. It represented less than a tenth of the Midwest Undead. But vampires, being the lone-wolf personality type, were intrinsically nonjoiners. Let the cabal call him crazy. V.A. was going to work.

He flipped the mike back on again. "A quick question for our

Jewish vampires: Are any of you experiencing any discomfort from our location? No? Good." He flipped the mike back off.

Obviously, a Christian church basement, the traditional setting for such groups, wouldn't work for Vampires Anonymous. The Baron had gotten the idea of using a synagogue from one of his recent victims. The old man had held up a Star of David to ward him off. One dead rabbi later, the Baron knew where to hold the meeting.

To the Baron Brad's knowledge, no organized research had been done to test the effects of other religions' accoutrements. He shook his head. The Undead just had to get organized before they were exterminated.

He joined the crowd at the back of the room to partake of a little refreshment and small talk.

"Baron Mooreland."

It was Lady Julia Peterson, of the Ft. Madison, Iowa, Petersons.

"Lady Julia, how good to see you," the Baron said, bowing low to kiss her hand.

She smiled and took his arm.

"As you know, Baron, I have supported this idea from the very beginning, and I've sent a number of letters saying so to the ruling cabal. However," her voice dropped to a whisper, "their concerns of security are entirely valid. I must admit I'm a bit uneasy having this many of us in one place. One raid by a wild pack of Van Helsings could wipe our community out."

Trying to regain her composure, she brushed back her feathered blonde curls with her fingertips and laughed playfully.

The Baron thought the laughter sounded forced.

"I don't usually think such grim thoughts," she assured him. "Perhaps it's our surroundings."

"Never fear, Lady Julia, there shall be no holocaust of the Undead tonight. We've taken many precautions to insure our security."

He led her into the hallway.

"Perhaps you noticed the oily substance on all the windows and door handles? They've all been treated with a potent mixture of poison ivy extract and unguent of chili powder.

"Outside, we have a spy manning a Demon Dog hot dog cart

on the corner. He's our early warning defense system. Also, we've hired a couple of panhandlers to spread out on the front steps."

He led her down the hallway to the long bulletin board that hung on the wall.

"I put this poster together myself," he said proudly, pointing at the yellow photocopied handbill. "Surely you saw them on all the doors?"

"I did wonder if I'd come to the right place when I saw the fliers for the amateur poetry reading," Lady Julia said.

"In the unlikely event that anyone actually shows up for that, we have a doorman positioned to collect a five dollar cover-charge."

Lady Julia giggled at the deviousness.

"And of course, we've covered the basics," he told her, as they wandered back into the meeting room. "We locked the parking lot and towed in old junkers to fill the metered spaces on the street.

"And several of us met for an early dinner in the neighborhood. The police are quite busy picking up the pieces of a couple of drunken vagrants who passed out on the railroad tracks. The Transit Authority had to completely shut down this stop for the night."

"Well!" Lady Julia said, "I'd like to see a bunch of Van Helsings try to get a bag of wooden stakes past a Cincinnati bus driver!"

Baron Brad laughed at her.

"Need I go on?" he asked her kindly.

"Not at all. Obviously, we're in good hands tonight," she said.

It was time to get started. The Baron started herding the group away from the refreshment table. He stood back and watched as the vampires shuffled into the circle. He smiled as he watched a couple of vampires pull some of the chairs out of the circle, to make room for the werewolves, who preferred to lay on the floor. It was heartening to see Furry Friends attending the meeting. Werewolves didn't become vampires until after they were killed, of course. But obviously, these creatures were planning for their future. The Undead needed just that type of long-term-picture people to guide the community into the next millennium.

He took his place at the podium and turned on the mike.

"Hi, I'm Baron Brad Mooreland. And I'm . . . a Vampire," he said, with just a hint of melodrama.

An unerring sense of dramatic presentation was one of the more important attributes gained when one was transformed into the Undead.

The group looked around hesitantly at each other. Then, in uncertain unison, answered, "Hi, Baron Brad."

The Baron nodded, pleased. Obviously some of the cadavers had belonged to a Program while they were alive. That made things much easier.

Brad wasn't really a Baron, of course, just as the cadaver sitting to Brad's left wasn't a real Count. Not by the living's legal standards, anyway. But it was part of the Undead's social structure that you took a title upon your rising. At each century's un-deathday, you were awarded the honor of upgrading the title. Who were the living—to deny them the use of the title Baron or Count?

In a way, that was what this whole meeting was about. Getting the Undead organized. They had been a repressed minority for too long, discriminated against and misunderstood.

"It is only through learning to accept ourselves, that others can learn to accept us. We must come out of our closets of shame, stand tall, and be proud of what we are," Baron Brad told them, his voice cracking with emotion.

"Remember, it is not God—but Christians—who are against us. We must learn to distinguish among the magic of Christianity, with all of its powerful talismans, and the power of God."

A murmur of assent passed through the room.

"For are not all things on this earth *His* creatures?" he said warmly. "Now, who among you would like to share his story first?"

There was a scraping of chairs and a low-pitched buzzing as the cadavers blushed and avoided his eyes.

"Oh come now," Brad said. "You're among friends."

Hesitantly, Count Chaney raised his blanched hand. The Baron traded places with him.

He tapped the mike. "Is this thing on?" the new speaker asked hesitantly, using the age old phrase of those who are stalling because they are afraid of the mike. The group assured him the equipment was working.

He cleared his throat and said, "Hi, my name is Count Ralph. I'm from Rockford, Illinois. And, I'm a Vampire."

"Hi, Ralph," the group responded.

Ralph's face lit up from the encouragement.

"I've been a Vampire for 236 years. In that time, I've seen some pretty awful things—and done even worse."

As Ralph came to the close of his statement, Brad led the group in a round of applause. Ralph's neighbors slapped him on the back as he returned to his seat.

Standing behind the podium again, Brad asked, "Ralph, how did you become a vampire?"

"Loss of blood," he mumbled.

The Baron nodded. "That's pretty common. Let's take a poll. How many here died from loss of blood when a roving vampire bit you? Raise your hands. Don't be shy."

Here and there a few hands went up.

"How many became vampires because you died in a state of sin? Suicides?"

Several members nodded or waved their hands. Looking closer, Brad could make out the razor-blade scars left on one woman's wrist, and the rope burns around the neck of an older man. Injuries incurred as a vampire would heal quickly, but suicide scars never went away.

"Any excommunicants in the group? Perjurers?"

"Before, or after, we died?" an anonymous voice wisecracked.

The Baron smiled tolerantly. A little levity was a good thing at this type of meeting. After all, if we can't laugh at ourselves, who or what can we laugh at?

"Who here was cursed by their parents? Dabbled in Black Magic? Were exceedingly wicked persons?"

Hesitantly, one cadaver raised his hand. His neighbors on either side moved their chairs away from him.

"Judge not lest ye be judged," Baron Brad admonished them.

With shame-faced grins, they scooted their chairs back, not quite as close as they had originally been.

"Any unavenged murder victims among us tonight? No? How about unbaptized children?"

The McGregor twins, who looked about six but had already passed their first-century mark, nodded.

Brad said, "I thought so."

A 12-Step Program

"How about corpses who did not receive Christian burial? People unlucky enough to be born on Christmas Day? Any seventh sons? The seventh son of a seventh son?"

A husky young man in the back of the room raised his hand. The group gasped. Brad made a mental note of it. Seven-sevens, as they were known, were incredibly powerful and equally bad-tempered.

By the Baron's accounting, there were still a few individuals unidentified. "Anyone born with a caul?"

He shook his head sadly as one young woman raised her hand.

"That's a shame," Brad sympathetically. "With advancements in prenatal care, those are completely preventable with dietary supplements."

"Anyone womb-cursed?"

This had always been a catch-all category for vampires who couldn't account for their condition any other way. It was hard to detect and harder to prove that a vampire had stared at a pregnant woman. In the few instances it was detected, the curse could be reversed by a priest's blessing.

"Now that we know each other a little better, who'd like to go next?"

The Baron stared expectantly at the crowd.

A young woman to his right raised a tentative hand. Obviously new to the world of the Undead, her skin still had a salmon tinge to it. She was just the sort of vampire who needed this group most. Brad smiled at her and motioned her to the podium.

"Hi, I'm Linda," she said, tugging nervously at the shoulder strap of her jumper. "I live in Wauwatosa, Wisconsin. Unlike so many here, I knew my sire. I was young, impressionable. Thought I was in love at the time."

There was a murmur of sympathy from the group.

"But being Undead wasn't what he said it would be. Three months after he changed me, he took off with a little tart—a ghoul that he'd met at the street fair in Madison during the Halloween festivities. That was two years ago. I haven't seen him since. I heard a rumor that he'd gone on a binge down in New Orleans during Mardi Gras last year. Supposedly he got drunk, passed out, and got fried by the sun. But I don't believe it. That worthless son of a bitch is out there somewhere, ruining somebody else's afterlife."

Brad laid his hand tenderly on her shoulder.

"No bitterness, Linda. Aren't you just projecting your anger outside yourself, when in reality, you're unhappy with who and what you are?"

She nodded.

"You must accept yourself, and make peace with your past."

The Baron turned to the group. "I think Linda needs a little extra support here tonight. Who has a hug for her?"

Count Ralph stood up, and she tottered into his arms. The group broke out in spontaneous applause.

Brad beamed. The meeting was going splendidly. Out of the corner of his eye, he saw Lady Julia wink at him.

It was going out on a limb, but he asked, "Seven-seven, would you like to share your story next?"

The burly cadaver, who, rumor had it, made his unliving as an All-Star Wrestler, barked once, then slunk down in his chair and looked the other way.

Ruffled by the response, Baron Brad said quickly, "No pressure!"

One of the werewolves "woofed" and padded up to the mike. "I'd like to say something."

His S's slurred into R's, the wolf's soft palate not being designed to utter the nineteenth letter of the American alphabet. Brad made a mental note to talk to the cabal about arranging speech therapy sessions. Perhaps that was a project Lady Julia would consider taking on.

"I'm Harold Raines from St. Louis, Missouri. Obviously, I'm not a vampire. Not yet. But I'm a realist, folks. I know it's just a matter of time. Some drunken hunter's gonna mistake me for a deer, or some ranger with the Wildlife and Game Department is gonna try to tranquilize me and relocate me in one of the state parks.

"I've been a werewolf for twenty years. But it hasn't been so long that I don't remember the culture shock. Back then, there wasn't anything like V.A. or W.A. to help you through it. And unlike you folks, the lucky ones, anyway, werewolves don't have any sires to explain things and help us through."

He sat back on his haunches and rubbed his nose with his front paw.

"One day you're walking around, minding your business as a human, and some wild dog on steroids knocks you down and bites your ass. You go to the doctor. The wound heals, and you think nothing of it. Until the next full moon—when suddenly you're sprouting hair and you've grown a tail and a whole lot of extra teeth."

The group murmured sympathetically.

"Don't get me wrong," Harold growled. "I'm not saying you vampires have it any easier. I think V.A.'s great! A group like this helps me prepare for the inevitable. I think we should give a big round of applause to Baron Brad, and all those cadavers who made this possible."

The vampires applauded and Harold wagged his tail.

The Baron stood up and waved his hands to stop the applause. His cheeks were tinted with just a hint of pink.

Just then, the doors flew open and a mob of angry young poets swarmed in, pushing the bouncer forward on the crest of the wave.

Clearly, they were going through their Gothic phase. The boys uniformly wore black jeans and black cotton turtlenecks, while the girls sported short black dresses. The jewelry was frighteningly unisex. Small silver hoops pierced their nostrils, oversized rosary crosses dangled from their ears, and intricately carved wooden stakes suspended from black cords around their necks.

But this wasn't a pack of rampaging Van Helsings. The youths were yelling something about First Amendment rights, free speech, and starving artists.

"We demand access to the mike!" one young rebel with spiked hair and multiple nose rings shouted.

The Gothic Gang fell silent as they noticed that thirty pairs of gleaming fangs and glowing red eyes were trained on them.

"Uh, wrong room?" the rebel leader asked, doubtfully.

"Why, yes," the Baron responded, his voice as silky and smooth as the Arabian boudoir where he'd spent his first Undead night.

"I believe your group is down the hall," he intoned. Silently, he willed the others to join him in invoking a group trance.

Slowly, the young poets backed out of the room, herded by the sheepish bouncer.

When they were gone, the Baron clapped his hands to get the group's attention.

"All right, folks, it's been a good meeting! Don't let the interruption get you down. Remember, when the afterlife throws you a tomato—make a Bloody Mary!"

"Before you go, I've got just a few announcements to make. Lady Julia is passing out membership fliers at the back of the room, so be sure and pick one up."

Baron Brad checked his notes.

"Next month, the Countess Bathory will give a talk entitled 'If I Had Him for Dinner—Do I Have to Go to His Funeral?' and other issues of Undead etiquette. And coming up in October, Dr. Harry Jekyll will talk about 'The Effects of Daylight Savings Time on the Vampire's Feeding Patterns.'

"To better accommodate our Furry Friends we'll hold it on the full moon. So mark your calendars. I hope to see you all next month, and why don't you all try to bring a friend!

"What's that Duchess Longtooth? Oh, yes," the Baron nodded. "Additional refreshments will be served in the next room."

Tina L. Jens short stories have appeared in many other horror anthologies, including *100 Victorious Little Vampire Stores, South From Midnight, The Secret Prophecies of Nostradamus, Shock Rock 2,* and *Phantoms of the Night,* among others. She lives in Chicago.

Even vampires need a little comic relief once in a while.

A Night At the (Horse) Opera

BY P. N. ELROD

The smell of buttered popcorn was a little sickening until I got used to it and I wasn't able to drink soda pop anymore and even the darkness wasn't really dark for me, but a movie was still a movie and it was rare that I didn't drop in on one of Chicago's shadow palaces two or three times a week to take in the latest show.

This particular one wasn't especially new; *The Plainsman* had been out for a while, but I'd somehow missed it, a sad comment on a Gary Cooper fan. Of course, I also liked Jean Arthur, who was mighty pretty done up in Hollywood cowgirl style. I lost track of some of the dialog at one point speculating how my girlfriend, Bobbi, might look in a similar outfit made of buckskins. Probably very good, I thought; then things started happening in the plot that I couldn't follow because I'd missed something during my lapse of attention.

"What's going on?" I whispered to the man next to me. Not taking his eyes from the screen, he obligingly leaned over and filled me in, speaking with a decided New York accent. I'd lived there for a long time before moving to Chicago and was interested to find out more about him, but decided to leave further questions until after the feature.

De Mille's epic danced over the screen with enough thrills and drama to keep the most jaded Western lover satisfied. If it was still playing here tomorrow, which was Bobbi's night off, I'd ask her to see it. She wouldn't need much persuading; she liked Gary Cooper, too.

The movie rolled to its end, and the lights came up. Other people rose to leave, uniformed ushers appeared, and the rest of us settled in to wait for the next feature to start. Bobbi's last show at the night club where she sang wouldn't be over for another couple of hours, so I was with the settling-in crowd. The same apparently went for my seat mate, who pulled out a crumpled sack of peanuts from somewhere and began shelling and eating them in a leisurely manner.

"Thanks," I said.

His bright eyes clouded slightly as he tried to recall why I was thanking him, then comprehension dawned. "Don't mention it."

"New York?" I asked.

"Ninety-third Streeter," he promptly replied. He had a sloping nose, wide at the base, a wide, expressive mouth, receding hair, and enough mischief packed into his mug for a dozen Christmas elves. He looked as though he ought to be somebody, and I had a sudden nagging feeling that I knew him. "You from there, too?" he asked.

"Not since last August. You ever hang out at a place called Rosie's? Across from the *Dispatch?*"

He shook his head solemnly.

"Thought I might have seen you there."

"You probably saw me here, is what I'm thinking." He tossed a peanut high and caught it in his mouth with the easy skill of long practice. "Want one?" He shook the bag, open end toward me.

"No, but thanks anyway." Maybe I'd seen him here before and just hadn't noticed him among the hundreds of other movie watchers. "Been away from New York long?"

"Long enough. California's my home now, least when we're not on the road."

"Salesman?" But that didn't seem quite right for him.

Another peanut flew high and dropped in. He chewed it slow-ly while his eyes, his whole expression, turned steady and serious. "Yeah. I'm a salesman, all right. I sell money."

"You what?"

"I sell money. You never heard of the business?"

"No . . ." I'd either stumbled across a counterfeiter or a lunatic. Now might be a good idea to make a graceful exit, but the guy put up his bag of peanuts, smiling at my expression.

"I know what you must be thinking, but it's no scam. I really do sell money. It's perfectly legal."

Okay. He'd hooked me. "What is it? Like coin collecting or something?"

"Nah, this stuff." He pulled out his wallet and fished for a five dollar bill, holding it out to me. "Take a look. It's real, right?"

As far as I could tell it looked just like any other used bill. "Right . . ."

"Okay, I'll sell you this five for four-fifty."

I shook my head. "Ah. No, thanks."

"It's not a scam," he earnestly assured me. "Think of the profit."

"What do you get out of it?"

"A sale."

"Maybe not this time, but thanks all the same."

"You sure? It's a great bargain you're passing up." At this point he looked too innocent to be believed. He read that I was too wise to fall for whatever gag he had in mind, gave a good-natured shrug, and put away the bill and wallet. He hauled out the peanuts again.

The nagging set in again with a vengeance. "I *know* you from somewhere."

"Go to the movies a lot?" he asked.

"All the time."

"You really don't know?"

"Not unless you tell me."

He chuckled, his whole face going into it and that's when the dawn started to break.

"Wait a second . . ."

He did, dropping his chin a bit and letting his mobile mouth hang slack in an exaggerated pause.

"Oh, jeez, you're—"

A hand clamped down heavily on his shoulder from behind and made him jump. He instantly gave up his miming game and looked around in mild irritation to the source of the interruption. I looked, too, and forgot all about the conversation. The man looming over us was big even by Chicago standards and he wasn't alone. He had two very large friends waiting in the aisle. The three of them looked as though they could take on the Wrigley Building and win. Their hundred-dollar suits were not well-tailored enough to hide ominous bulges under their left arms.

The man's hand flexed, and my seat mate rose like a puppet.

"Oh, hell," he said, irritation suddenly replaced by fear. The smell of it fairly jumped off him.

"You don't know the half of it yet," the man told him.

"Wait a minute . . ." I began. "Aren't you Guns Thompson?" I'd heard he was working as muscle for a West Side mob these days.

One of his goons dropped a meaty hand on my shoulder.

"Or maybe not. I could be mistaken."

"Shhh!" someone down the row advised us severely.

"Out of here," said Thompson, and the five of us were abruptly marching toward the lobby just as the next show began. The noisy barrage of a newsreel theme song was enough to drown out any protests we might have made at this treatment. I could have made an issue of things, but I'd heard that Thompson was a rough customer and wouldn't put it past him to open up with his heater right then and there. No, it was a much better idea to go along and put a few walls between the other theater patrons and whatever caliber of bullets he and his cronies were packing that night.

We threaded past ushers with flashlights guiding people in; no one noticed us, or if they did, they were going to mind their own business and watch the movie. We were urged through the open doors and spilled into the lush lobby. The popcorn smell hit me all over again with a fresh wave of nausea, but I had other things to think about as they hustled us past the bank of doors leading outside. I'd been expecting a quick exit and maybe a car trip to somewhere unpleasant, but Thompson instead headed for the men's room.

We trooped in as though we had business there. A couple of guys were washing up, and some instinct told them to hurry the job and leave. The last one out didn't hang around long enough to dry his hands before he bolted.

Couldn't blame him. The brightly lighted background of patterned tile did nothing to improve Thompson's looks. Despite their flashy clothes, he and his friends were as out of place as a trio of gorillas at a Sunday school picnic. It showed in their hard, impassive faces and the way they moved like intelligent bulldozers.

"You've got the wrong man," protested my seat mate. "You're after Chico, aren't you?"

"Not anymore," sniggered one of the goons. He went to stand by the door, jamming his foot against the base to keep out unwelcome interruptions.

"But I'm his brother Harpo, I'm telling you. You've got the wrong man!"

Thompson stared, eyes all narrow so you couldn't read them.

"It's true," I put in, trying to be helpful. "This is Harpo Marx."

"Oh, yeah, then how come he's talking?" demanded Thompson.

"Yeah," said the goon at the door, suddenly giggling. "An' if you're Harpo, where's your harp?"

"Back in my hotel room," came Harpo's logical answer, but his voice was thin and nervous. He was still clutching his bag of peanuts in one tight fist. They rattled a bit against the paper because he was trembling.

"Besides, everyone knows that Harpo's a dummy."

"I am not—that's just a character I play!"

"Stop wasting time," Thompson growled and pulled out a forty-five that looked like it could drop King Kong in one shot.

He wasn't pointing it at anyone just yet, so I thought I'd try once more. "C'mon, Guns, give the man another look and you'll see he's not the one you want."

He looked again but couldn't see any difference. Then he looked at me, and that's when he started pointing the gun. "Where do you get off knowing me?"

"Hey, everyone in town knows Guns Thompson." All you had to do was walk into a post office and study the portraits left there by an FBI that hadn't gotten around to collecting him yet, but I wasn't going to mention that. He'd gotten his nickname during the Prohibition gang wars for his talent at handling a

Thompson machine gun. It was about his only asset, since he and his friends apparently didn't have enough brains among them to fill a coffee cup.

"Who the hell are you, anyway?"

"My name's Fleming and I'm nobody special, honest."

"Fleming?" Thompson's face screwed up in an effort to think. "Where do I know him from, Higgs?" he asked the guy by the door.

Higgs shook his head.

"Rinky?" This directed to the thug guarding Harpo.

Rinky shrugged.

Since my arrival in this town I'd been reluctantly bumping heads with its criminal element, so it wasn't too surprising that Thompson had heard of me from somewhere. Most of the time I do whatever's needed to cover my tracks; on this occasion, I was fervently thanking God for Thompson's poor memory. He growled and dismissed me as unimportant and turned his attention and his gun on Harpo.

"Okay, Marx, you ran up a bill with Big Joey, and it's past due. I can take it out of your pocket or your hide."

"This is a pretty public place for that kind of business," I said. I wasn't crazy about putting myself forward but figured I had a better chance of surviving it than Harpo.

Higgs giggled again. "Big Joey *owns* this joint, bo. Make noise if you want. Ain't no one gonna come in to see why."

Which made for a pretty disgusting situation, I thought, as the three of them laughed at my reaction. I checked on how Harpo was doing, but he wasn't doing much of anything. He was frozen, staring hard at something behind me, his mouth sagging a lot. The back of my neck began to prickle as I realized what he was looking at. Hells bells, why couldn't these jerks have taken us for a ride, instead?

"Marx?" Thompson said, moving a step closer and raising his gun an inch.

Harpo continued to stare until Rinky gave him a shake, then he looked vaguely at Thompson.

"Stop playing the dope. Pay up, and we'll let you go back to the movie."

"H–how much?"

"Five grand."

The mention of such a large sum got Harpo's attention as nothing else could, given his circumstances. He gulped. "My God, how long was he playing?"

"Who?"

"Chico."

"*You're* Chico, you dope."

"Sorry, I forgot."

Thompson tapped him lightly on the side of the head with the barrel of his gun, just enough to jar him. "Pay up, or get busted up. I don't want no more shit from you, sheenie."

Harpo had been drained of color up to this point; now he flushed a deep red. There was a lot going on all over his face, subtle stuff, but strong; anger, resentment, and outrage were now mixed in with his fear. I'd seen comic exaggerations of them on the screen, but he'd been acting then, working hard to make people laugh. I'd been one of them. This took only a second, maybe less than a second, and then he exploded. It was almost too fast for me to follow. Harpo's fist came up, connected, and Thompson staggered away, clutching a suddenly bloody nose.

The blood smell hit me all over like it always did, but I didn't have time to spare for it. Rinky had surged forward to slam Harpo back into one of the stall doors. They were designed to open out; this one's hinges gave way and it crashed inward, stopping abruptly when its edge struck the toilet inside. Off balance, his bag of peanuts scattering, Harpo fell against it and dropped, but he was still mad and scrapping. From the floor he kicked at Rinky's ankles, but Rinky danced out of the way, reaching for his gun.

Before he could haul it out, I was on him. I grabbed handfuls of Rinky's coat and maybe some skin under it because he yelped loud enough. One solid pull and turn, and he was flying across the length of the room, crashing into the tiled wall. He bounced and went down, staying there.

Then something roared out, a horrendous explosion, stunning in the confined space. The sound was as solid as a bowling ball, and it struck me high up, square in the back. I saw a burst of blood leap from the middle of my chest, and then the floor was flying up too fast to dodge.

I couldn't tell if the silence that followed was a result of their shock at what had happened or my inability to hear anything. My ears felt stuffed and when the stuffiness wore off, it was replaced by a hot, unpleasant ringing. Negligible, though, it was nothing compared to the reaction my body was having to the slug that had just torn through it.

Couldn't move. The pain was searingly familiar, which did not make it any easier to bear. My initial, involuntary reaction to getting shot is to vanish. Once incorporeal, I would be free of the pain, floating in a unique pocket of existence that's always given me healing and comfort.

Great stuff, but the drawback is that it always scares the hell out of anyone who sees me doing it. The situation had gotten nasty enough; I wasn't about to add to it, so I grimly hung onto solidity, gritting my teeth as flesh, bone, muscle, and finally outraged nerves knitted themselves back together into a shaken whole again.

"Oh, my God," whispered Harpo, somewhere behind me. He was probably staring at my apparent corpse. I wasn't moving and, if necessary, I can lie very, very still indeed. It was a necessity now, if only to allow myself a moment to get over the worst of it. That moment came and thankfully went, but I stayed where I was, straining to listen, hoping to figure out some way of helping Harpo without getting him killed.

Someone shifted, his shoes crushing and crunching the peanuts that were all over the floor. It was Higgs, coming over to check out Rinky.

"He's out cold, Guns," he reported.

"Throw some water on him."

Higgs complied, running water in one of the sinks. He cupped his hands together to carry it over to his friend. I could see only just that much from the corner of one eye, having fallen at an inconvenient angle. Higgs never bothered to glance at me. I was just another mess on the floor to be ignored, like the peanuts.

Someone was having a hard time breathing, probably Harpo. I heard a series of little sick gasps, then a sudden rush of movement. The next thing I heard was him throwing up in one of the stalls.

Thompson thought it was funny. "The little sheenie shit can't take it, Higgs."

Higgs grunted amused agreement and made a second trip for some water.

"Jeez, that puke stinks. Flush it, Marx."

After a moment, the toilet was flushed.

Rinky began to show signs of reviving. He groaned, snarled at the latest faceful of water, and was hauled to his feet by Higgs.

"Rinky, go wait in the car," Thompson ordered.

Rinky made an unsteady exit. Just as he got to the door, someone must have poked his head in.

"Hey! What's going on h—"

"Never you mind, bo," said Higgs. He'd been following Rinky and now kept on going, keeping up a patter of tough talk to convince the newcomer to butt out. It must have worked; no one else came through to investigate things, leaving Thompson alone with Harpo . . . and me.

"Come outta there."

Footsteps dragged reluctantly over the floor as Harpo emerged from the stall.

"You see what happens when I get pissed? Well, I'm startin' to get pissed with you. You come up with the money, or you end up just like him."

"Okay." Harpo's voice had dropped lower than a whisper, as though he had no air left in him to use.

"So fork over."

"But I—" Harpo broke off.

"Don't tell me you don't have it. You movie people always carry a wad with you."

Okay, he'd be concentrating on Harpo now, as good a time as any for me to make a move, even better with Higgs and Rinky out of the way. I stopped being me for an instant, slipping into that nonplace where I had no body, no weight, no sight, only mind and will. I sensed the hardness of the floor and, as I drifted over it toward them, could determine just how close they were to each other.

Very close. Thompson and Harpo backed up against the stall doors and I could guess he had his gun right in the poor guy's face.

"C'mon, move it."

If Harpo came up short of cash—and it was very likely he would—Thompson was just crazy enough to scrag him as casually as he'd scragged me. There was no way I could be subtle about this. I had to hurry and break things up now and figure out how to cover my tracks later.

Thompson, at least, never knew what hit him. I materialized with my hands already reaching for him, one to push his gun out of the way and the other flowing smoothly into a solid sock to his jaw. He reeled back, eyes rolling up, and careened off a urinal before making friends with the peanuts on the floor.

I turned to check on Harpo. He wasn't moving much. If he hadn't been braced against the stall dividers, his legs might have given out. His eyes were wider than they'd ever been in the movies as they traveled from me to Thompson and back to me again, finally resting on the hole in my shirt and its surrounding bloodstain.

A hundred questions raced over his face, but not one of them could get out. He was just too damned scared.

It's not as though I hadn't seen his reaction before on others, but it was like getting shot; familiarity never made it any less painful. I backed away and said something stupid to him about taking it easy and that everything was all right. I could hear his heart pounding fit to bust and felt a stab of worry about the ashy color of his skin.

"You okay?" I asked.

He stared.

I repeated my question.

He gulped, grimacing perhaps, on the vomit taste left in his mouth. "I'm . . . fine," he squeaked.

"You sure? You don't look so hot."

His mouth twitched. "Dead. I saw. You."

I gently put a little more distance between us. "Yeah, I know. I'm sorry."

Now he seemed to twitch all over. "Sorry?"

"I didn't mean to scare you. I really didn't. I don't want to now." I'd backed off as far as I could. He could run out the door if he wanted. I wouldn't stop him. I certainly wasn't going to try hypnotizing him into forgetting his fear or into accepting me or anything like that. It's a really shitty, dangerous thing to mess around inside people's minds in that way. These nights I never did it unless at the time it seemed more shitty and dangerous not to; this wasn't one of those times.

"Is this some kind of a trick?" He was looking pretty hollow and lost.

"No trick. Houdini I ain't. Nothing up my sleeve but arm." I couldn't lie to him, even when the temptation was there to explain it all away as an illusion.

"Then how?"

It got real quiet as I considered just how to answer. Even a short lecture on Rumanian folklore and how it differs from actuality would take a while to get through, and I couldn't stand there and deliver it in the men's room with peanuts and Guns Thompson all over the floor.

I said, "You ever see that Bela Lugosi movie that came out a couple of years back?"

Maybe he'd seen it or not, but he suddenly understood.

"It's sort of like that for me . . . only I'm . . . a nicer person." I spread my hands, giving a little shrug, probably looking a little hollow and lost myself.

Harpo stared for a time, then his eyes switched over to the bank of mirrors on the wall over the sinks. They'd given him his first clue, after all. A few minutes ago the surprise had been enough to take his attention right off of Thompson's threat. From where I was standing, I could see his reflection. It peered hard at the spot where I should have been, but nothing was there, or course. After a time, it looked down to where Thompson lay.

Then Harpo straightened himself a little to look directly at me. "Yeah, you're right. You *are* a nicer person than some people I could name."

Life's damn tough, but every now and then it allows you to work yourself into having an impossible hope for something you want more than anything else. It flashes up so fast and so hard that you can see and know *exactly* what it will be like for you to have that hope fulfilled. For a second or two it's absolutely real, and it's the best feeling in the world—while it lasts, until the bright instant passes and you have to face the black disappointment.

But this time the disappointment didn't come. Harpo Marx spared me that, giving me what I'd hoped for, wanted, needed.

Acceptance. Just like that. No fanfare, no more questions.

God bless him.

"Thanks," I whispered.

"Does that hurt?" he asked cautiously pointing to my chest.

I shook my head, to0 full to talk just yet.

"What are you going to do with him?" He pointed at Thompson.

I coughed to clear my clogged throat. "Damned if I know. Got any ideas?"

His face had begun to take on more normal lines as the tension melted off, and now I saw a ghost of his character's elfin mischief flit past. He walked over to Thompson and studied him, then stepped to one of the sinks, turning on the tap. Cupping his hands like Higgs before him, he slopped water onto Thompson, who jerked and jumped and rumbled an obscene protest.

Harpo stooped and solicitously helped Thompson to his feet. Thompson was just awake enough to see and vaguely understand what was happening. He was just getting to the point of snarling at his benefactor, but Harpo cut him off by landing as neat and as forceful a gut punch as had ever been my privilege to see. He all but buried his arm up to the elbow in Thompson's middle, and the man immediately folded. His breath whooshed out and was slow to return.

Harpo stood over him, anxiously watching and waiting. After a minute, Thompson, being fairly tough, had recovered enough to straighten up again. The second he was up, though, Harpo let him have it once more. Thompson grunted and dropped to his knees. It took a while before he was able to breathe regularly, and it took even longer for him to find his feet.

Harpo helped him.

Thompson should have known better.

This time Harpo's gut punch was followed up by a hard, crisp uppercut with just enough force behind it to finish the job. No gasping for air for Thompson. He simply dropped. Next Christmas was about ten months away. Maybe by then he'd wake up.

Harpo shook his hand, blowing on it, then returned to the sink to let the cold water run over his bruised knuckles. He was grinning. "I shouldn't have done that. Any more and I couldn't play the harp for our show. We're touring, you know, trying out some acts we're going to use in a new movie," he explained.

"Where'd you learn to sock like that?" I asked.

"Benny Leonard," he answered, dropping the name of the lightweight champion of the world in a most unaffected manner. "We did a tour with him once, used to take turns sparring with him. Great guy." He cut the water and toweled off. "Wish he could have been here to see this."

I picked up Thompson's .45 which had fallen when I'd hit him. It probably wouldn't hurt to call up a homicide cop I knew and ask if he was interested in an easy collar. Lieutenant Blair didn't like or trust me much, but he wasn't above accepting a favor when it was offered. Putting the gun in my overcoat pocket to give to him later, I buttoned the front together to hide the bullet hole in my bloodied shirt. I'd have to remember to keep my back to the walls to hide the matching entry hole there.

The first cold tickle of hunger plucked at my belly and throat. It wasn't really critical yet, but I'd have to make time tonight to stop at the Stockyards to feed, to replace what had been lost. Some of it still smeared the floor. Frowning, I went to a stall, ripped away a length of toilet paper and swabbed my blood from the tiles, tossing the waste in the trash.

Harpo watched without comment, his face solemn.

"I know you've been through a lot," I said, "but would you mind doing me a favor?"

"Anything you want, buddy."

I got out my notebook and scribbled a name and number on a page and gave it to him. "Could you call this guy for me? Tell him Jack Fleming is baby-sitting Guns Thompson here and for him to come over right away."

He looked dubious. "This a cop?"

"Yeah, but I can leave your name out of it if you want."

That made him happy. "But what about his friends?"

"They'll clear out the moment a patrol car pulls up. They're dumb, but not that dumb."

"I owe you."

"Let's call it even if I can have an autograph."

He laughed in a big way. "I'll go you one better. How 'bout I take you back to where I'm staying so I can introduce you to my brothers?"

This was almost as much of a shock as catching that bullet, only without the pain. "Really? You mean it?"

"Yeah. I'd like them to meet the guy who saved my life."

I sagged a little. "You won't tell 'em how, will you?"

He pulled in his lower lip, considering. "No, I don't think that would be a good idea. We'll talk around it somehow."

"That'd be great, then. Just great."

He grinned. "Grouch'll be there and he might know where Chico is, I think," he added darkly, "I need to talk with Chico. When we were kids we were always being mistaken for one another, like twins. I never imagined anything like this would happen because of it, though."

"Maybe you could wear the wig and raincoat—at least while you're still in Chicago."

He grinned. "There's an idea. I'll go make that call for you, okay? Think it'll take long?"

"I'll make sure it doesn't," I promised. He started to go. "Wait a sec."

He paused at the door.

"That stuff you were giving me about selling money—is that part of your show?"

"Nah, that's just something Chico and I do for the hell of it. People try to figure out the catch, only there isn't one. It drives 'em crazy."

"Was I crazy enough for you?"

"Brother, you were a pip." He flashed another broad grin and left to make the call.

I looked at the closing door and decided that I'd been given the privilege of a lifetime. The Marxes worked their butts off to give people like me a good laugh and the chance had fallen my way to give one back in return.

And it felt pretty damned good.

P. N. Elrod is the author of the *Vampire Files* series, featuring undead detective Jack Fleming. She is also the editor of the anthology *Time of the Vampires*. She lives in Fort Worth, Texas.

Everyone needs a friend to watch their back,
especially when there's a vampire around!

Harvest Moon

BY MARK A. GARLAND

*T*he body was barely recognizable, but the boy's face was nearly intact. It was the same boy who had been there in the street with the others the night John Parsner had crashed into the light pole—and died. Tessi handed the photograph back to the lieutenant and nodded. "No," she said. "I didn't really know him. He lived down the street. I saw him walk by now and then, sometimes with friends. That's all."

"He ever bother you?" Lieutenant Adkins asked, handing the photo to Larry Wells, the handsome young officer with him who seemed to be mostly along for the ride. Adkins seemed a competent man, Tessi thought. A career officer, fifty and growing a paunch, weary of the routine but sharp enough when he chose to be. Dangerous, potentially. To Adkins, the matter of the teenager's murder was especially important; Tessi reasoned it would be unwise to take either of them too lightly.

"No," she said. "Never. Why?"

"Well, you know, kids that age and senior citizens don't always mix. I wondered if he might have been some sort of troublemaker. He ever hang around with trouble? Anyone unusual you might have seen him with lately, strangers in the neighborhood, going to his house or talking to him?"

"Not that I know of," Tessi answered, then let the silence hang between them. While she was resolved to be affable, she had no wish to prolong the encounter, for any number of reasons. Adkins turned and walked slowly about the room, looking at everything, apparently seeing nothing.

Ingrid chose that moment to poke her head in the front door at the top of the stairs. She glanced briefly about, then silently invited herself in. Ingrid owned the two-family, was Tessi's landlord and downstairs neighbor since spring. A quiet old woman in her own right, not as nosy as most, which Tessi liked. Though certainly Ingrid had her moments.

"No motive yet?" Ingrid asked, a grin bending the many neat wrinkles of her face. "I read the morning paper."

Adkins shrugged. "We're working on it."

"Strangest thing," Ingrid said. "And awful. Just awful."

"Good kid, as far as I can tell," the Lieutenant said, shaking his head. "Doesn't make much sense. But we'll stay with it."

"So brutal," Ingrid remarked. "They must have killed that boy at least ten times over."

"They?" Adkins asked, looking up.

"Well, you know," Ingrid said, blushing. "I don't know. Hard to imagine just one person doing all that."

Adkins stared a moment, then nodded. "Did everyone around here get along with him?"

Both women nodded.

"And you folks—would you say all of you get along with each other pretty well? Friends and neighbors?"

More nodding, though Tessi was not being entirely sincere. She hadn't had many friends in her lifetime, and mostly that had worked out for the best; the term did not necessarily denote anything permanent or reliable or safe.

"We'll talk again," the lieutenant said. "Meanwhile, if you think of anything or remember anything you think I might be interested in, just call."

Adkins and Officer Wells took a last look about the dining and living room area, ending near the door. "Thank you for your time," he said, and then they were gone.

"He questioned everybody on the street," Ingrid said.

"Especially those of us that were there. Waste of time, of course. Nobody around here would know anything."

There had been five of them "there" altogether: the old fellow Rawley and Mrs. Kip the hair stylist, then Ingrid and Tessi herself—and Roger Long, the dead paperboy. The kid was always late with the papers, and the rest of them had cornered him in the street, just under the street lamp in front of Ingrid's two-family. Tessi had simply been passing by on her way into the house when she'd been called into the huddle for possible testimony.

Then John Parsner had come breakneck around the corner in his pickup, the police just behind him. He swerved to miss the huddle, hit the light pole, and died. The police said Parsner had ended a domestic dispute an hour earlier by stabbing two holes in his girlfriend's throat with a weapon the police had not identified. She'd bled to death, apparently. Though Parsner had somehow cleaned up the mess. At least that's what the paper said. The authorities were still trying to find out something about John other than his name, but without much success.

"Maybe Lieutenant Adkins thinks one of us killed the paperboy. You know—kid's late once too often and . . ."

"Tessi!" Ingrid made a face, indignant. "Don't even *say* such a thing!"

"Sorry." Tessi turned and went out into her kitchen, leaving Ingrid standing there. She glanced out the window at her garden, then to the far edge of the back yard where she kept her small traps set up. The garden was doing fine, but the traps appeared empty. She could grow pretty much whatever she needed, but rodents and such, hereabouts, were not so easy to come by. She got a glass and ran some water. When she looked again, Ingrid wasn't there.

◊◊◊

Mrs. Kip's body looked much the same as the paperboy's: gaping, multiple stab wounds. But very little blood, Tessi noticed as she looked at the photographs. Lieutenant Adkins seemed almost apologetic.

"I have to ask you if you know anything about this," he said, looking at Tessi. "Anything at all. Anybody you know of that might have known the kid and Mrs. Kip? Anybody unusual you might have seen talking to *both* of them, especially recently?"

"No," Tessi replied. Adkins took back the photos and handed them to Officer Wells. This time they sat on the sofa and matching armchair that faced each other across the glass coffee table. The flat had come furnished. "I don't know of anyone." *I don't want to know,* she thought. *I just want to be left alone.* The whole affair was quite distasteful. Too much activity, too many people, too much blame to be laid, too much strange death.

"How well did you know Mrs. Kip?"

"I didn't, really. I don't know anyone here that well."

"Who does your hair?"

"I do it myself."

"I thought so."

Tessi wasn't certain what he meant by that. She doubted he was being facetious.

"We're working on the assumptions that the same person killed both of them and that this person probably knew both of them. Mrs. Kip was alone in her home, just like the boy was. Not much sign of a struggle or forced entry. I noticed you can see her house, right out your front window there, and about half of Roger Long's house up the block. Funny you wouldn't have noticed anyone."

"I don't look out that window very often. I like to keep to my own business."

"No offense, but I thought older women were famous for looking out their windows." He raised his eyebrows.

"Some of them."

"Your neighbor downstairs does. She says she's seen a strange man around once or twice lately, maybe the night before Mrs. Kip's murder. Dark slacks and jacket, bald head, just walking."

"I couldn't say," Tessi told him.

"Again, you'll let me know if you do see anyone."

"Of course."

The lieutenant rose and nodded to Larry. They left in no particular hurry. Not a minute later Ingrid let herself in. Tessi saw this as inevitable.

"They ask a lot of questions, but they don't have any answers," Ingrid said.

"The lieutenant said you saw someone."

"I don't know. I mean, I saw a man, but it was dark and in good weather you see people out walking anyway. He could have been selling encyclopedias for all I know. I'll tell you something, though. I've lived in this neighborhood for twenty-nine years, and we never had anybody murdered before, let along two people—and in the same week! And that's not to mention that fellow that crashed his truck into the pole. It's enough to make you see monsters in your closets. I'm even thinking of going to stay with my son over in Terre Haute for a while, just to get away from it. Better not to be alone in times like these."

"I suppose you're right."

"He's a good boy. We get on each other's nerves, though."

"Still, it's nice to have that," Tessi said.

Ingrid looked up. "You got anyone you can go stay with?"

"No. I'm fine."

"Nobody at all? No family, no . . . no guy or anything?"

Tessi shook her head. "No guy; not lately anyway. There was a woman who took care of me when I was young. She died a very long time ago. I guess she was all the family I had left."

"No friends?"

Tessi shrugged. She didn't want to say that friends were much too dangerous for someone like her, that they could turn on you if they learned too much about you. That you could help them one day, work a little magic, and find them pointing a finger at you the next. A finger of fear. A finger of death. It had always been that way, hadn't it?

"Well, I don't know when I'd go to Myers'. Maybe not for a while yet. Don't think I'm quite ready for that. I'll probably be right downstairs. If you need someone; you know, any time."

A brave woman, Tessi noted. And thoughtful. And she was right, about being alone. But Tessi had learned that given enough reasons, time, and practice, you could get used to most things, including solitude. Besides, Tessi reminded herself, people had never given her much choice.

"I'll be sure and let you know if I need someone to talk to," Tessi said. "Really."

"Good. You know, I hope you don't mind my saying, but I

always thought you were kind of a strange thing—so quiet all the time, so dour, staying in so much of the time or tending to those herbs and whatever else you've got growing in that garden of yours." She smiled. "But I guess you're not such a bad egg."

Tessi smiled too. She couldn't help it. "Thanks."

In a few minutes Ingrid was gone, back downstairs. Tessi sat for a time, thinking too much, trying to get a grip on the uneasiness she felt, wishing she could recover some of the perspective she had enjoyed in her youth. This John Parsner thing was going to be a problem, and who needed that.

She made a small dinner for herself: warmed pork roll and cabbage and a glass of wine. After that she made some tea and phoned Ingrid and invited her back up.

◊◊◊

The lights and radio messages from the police cars kept everyone else in the neighborhood up half the night. Rawley had lived right on the corner, two doors up. The photographs were the same; perhaps even more graphic this time. She looked at them, especially at the dead man's neck, but you couldn't tell anything. There were too many knife wounds. And very little blood.

Tessi felt Lieutenant Adkins watching her closely across the little dining room table. "Rawley had a gun," Adkins said. "A loaded automatic pistol he kept in a nightstand next to his bed. The clip had been emptied. He apparently fired every round last night. We found a few bullets in the walls. We're looking for the rest of them. I'd like you to tell me everything you heard and saw."

"Police, police cars, a TV news minivan, the neighbors, and a lot of people who must have wandered over from—"

"I mean before we got here." Adkins made an ugly face. "Your downstairs neighbor said she had a dream about gunfire before she woke up. She thinks that must have been Mr. Rawley. I'm hoping someone might have been up earlier, say about two A.M."

"Sorry," Tessi said. She had been up, and at just that time. She liked to nap in the afternoon, then get up during part of the night. There were things you couldn't do any other time—books that were best kept away from sunlight, creatures that could only be collected after dark when there was moonlight. Besides, there weren't usually any people about to worry over.

The moon had been especially full and bright last night, she recalled. Especially lovely. But the sound of gunfire had spoiled the mood completely. Tessi just wanted all the police and murders and *other things* to go away.

The lieutenant seemed to brood a moment. "There were five of you out in the street that night when John Parsner came around the corner, missed you, and killed himself," he said. "So you're all lucky on the face of it . . . until one by one people from that group start to die. Two weeks later you and Ingrid are the only ones left. Now, I don't know what's going on between you people, or why you were all out there that day, but I don't believe this story about the kid delivering late papers. And I don't believe you personally were just happening by either. I thought maybe there was some connection between one of you and Parsner, but we've pretty much ruled that out as well.

"Something happened among you, or you all got involved over your heads somehow and burned the wrong lunatic—I can't say what as people keep getting murdered before I can get to know them. But whatever happened was worth killing over, and since you and Ingrid are the only ones left, we have to assume that the murderer is after both of you—or that the murderer is one of you. You see that, don't you?"

Tessi looked at Larry, who was looking at her with wide, simple eyes, then at Adkins, who had one eye drawn nearly shut.

"Ingrid has lived here for years," Adkins went on. "You've only been around for a few months. And I can't find out much about you either—just like John Parsner. I've got people checking into that. Tell me, what will they find?"

Tessi didn't say anything. What was there to say? No, I'm not a murderer. Or No, Ingrid would never hurt a soul. No, you won't find anything, not really. And No, she didn't have anything to do with John Parsner, nor would she; not if she had any choice in the matter.

She had been blamed for a great many things in the past, good and bad (*They've always tried to blame me,* she thought), but she hadn't been responsible most of the time, even years ago.

"What are you going to do?" she asked.

"Ingrid mentioned possibly going to stay with her son on the other side of the state, but she tells me you already know about that. And if you're the murderer, then what's the point? And if you're not, maybe the murderer would decide to kill everyone there along with her. It's not something I'd care to predict.

"No, I'd rather keep both of you here under police guard for a couple of weeks or so. There will be an officer stationed outside around the clock. Are you comfortable with that?"

"Yes," Tessi told him, nodding. "Thank you."

Adkins' eyes jumped just noticeably, a hint of surprise, perhaps. "Good," he said. "If you see or hear anything, just tell the officer. I've explained all this to Ingrid, and she's fine with it too."

"Good."

"She says you two are friends."

Tessi looked at him a moment. "Yes," she said.

Adkins nodded slowly to Officer Wells, then he got up from the table. "We'll be in touch," he said. They let themselves out. Tessi breathed a shallow sigh. She hoped the lieutenant was wrong—about the murders, about the gun, about how long the surveillance might last; she wished none of it had happened, that nothing else would. She wished she was wrong, but that wasn't likely. Still, it was too soon to throw fits. You couldn't know the future—at least she had never been much good at it.

She had a fair enough sense of the present, though, and that was what bothered her the most.

◊◊◊

The rain fell steadily, mixing with dusk, gray on gray. They stood at the front window of Ingrid's downstairs apartment watching an unmarked car pull up across the street, watching another pull away. Changing of the guard. The replacement got out of his car and ran, navigating the worst puddles, to knock at the door. It was Larry Wells, wearing his usual polite smile. He'd been there the last four nights. Ingrid let him in.

"You're getting soaked," Tessi said, shaking her head, tugging her own light jacket around her against such chilly thoughts.

"I know. Just letting you know I'm here. Everything all right?"
Tessi nodded.

"Why don't we invite him in for coffee?" Ingrid offered, glancing over her shoulder. Tessi nodded again. What could it hurt?

He refused at first, but that proved quite futile. "Okay," he said finally, surrendering to Ingrid, "just one."

They sat in Ingrid's front room and talked. Ingrid told the officer about a cousin who'd been a policeman in the forties when they'd lived in Maryland. Larry was from North Carolina. Ingrid said he didn't have a trace of the accent.

"Not sure if that's good or bad," he said. "The rest of my family, they still sound southern." He got up after that, put down his empty cup. "Thanks," he said then. "Got to get back out to my car."

They let him go. He opened the door and there was someone standing there. A man slightly taller than Larry, slightly wider, dark slacks and dark jacket, a balding head. He stepped through the doorway, put an open hand on Larry's chest, and pushed him backward. Tessi recognized the face from the pictures in the papers—the man who had been driving the pickup truck, John Parsner. He was soaked with rain. He stood dripping on the living room rug, hands and face cold white like wet chalk, one hand clutching a rather small hunting knife.

Larry had his gun out. "Don't move," he said, stepping back two paces. "Not a muscle. Throw down the knife."

"You're supposed to be dead!" Ingrid said, blurting it out.

John Parsner looked at her and nodded very slowly. "So are you," he said, a thin voice, barely audible.

"No, I saw the body at the morgue," Larry said, shaking his head. "You *are* dead! And the body's not missing."

"No one looks at night," John Parsner said and stepped forward. Larry pulled the trigger. The police revolver boomed in the small living room. John took the slug high in the abdomen. He closed his eyes, then opened them and came forward again, taking two more rounds in the middle of his chest. John grabbed the other man's arm and pulled him into the blade of the hunting knife.

The young officer screamed, a sound joined by Ingrid's scream only feet away. Larry went to his knees as John pulled the knife back and let go of him, then he fell to one side and lay still. John

Parsner knelt down, leaned over the officer's body, and put his mouth to the man's neck. After a few seconds John sat up again, and got to his feet.

Ingrid and Tessi had backed up against the living room wall just behind them and were inching toward the doorway to the kitchen. John stood, still dripping rain, the knife dripping Larry's blood. He brought the blade up and licked it clean, then he came ahead. "This way!" Tessi barked, and she headed for the living room door.

Ingrid screamed again and tried to run for the kitchen.

John showed a sudden, remarkable ability to move and cut Ingrid off. They stood by the door, inches apart, both frozen in place, both staring. Tessi was at the front door. She had hold of the knob, had the door partway open already. Every instinct told her to step outside. Just go. That thing in her living room had gone insane—had gone on some sort of vengeful killing spree that saw no purpose—but you didn't give his kind therapy.

Rain fell on her hair and one shoulder as she stood half out on the step. *Go . . .*

Then she heard Ingrid screaming—short, breathless screams, one after the other. Tessi had heard a person scream only once like that in her life. At a public burning, the execution of the woman who had been Tessi's mentor. There was no choice but to run then. Tessi had been young, inexperienced, terrified, and so, so alone. . . .

She'd been alone ever since. Safe.

She took a breath, then turned and went back through the doorway.

John had Ingrid by the arm, the same way he'd had the young officer. He had the knife up. Tessi could see his teeth now as his lip curled back, especially two of them. She shouted a phrase neither John nor Ingrid would have recognized and the kitchen door flew open, catching John squarely across the back. He turned and let go of Ingrid to swipe at the door as it swung away then came back harder, crashing into him again. As he fought with it Ingrid stumbled backward, moving away.

"Here!" Tessi called to her. "Come to me!"

Ingrid heeded, though she barely had her legs under her as she reached the front door. Tessi caught her, helped her step out onto the rainy step. "Go to the neighbors and get help," she said and closed the door before Ingrid could reply.

John was finally out of range of the door as Tessi turned to face him. He started for her with slow, deliberate steps.

"The dead have their place," Tessi told him, "and this is not it. Go where you must, but leave here."

"When I'm finished," John Parsner said. "When both of you are finished." He was close now, almost within reach.

"You *are* finished," Tessi said. She glanced to one side, speaking softly, waving one hand, and Ingrid's dining room table abruptly slid across the room. It caught John at the hips as he turned toward the commotion. He doubled over onto the table, which kept going, accelerating until the sounds of popping plaster mixed with that of crumpling bone as both of them slammed into the wall.

The knife lay loose, halfway across the table; John stared at it, then tried to reach for it. He began pushing at the table, working himself free.

"If you want your knife, you shall have it." She put her hands out in front of her, began working her fingers. The knife spun, point first, then leaped. At the last moment, John jerked his head left. The knife buried itself into the wallboard behind him.

"What are you!" John howled, as if it made all the difference.

"It's a little late for introductions," Tessi said.

"You can't hurt me," John said, grinning, showing off those pointed teeth. "And you can't kill me."

"That's not what I hear," Tessi said.

"You hear wrong. The tales aren't true."

"Spikes and crosses?" Tessi asked, innocent.

"Hardly," John said. He turned to get the knife.

Tessi wiggled her fingers once more. The knife freed itself, flipped over, and came straight down, cutting deep into John Parsner's arm just below the shoulder. He barely blinked as he caught up with the blade and pulled it free again. Very little blood appeared.

"There," he said, pushing free of the table now. He raised the damaged arm in presentation. "You see?"

Tessi waved and the knife switched targets, pulling John's hand with it, as it began hacking repeatedly at various parts of his upper torso. A strange look of puzzlement crossed John's dull-white face, then one of intense concentration. He waved the knife back into the wall finally, but the instant he tried to relax his grip it began attacking him again.

Tessi left him then and hurried as fast as she could up the stairs to her own flat. She went into the big closet in her bedroom, into the small cedar chest she kept there. The spell that kept the lock was stronger than any key and beyond the talents of most any conjurer that might find it. She spoke the words too quickly at first, then tried again, and the lid pulled open. Inside she kept everything she might need: the plant and animal and mineral essentials she had collected, all carefully dried, labels carefully written. Some recipes had already been prepared, cooked on the stove—some in the moonlight through the kitchen window.

She found a small baby-food jar first and stuffed it into her jacket pocket. Next she took out three mayonnaise jars, two of them nearly filled and one empty, and removed the tops. She poured half the contents of each full jar into the empty one, and an immediate reaction took place. Colors, blues and greens, grew bright, then darkened again. Foam rose to the top. She covered all the jars, took only the mixture, and ran back to the stairway. John met her coming up as she started down. He seemed to have the knife completely under control again. Well, that had only been intended to slow the beast down.

"No more," Tessi said. "You can't do this. Even the living dead must know their bounds."

"Yes, of course. No more," John Parsner said, rising another step. "After you are dead, and the other. No more for a long while."

Tessi backed up one step, keeping five stairs between them. She turned the cover off the jar. He was right, of course; you couldn't kill his kind, not even with a wooden stake through his lifeless heart—she splashed the gray liquid down the stairwell, soaking John Parsner's face and shirt, and twice recited the words of the spell—but you could make some considerable alterations.

John made a gurgling sound that faded as the flesh of his body grew taut, then porous, as his muscle and cartilage withered. His gasp fell silent as his features went flat and his eyes disappeared. His body crumpled abruptly, already brittle, onto the stairs, still clutching the knife. Tessi waited while the remaining flesh shrank away further, while the bones turned finally to a powdery dust, like the rest. The stench of rot rose in a sudden wave, then passed.

She made her way down, careful not to collect dust on her shoes, and went back to the living room, to the side of officer Larry Wells. *Not quite dead yet,* she saw. She pulled the jar from her pocket, got it open, and used her fingers to spoon the salve onto the young officer's wound. Then she talked to him, carefully choosing the ancient words and watching as his nearly absent breathing began to grow stronger. She rose, then went back upstairs, collecting the knife as she passed. She carefully rinsed the jar out in the kitchen sink. Next, she got her broom, and a dust pan. She'd have to put the dry remains in a zip-lock bag, she thought, before she threw them out. *Do not add water,* she thought, which almost made her smile.

◊◊◊

They stood drying off in Helen and Ray Stanford's living room, both of them still shivering despite being wrapped in thick afghans Helen had knit herself.

Lieutenant Adkins stood near the door, talking to yet another officer that had just come in. They'd found Officer Larry Wells unconscious on Ingrid's living room floor. He had a small flesh wound in his abdomen, nothing too serious. But he apparently had quite a story he was telling, and it matched those of the two women. No sign of the intruder, other than the knife that had turned up in the side yard. The Stanfords had seen Ingrid run out the front, then Tessi, a short while later, running out the back. "I climbed out a back window," Tessi explained.

No one had seen anything after that.

Adkins put his notebook away and shook his head. "At least we have a description," he said. He looked up at Ingrid. "How do you feel?"

"Sick," Ingrid said. "And about ready to collapse," she added, taking a breath, waiting several seconds to let it out. "But I'm afraid to close my eyes. If Tessi hadn't been there to help, if she hadn't yelled to me when she did, I don't know what would have happened."

"I've got a big mouth, that's all," Tessi said.

"And a friend for life!" Ingrid replied.

Tessi looked at Ingrid, fought back a grin; she felt tired, too, and a bit shaken, of course. But there was something else—a buoyancy she had not felt in far too many years. She turned and looked out through the Stanford's big front bay window. The rain had stopped. The night sky had nearly cleared, ready for dawn, and the street was bathed in brilliant moonlight. She felt lucky to be alive.

"You okay?" the lieutenant asked.

Tessi nodded. "I'll be fine." Unless the good lieutenant had ideas to the contrary.

Ingrid's son poked his head in the door. He'd been waiting for an hour.

"Okay," Adkins said. "I guess you both can go."

Mark A. Garland is the author of five novels, including *Sword of the Prophet*, and one young-adult book. His stores have appeared in many anthologies and magazine, including *Tarot Fantastic, The Fortune Teller,* and *The Random House Book of Science Fiction Stories.*

Who better than a vampire to appreciate eternity?

The Tenacity of the Dead

BY JOHN HELFERS

arten drained his mug of beer and placed it on the table. The young man across from him did the same. He fumbled the mug as he set it down, nearly knocking it over. Marten watched various waitresses move among the tables in the crowded bar, let a Hispanic go by, then caught the eye of a blonde-haired one.

"Two more," he said. She nodded and left for the bar.

"That's what I'm saying," Marten's companion said loudly, slurring his words and drawing dark stares from a few of the tables around him. "Look't all them spics, kikes, niggers. All takin' jobs away from righteous God-fearing Americans."

Marten leaned over conspiratorially. "Hey, Bobby, I don't think this is the place to start anything, know what I mean?"

Bobby turned from the group of factory workers he had been glaring at to stare at Marten. "Yeah, yer prob'ly right. Maybe me an' the boys should pay this place a visit later, show these mud people the power of the Aryan race."

The beers arrived, and Marten reached for his and took a sip, not because he wanted to, but to mask the disgust he felt. He set the ice-flecked mug down and leaned forward. "I overheard some of your boys at the rally talking about 'making a statement.' Is that something I could get in on?"

Bobby was gulping his beer like it was water, and his mug was only a quarter full when it hit the table. "Tha's a secret. Only a few people know what's goin' down."

Marten looked around as if afraid someone might be eavesdropping, then lowered his voice to a whisper. "But *you* know, right?"

"Damn right I do. I'm a trusted man in the South Dakota chapter—loyal 100 percent."

"And you know I am too." Marten was insistent.

"I dunno. I mean, I jus' met you today." Bobby whistled loudly and held up his now-empty mug.

"Yeah, but we share the same views, right down the middle, right?" Marten said, smiling.

"Damn right we do." Bobby's refill arrived, and he polished off half of it in one gulp. Wiping foam off his lips, he leaned forward. "Okay, I'll give you a hint. You know that big statue of that fuckin' redskin outside of town?"

"The statue of Chief Sitting Bull?" Marten asked.

"Tha's the one. Well, by tomorrow it ain't gonna be there no more." Bobby leaned back and grinned, showing yellow, crooked teeth.

Marten's brow furrowed. "You don't mean? . . ."

Bobby nodded. "Boom," he said.

"No shit. They're gonna blow it tonight?" Marten asked.

"Yup, at 'bout two in the morning," Bobby said, then clapped a hand over his mouth. "Oops, I should'na told you that."

Marten put his finger to his lips. "Shh. It'll be our secret. Hey, isn't that some of the guys coming in?" He pointed towards the door behind the young skinhead. When Bobby turned to look, Marten dropped a small white pill into his beer. It dissolved by the time Bobby had turned back to him.

"I didn't see nobody," he said.

Marten shrugged and raised his mug. "Oh well, let's drink to . . . an early Fourth of July."

"Goddamn right," said Bobby, slamming his mug against Marten's, then draining it. A few minutes later his head was drooping down as the drug took hold. Marten eased his empty mug aside as Bobby slumped over the table. He peeled a few bills off a roll from his pocket and dropped them onto the table next to the unconscious form, then got up and walked out.

They're moving faster than we'd suspected, he thought as he walked to a black Cadillac. *I wonder who their connection is that can get them so much explosive. That bears investigation. There can only be three or four dealers with that much inventory.*

Marten got into the car and drove toward the far side of town. He was confident the racist group would be stopped before they could destroy the monument. Victor and he would see to that. *Victor should be awake by the time I get there. I can brief him and we can get going,* he thought. It was going to be a busy night all around.

◊◊◊

Victor strode briskly down the corridor, his shoes clicking on the polished marble floor. As he walked, he could hear the faint whistle and thump of artillery shells landing outside the city as the Germans advanced. Soon Paris would fall. But they would not get everything.

As he walked by the empty walls, names came unbidden to his mind: Picasso, van Gogh, Monet, da Vinci, Michelangelo. *He glanced at the spots where the masterpieces, now safely packed away and headed for Switzerland, had hung just hours before. He allowed himself a small smile of satisfaction before his lips tightened. Better to wait until they were safely outside the city.* This time, history does not repeat itself, *he thought.*

Soon he could hear noise up ahead. Men running, moving boxes, cursing as they quickly loaded the trucks that would leave the Louvre with their priceless cargo. As Victor walked in, one of the men cried out as a crate labeled medical supplies slipped from his grasp and started to slide off the truck bed.

Before anyone else could react Victor leaped to the box, grabbing it just before it hit the floor. Hoisting it back onto the truck, he snapped at the loaders, "See that it doesn't happen again."

The man pushed the crate and nodded, motioning to another partisan to help him. Victor looked around, spotting a small, wiry man with crew-cut black hair checking boxes against a clipboard he held. Trotting over to him, he asked, "Rico, how are we doing?"

The shorter man didn't even look up. "It's about time, Victor. We're barely ahead of schedule, although with the Germans this close, that doesn't mean much. Did you get the papers?"

"Of course." Victor patted his breast pocket. "When do we leave?"

"Hopefully in the next half hour. If you help, it will go even faster."

"Consider myself at your disposal." Victor took off his suit jacket and threw it in the lead truck, then helped the men finish. Fifteen minutes later the last of the tarpaulins was tied down, and the men scattered to their assigned vehicles.

Victor was walking to the lead truck when he stopped, his ears registering a noise back in the halls of the museum. He told Rico he had forgotten some papers in the office and would be back in a minute.

Once out of sight, Victor slipped out of his shoes and picked them up, then started walking silently back toward the main gallery. Standing at the entrance to the large hall, he was rewarded with the scuffle of feet trying to move quietly on marble mixed with voices whispering in accented German.

Could the Gestapo be here already? *Victor wondered, puzzled but not overly concerned. After all, spies were everywhere. Some were simply better at their job than others. He waited for the men to come to him, planning his attack. Although he didn't carry any weapons, he was confident the intruders wouldn't advance any farther.*

The two men were skilled; Victor had to give them that. One would advance, then the other, each covering his partner's movements. They reached the double doors leading into the smaller hallway. Victor remained where he was, cloaked in shadow. The barrel of a pistol poked into the room, then the hand holding it. A dark form took a step in, then another.

On the third step, Victor moved. His fist slammed into the man's neck, killing him without a sound. With his other hand, he snatched the dropped gun before it hit the marble. As the limp body crumpled to the floor, Victor set the pistol down, straightened up, and faced his other opponent.

The man stared back at him, holding a slim knife by the blade as if to throw it. The guy had olive skin and black hair and moved with uncommon grace. He flipped the dagger and caught it by the han-

dle, the blade carving a pattern in the air. Professional, *Victor thought,* and probably not half bad. *Knowing he had to end this quickly, Victor let him make his move.*

The man was good, his stiletto held in the classic fighting position, able to slash or stab without changing his grip. He feinted low, then reversed direction and aimed straight for Victor's chest. Victor stood his ground and took the blade all the way to the hilt just to the right of his sternum. He didn't fall, gasp, or cry out. He just smiled, revealing pointed, elongated canines.

The Italian staggered back, gasping at what he saw. "You."

It was the last noise his throat could utter before Victor was upon him, sinking his fangs into the man's neck. Drinking rapidly, Victor savored the mingled flavors of adrenaline and fear in the Italian's essence. Then, dropping the drained body, he knelt beside it, pondering the man's last word. "You." He pulled the dead man's shirt open. On his chest was a small tattoo in blue ink—an arcane symbol only those in his business would understand.

Or those he hunts, *Victor thought, recoiling in shock.* They've found me again. *Picking up the dagger, he slashed the Italian's throat, obliterating the puncture holes. He left the body and trotted back to the trucks, pausing only to slip his shoes back on. As he walked, he tried to figure out how the hunters had located him. The Italian obviously hadn't expected to run into him; otherwise he would have had a more effective weapon.* Another hijacking . . . *he thought. A similar occurrence rose in his mind, but it sank back into his unconscious without revealing any more details.*

Victor opened the passenger door and got into the drab green three-quarter-ton truck. Rico sat in the driver's seat, dressed in tan fatigues with a red cross on his arm. The Frenchman's mouth crooked in a half smile. "I thought you were fast."

"When we get out of here, I'll show you just how fast I can get to a bottle of Bordeaux." Victor smiled back as he changed into a similar uniform, turning away to hide the blood-stained shirt. What had been a deep stab wound on his chest was now a white line, and by the next evening that would be gone as well.

Rico drove the truck out of the small yard and into the street. As Victor looked around, his face tightened in anger. The streets were deserted, houses and shops tightly closed against the incoming mael-

strom. Between the buildings he could see dots of fire on the horizon where the Germans were decimating the last of the French armies.

The small convoy slowly crept out of the city, trusting the night to protect them. But on the outskirts of Paris, their luck deserted them.

"Mon Dieu, they have a checkpoint up already," Rico cursed, slowing the truck to a crawl.

"Keep driving. The papers we have will see us through," Victor said. I hope, he added to himself.

One of the jackbooted men held up his hand, stopping the convoy. He approached Victor's side of the truck. "Cargo and destination?"

"Medical supplies for hospitals at Cologne," Victor answered in fluent German as he handed the soldier the papers clearing their route.

"Hmmm. . . . I was not informed. Your papers are in order, but all convoys leaving the city are to be checked. Let me see your cargo."

Victor turned to Rico and said in French, "They want to see our cargo. When I give you the signal, we move." Rico nodded tightly.

Victor swung down from the truck cab and led the officer to the rear of the truck. Starting to untie the ropes that held the boxes, he looked up at the officer with concern. "Yes, sir?"

"I didn't say anything." The officer's handsome features clouded with confusion, giving Victor the break he needed.

"Yes, officer, I think you did." Victor's brown eyes flashed as they bored into the German's cobalt blue ones. "You just said that our cargo and papers are in order and that we're free to continue."

"I said that . . . your cargo . . ." the officer trailed off uncertainly, his gaze still locked by Victor's mesmerizing eyes.

"Was in order, along with our papers, and that we're free to go." Victor intensified his stare, concentrating his willpower to drive past the man's natural suspicions. Nazis were harder to control, given their fanatical brainwashing for the Führer. Another unfortunate side effect of that fervor was that his commands didn't last as long. But after a few seconds Victor sensed the last of the man's protests die away, and he relaxed and repeated the orders. Victor retied the rope and clapped the officer on the shoulder, smiling all the while. The officer shook his head, then smiled back and walked towards the front of the truck, signaling a soldier to open the barricade.

Still smiling, Victor got back into the truck. "Go. Now."

Rico engaged the truck's gears. "How did you—"

"Don't ask. I have a feeling he won't be fooled for long. As soon as we get out of sight, go as fast as you dare."

"Hey, mon ami, I know these roads like the back of my hand," Rico said.

"Just make sure it isn't the back of your head," Victor replied, watching the rearview mirror. He saw the officer watching the convoy pull away, the man still shaking his head slightly. He started walking towards the tent at the side of the road. Victor grimaced. "How far to the turn off?"

"Just a few more kilometers. We're almost there," Rico replied.

The convoy traveled in silence for a few minutes, then Victor leaned out the window and blinked, reveling in the wind washing over his face, his eyes adapting to accommodate the pale light from the moon. He spotted the turnoff just ahead. This time they had been lucky. With the war intensifying, it was doubtful many more recovery missions like this could be made.

Victor relaxed and pondered the two men in the Louvre. They definitely bear investigating, *he thought.* Perhaps after he left France he could start tracking those hunters again. The war might loosen a few tongues more easily. . . .

A thunderclap split the night, and Victor saw a row of explosions walk up the road and envelop the rear truck in an orange fireball.

"Step on it, Rico!" cried Victor. Even as he spoke, the truck lurched forward, picking up speed on the mountain road. More salvos followed; they slammed into the hills around the convoy, showering dirt and rocks on the trucks but causing no damage.

As they climbed higher into the hills, Victor looked back at the burning truck, tears blurring his vision as they streamed down his face. One trickled to the corner of his mouth, and he tasted coppery blood on his lips. He wept not so much for the men who had died—they had known the risks when they volunteered—but for the irreplaceable antiquities the truck had been carrying, now destroyed forever. Once again, *he thought bitterly,* history does repeat itself.

◊◊◊

Victor returned to consciousness, his body telling him night had arrived. He rubbed at his eyes, felt the stickiness there, and taking his hand away, saw the smears of blood where his tears had fallen. Then the hunger hit, convulsing his body. Fumbling for the walkie-talkie on the nightstand, he clawed at the switch.

"Marten, I'm awake," he whispered.

"Yes sir," came a quiet reply.

Scrabbling, Victor rolled on his side, every movement sending needles of pain through his body. He opened the small refrigerator next to the bed. Small, red-filled plastic pouches hung there, neatly labeled. Victor grabbed one and greedily drank the cold, coppery-tasting liquid until the hunger pangs were driven back. Never sated, never stopped, just pacified for a while. He opened another and drained it as well; it was going to be a long night.

Rising from the bed, he padded to the bathroom, a shudder passing through his body as he walked. He turned on the light and looked in the mirror, his eyes following the tracks of the tears he had cried while in hibernation. Victor never called it sleep, it didn't seem right. He hadn't "slept" for almost eight hundred years.

He examined his unlined face closely, seeing it as he had in pools of water or polished steel centuries before the mirror was invented. *The myths say we cannot be seen in mirrors because we have no soul*, he thought. *They're wrong. It is for precisely that reason we can still see ourselves—so we can look at our faces every day and be reminded of what we've lost.*

Stepping into the shower, he turned the knob to its hottest setting, as if it could wash away the sins he'd committed over the centuries. He didn't need to bathe, but he enjoyed showering. It was one of the few things that made him feel relatively human.

As he washed, Victor thought again about the dream he'd had. After Paris had fallen, he had tried to track down anyone who hunted vampires. It had not been the first time people had found out what he was. Usually they were individuals who had accidentally pierced the illusion of humanity he wrapped himself in. The loners were quickly dealt with, quietly and permanently.

These hunters, however, were nothing like the rogues he'd dealt with before. Well-organized and well-informed, they appeared anywhere, anytime, trying again and again to kill him. He'd seen that symbol before, but finding out anything about it or those who wore it was next to impossible. Victor had spent countless months and even more amounts of money trying to track down anyone who could tell him something. All he had to show for his efforts were rumors, half-truths, and midnight meetings where he was the only one who showed up. Whoever those people were, his contacts were more afraid of them than of him.

The nightmare itself bothered him, though not as much as the hunters. Victor "lived" in the past during his hibernation, linking the time he had passed through with the present day, drawing similarities and differences from each, comparing and contrasting, but most of all living both there and in the present. Because he did not age he didn't forget things, and the smallest details were forever stored in his mind. Finding certain events to compare to the present day, however, was sometimes difficult, there being almost eight centuries of them. But the reverie gave his current life focus and helped him retain his true identity. It also helped keep him sane.

With these visions of the past came flashes of precognition—disjointed images of the future, or at least what might be. Victor was adept at sorting the clues of his subconscious and relating them to the present. A few days ago he had dreamed of standing before the ruins of a once-mighty stone statue. From its shattered mouth echoed the words, "Look on my words, ye mighty, and despair!" Discussing the dream with Marten, they had narrowed down the meanings and possibilities, and that had brought them here, to a hotel in South Dakota. Hopefully, this would not be another dead end.

Usually, however, Victor had some control of his hibernation dreaming. He had not intended to relive the German takeover of Paris, nor the nearly failed evacuation of the museum. As it was, they had lost another truck to sloppy driving before getting off that road, though the art works had been recovered from that one.

Victor ran his dry tongue over his lips, savoring the Italian assassin's sweaty fear, tasting it as if it had happened yesterday. Packaged blood never came close to fresh.

Remembering the fight brought a new possibility to mind. *Is it a warning? Am I heading into a trap?* That was the problem with the visions: They only hinted at what *could* happen, not what *would* happen.

Victor Renko, Victor mused, *It feels good to use this name again. It reminds me of my original title.* How many lifetimes ago, how many dead? Just names, false histories, nothing more, taken for a few years, then discarded. . . . Every fifty years or so, Victor changed his name and identity, but he always came back to this one. It reminded him of the past, of when it all began.

Fire, marble engulfed in flames, papers burning. . . .

"No," he whispered, his voice drowned out by the rushing water. The memory that sprang unbidden to his mind was just as quickly repressed. Unfortunately, the names he used often brought back memories of the times when he existed under that name. Finishing his shower, Victor reached for a towel and wrapped it around himself as he left the bathroom.

Marten was waiting there, sitting beside the neatly made bed. Six years ago, Victor had found him breaking into art museums in Italy, a cunning thief for hire. Until he ran into someone even more cunning. Instead of killing him, Victor had made Marten an offer he didn't think twice about. After all, what human would pass a chance at immortality? That and the other option—death—had made it no choice at all.

That had been the beginning. Marten had convinced him to invest some of his vast fortune into building a headquarters in Victor's native Greece. Staffed with personnel who talked only to Marten, they were his eyes and ears around the globe, keeping him updated on important news in the art world. For even with the advances in security and authentication techniques, there was still no substitute for firsthand knowledge. That was what Victor had centuries of. It seemed the more time that passed, the busier he was.

A black turtleneck, close-fitting black pants, and steel-toed combat boots lay on the bed. He nodded to Marten as he began to dress.

"You found them, then?"

Marten smiled. "It was too easy. I befriended one of the younger protesters this afternoon at their demonstration. When the police moved in, I took him out of there. We went to a bar, and the rest is alcoholic history. Apparently skinheads have a low tolerance for liquor."

"When?"

"Tonight."

"They move fast," Victor said.

Marten nodded. "Apparently they feel their demonstrations aren't attracting enough attention. They want to up the stakes."

"Not if I can help it. How far to the site?"

"About an hour's drive. He said they won't start until about two A.M., with the demolition to happen near dawn."

Victor grunted, "Let's go."

◊◊◊

It was a cold night in St. Petersburg, and Victor was acutely aware of the effects the chill winds were having on him. The heavy wool cloak and layers of nineteenth century clothing were only for show, as he had no body heat to retain. Unfortunately, that also meant his limbs were slowly freezing in the winter air, leaving him sluggish and clumsy.

Victor spotted the sign for the shop he was looking for on the next block. Pulling his cloak more tightly around him, he hurried to the store front, which advertised rare books and collectibles, a luxury few could afford in these times. The shop was also distinctive because of the horses tied outside. Usually only the nobility could afford such animals.

Or the black market, *Victor thought as he approached the animals. They nickered and shied away from him, sensing Victor was no ordinary man. He entered the building before the horses attracted attention.*

Unlike most vendors in Russia, this store was lined with shelves from floor to ceiling filled with a mix of odd items, actual valuables, and junk, with the junk predominating. The room was a testament to either the lethargic economy or the shopkeeper's exceptionally active business suppliers.

"Ahh, Mr. Pardon, you have arrived. Wonderful weather we're having, yes?" the shopkeeper joked, a large smile on his face.

"Yes, a fine night for shopping," Victor replied. The owner nodded happily as he closed the shop for the evening. He motioned for Victor to follow him through a doorway behind the counter.

The odor of imported cigarettes and cigars fogged the room in a pallid haze. Victor saw four other men in rich clothes, their great-coats and cloaks draped over their chairs. It was comfortably warm in here, the heat coming from a fireplace on the south wall. Another door opposite Victor's place at the table was the only other exit in the windowless room. Victor removed his cloak and placed it over the back of his chair, then sat down.

The shopkeeper stood at the head of the table, rubbing his sweating hands together. Victor's senses, now accustomed to the room, smelled the familiar tang of something else almost hidden by the smoke: the scent of metal and oil. He listened as the small man spoke.

"Gentlemen, you all know why you're here. Each of you has received an invitation to bid on a single, most spectacular piece of merchandise, one not known to exist in the world. A treasure that, if its existence were made known to the art world in general, would cause an upheaval greater than any we've seen in years. Gentlemen, I give you the lost Fabergé egg."

With a flourish he removed a black cloth from a display column at his side and let the bidders admire the prize.

The egg was like the others in size only, slightly larger than a grown man's fist. It seemed to have been carved out of a single piece of flawless jade that caught the light in its emerald-green depths. It was bisected by two bands—one gold, one silver—braided together. The shopkeeper touched the hidden catch on the side, opening the egg so all could admire the scene within. A tiny sleigh holding a man and a woman seemed to skim across a forested landscape, pulled by six miniature reindeer. The sleigh, occupants, and team were crafted from pure platinum, and the snow they rode across was diamond dust that glittered in the dim lantern light.

Victor planned to acquire the egg and return it to the Russian government for display in their museum. Doubtless the other men in the room had less humanitarian motives in mind.

"Exquisite, yes?" the shopkeeper asked.

One of the men stood up, removing his hand from his suit coat pocket as he did so. "Quite. It will bring a handsome price when I sell it myself." The pistol he held left no room for argument.

The shopkeeper gaped in shock. "Sergei, what are you doing?" The other men stayed where they were as realization of what was happening dawned on them.

"Step away from the case, Marco. This piece will finance my companions and me for months."

One of the other men growled low in his throat and started reaching for his coat. The muzzle of the revolver swung to cover him instead. The man stopped moving but kept staring at Sergei's face as if memorizing it. The other two ex-bidders kept staring at the gun.

Victor also looked at the man's face. Sergei looked confident, in control. He's got a plan, *Victor thought.* Sergei walked to the case, shut the egg, took it, turned around, and calmly shot Marco between the eyes.

As the shopkeeper collapsed, the other men, seeing their fate lying in a bloody heap on the floor, tried to save their own lives. The first one scrabbled for his coat pocket again. He never had a chance, receiving a bullet between the shoulder blades for his efforts.

The other two men bought themselves time by upending the table and using it as a barricade. One bolted for the door, while the other stayed under cover. The runner hit the back entrance and almost made it out of sight before being shot down, Sergei coolly sighting down the barrel as he sent a finishing shot after the staggering form.

By this time Victor had gotten to the man behind the table and, with a quick twist, he broke his neck. Dropping the body, he looked at Sergei and smiled. "We work well together, eh?"

Sergei also smiled coldly and said, "An arrangement that has outlasted your usefulness." He pointed the pistol at Victor's head and fired.

The shot slammed Victor's head against the wall. He felt liquid oozing down his cheek, and knew he had lost an eye. He remained fully conscious despite the neat bullet hole in his face. Unfortunately, the impact had short-circuited even his undead limbs, and he was temporarily paralyzed. More often than he liked, Victor was reminded that he wasn't as invulnerable as the myths claimed.

With his one good eye, he watched Sergei wrap the egg and put it in his pocket. While he observed this, Victor contemplated two things: First, he couldn't use any more blood to heal himself, as he was too depleted by the gunshot. Second, if he didn't stop Sergei before he escaped, Victor was a dead man in more ways than one. He didn't have the strength to get to the other bodies and, more importantly, the blood in them. As Sergei walked past him to the exit, Victor made a final, desperate move.

Using every last ounce of willpower, he lashed out, his pointed fingernails digging into Sergei's ankle. Sergei staggered, his hand instinctively covering the pocket with the egg in it. At first, he thought he had snagged his foot on one of the bodies, but looking down, he saw the hand clamped around his leg. He then looked at the face of the man whose hand had grabbed him—straight into Victor's one good eye, which stared back at him and winked.

Upon seeing the not-so-dead man, Sergei wet his pants. With a high, keening wail, he frantically beat at Victor's hand with the butt of his gun, its other more deadly purpose forgotten at the moment.

Even though he felt several bones in his hand crack, Victor didn't loosen his grip. His hand locked around Sergei's ankle, slowly splintering the bone as the fingers gripped with all their unnatural strength.

The pain grew to be too much for the stocky Russian, and Sergei fainted, relaxing with a soft sigh. His last conscious act was to feebly move his hand to his coat pocket to clutch at the treasure within.

Slowly, laboriously, Victor began the maddening task of dragging the leg to his mouth. The stench of blood was everywhere, nearly driving him mad. Even the egg didn't matter so much as getting at the one thing that meant life itself to him. Dispelling his ravenous thoughts, Victor kept at his task, working the leg closer until he could finally feed. Long minutes passed as he absorbed what he could bit by bit. He felt his strength slowly returning, and he attempted to sit up. He dragged himself to the nearest body, which he tore into to get at the life-giving liquid inside.

When the body was white, Victor felt much better, although he knew he would have to feed again to fuel his regeneration. But first he needed some questions answered.

Crawling over to the unconscious, but still living, Sergei, Victor knelt beside him and slapped his face three times. The stocky Russian's eyes fluttered open, focusing on Victor's face.

"Who do you work for?"

It was several seconds before the man answered, "Didn't . . . expect you here. Not supposed . . . to know about . . . this egg."

His words chilled Victor more than the storm outside ever could. "What do you know of me?"

Sergei's eyes were fluttering closed again. Even Victor had to strain to hear his last word. "Vam . . . pire."

With a snarl, Victor tore open the man's shirt. There it was again—the blue marking of the hunters. Victor obliterated the tattoo with his teeth and drank, his mind racing. A trap or not? He said he didn't expect to see me or he would have been ready. If this wasn't so dangerous, it would almost be funny: A vampire and hunter working together to buy a stolen Fabergé egg, each unaware of the other's true identity. But if they have operatives in Russia, then I'm in even more danger than I thought. There's nowhere I go that they cannot follow.

With Sergei's blood warming him, Victor tried to stand. I hate dealing with the black market, *he thought.* You can't trust anybody. *He rose unsteadily to his feet and looked at the other bodies in the room. It gave him a strange feeling, knowing he was mortally wounded and still standing. Already his skull was slowly knitting back together, the nape of his neck prickling dully as the restoration began. Each time this happened, Victor felt the same odd sensation, as if he was standing outside his body watching it repair itself. Right after that, the hunger renewed itself, and this time Victor didn't even try to resist.*

When he came out of the frenzy, he wiped his mouth on his sleeve, leaving a deep red smear on the white cloth. The pale corpses around him now sported ragged bite marks on their necks and chests where he had fed. Victor, however, had more important things to worry about than the evidence of his being here.

Reaching into Sergei's coat pocket, he removed the egg, wrapped it in a linen handkerchief, and placed it in his suit pocket. Then he picked up the fireplace poker and raked the fire onto the rug. The flames spread rapidly, licking at the table, the display stand, and most importantly, the bodies.

Taking a last look around the burning room, Victor walked out the door and into the raging snowstorm. . . .

◊◊◊

A light touch brought Victor out of his reverie. *That's what I was trying to remember about France.* He had planned to track the hunters once more but had become involved in one of the bloody land wars that had shaken Europe. By the time it was over he had lost their trail. Filing those thoughts away, Victor looked at Marten, who pointed straight ahead.

The sculpture rose majestically out of the mountain, Sitting Bull's arm pointing toward a land free of oppression and prejudice. A land he and his people never found. Marten shivered as he gazed upon the monolith rising from the ground. Victor didn't shiver, but the statue affected him in much the same way.

Who would destroy this gift to the earth? Those who cannot see its beauty, who only see it as a tribute to someone who does not fit their view of what is acceptable. They do not understand its purpose: to exist in harmony with nature, side by side, a tribute to man and the earth living together. Victor felt anger build within him as he thought about the people who planned to destroy such a monument. The racists he was up against were the worst kind of group, willing to destroy a statue labored on for more than thirty years just to make an ill-conceived point.

"This will not be allowed," Victor said under his breath. He felt liquid on his palms and, opening his clenched hands, saw the crescent-shaped marks where his claws had bitten into his pale palms. As he watched, the cuts began to scab over, healing themselves. The familiar rage quickened, the warmth that flared within him just before he began his work.

"Save some of that anger, my friend." Marten's calm voice brought Victor's head up, teeth bared. "You know who your enemy is. Find them. Stop them. You know where I'll be."

Without looking at Marten or saying a word, Victor exited the car, slowly walking towards the construction site. The night was warm, with a heavy ground fog obscuring the damp earth. Victor melded with the mists, creeping ever closer.

A muffled cough alerted him to a human presence nearby. The slick smell of human sweat and nervousness reached him along with the ever-present blood scent. Victor moved closer, one with the fog, until he was right behind the lone sentry. He rose from the mist, his arm slipping around the guard's throat and constricting like a steel collar. The man didn't even cry out, just quietly passed into unconsciousness, and Victor let him gently slip to the ground. Walking to the base of the mountain, he looked up, his senses picking out three forms on Sitting Bull's pointing arm, one looking around as the other two huddled over something. Grimacing, Victor began to climb, his undead strength carrying him up the rough rock wall faster than any human could hope to go.

He reached the slope of Sitting Bull's leg, where the artisans were carving out the back of the horse the Dakota chief sat upon. Walking up to the stone statue's massive hip, he crouched down and leapt, sailing into the night to land on the statue's immense arm. He didn't land perfectly, his foot slipping in the dust left from construction. The three figures looked up, and the one standing started walking toward Victor, a gun of some sort pointed vaguely in his direction.

Victor stood waiting for him, confident in his ability to kill the guard before he could shoot. The man stopped about ten feet away, still holding the gun at his waist. He was dressed in black fatigues with an ammo belt and harness crisscrossing his chest. The shotgun he held drifted over to point at Victor's chest. Victor tensed to spring, his eyes targeting the man's throat. Then the man spoke, his voice calm. "We've been expecting you."

It's a trap, Victor thought, trying to assess the situation. "Who are you?"

The man seemed to be waiting for something before he answered. At last he said, "I know all your guises, despite having only seen you for the first time tonight. My people have been tracking you almost as long as you've been alive."

Victor's mind raced as he tried to discover where he had slipped up, what mistake he had made that had put these trackers onto him. "Then you know what I am."

"You are an abomination against nature, an unholy creation that must be destroyed. Look down."

Victor did so. Three small red dots were centered, unwavering, on his chest. "You see," the man continued, "we've known of your kind ever since your introduction into this world. Unlike the majority of the population, who think you exist only in myths and legends, we discovered, often fatally, that you are real.

"Our surviving ancestors recorded every bit of information we could find about you and your ways, your pathetic attempts to live parasitically among us, taking what you want without giving anything in return. Each generation they recruited new members, sometimes family, sometimes those who had lost their family to your appetite for blood. I can trace my bloodline back over seven centuries of hunters. We've dedicated our lives to stalking the shadows you live in, finding and destroying you."

As the man rambled on, Victor realized he was referring to him in the context of all vampires, however many of them there were. While this made him feel a bit better, knowing they weren't after him specifically, the idea of a centuries-old cabal of vampire hunters didn't appeal to him very much. Unfortunately, stuck as he was out in the open, there wasn't much he could do. Doubtless the three laser sights were attached to submachine guns, and even his unnatural stamina could not protect him from ten or twenty nine-millimeter rounds through the chest. Victor had to stall, buying time until Marten could get into position and hopefully see what was happening.

◊◊◊

After Victor headed for the monument Marten walked to the Cadillac's trunk and opened it. Taking a long, black case out, he removed a high-powered German sniping rifle of the type usually available only to the military. Affixed to it was a Starlight scope specially designed for night shooting. Marten screwed on a long, black silencer, loaded a twenty-round magazine, and chambered a round. Closing the case and the trunk, he trotted to a position about fifty meters away from the car on a small rise that gave him a clear view of the site. Unfolding the portable bipod attached to the barrel, he lay down and rested the rifle in front of him, turning the scope on and looking through it at the now green statue of Sitting Bull. Scanning the base, he saw Victor starting to climb up the rock face. Marten started to look around the rest of the monument for any other enemies. He located the trio on the arm and sighted in on the one standing up.

"Good-bye, buddy," Marten said when he had the guy's head in his cross hairs. He was just about to squeeze the trigger when he heard the click of a pistol being cocked.

"Freeze," a familiar voice said.

Marten exhaled and looked up. Standing over him was a familiar shape. "Bobby?"

The man smiled, his pistol aimed at Marten's chest. "Yup. Welcome to the party, pal."

"Jeez, you sound a lot more intelligent than this afternoon," Marten said, carefully taking his finger off the trigger of his rifle.

"Funny how that works, isn't it? You fell for that line like a lead balloon." Bobby stepped away from Marten and motioned with his pistol. "Get up, slowly."

Marten rose to his feet, hands in the air. He noticed Bobby's pistol had a silencer attached to its barrel. He also saw another black-clad man a few steps away with an assault rifle slung over his shoulder.

"Damn, you boys come prepared," he said.

"In our line of work, you're either prepared or dead. Now turn around and start walking toward the statue," Bobby ordered. The men started walking.

"Nice little setup you got here," Marten commented.

"We've had years of experience. You weren't half bad at the bar either. What was in my drink—chloral hydrate?"

"Something like that. You guys aren't the only backup team, are you?"

"Maybe we are, maybe we aren't. In a few more minutes you won't care either way. Sure is a shame though. We could have used you. Instead you chose to sell out your race to that bloodsucker. I'm not sure who's worse."

Marten stopped walking. "Now, wait a minute—"

"Shut up and keep moving." Bobby walked up to him to prod him in the back. As soon as Marten felt the pistol jab him he pivoted around, knocking the pistol aside with his left arm. His knee shot up directly into Bobby's crotch. As Bobby started to collapse forward, Marten reached for his gun hand while jamming his knee into Bobby's face. He grabbed the pistol and pointed it at the other man, who was fumbling with his slung rifle while opening his mouth to yell a warning. Marten sighted and fired twice. The man dropped without a sound. Marten shook his head.

"I respect him a thousand times more than I do you." Using the other man's shoelaces, Marten made sure Bobby was secured and trotted back to his rifle. Lying down again, he scanned the statue, looking for likely sniper positions. In a few moments he found two forms huddled on Sitting Bull's shoulder aiming submachine guns down at the outstretched arm. Marten steadied his breathing and prepared to fire.

◊◊◊

Victor felt his confidence faltering as the seconds ticked by with no shot from Marten. Desperately he kept talking. "So the racists weren't going to destroy the monument?"

The man smiled. "Of course not. They demonstrate and bluster, but they don't have the balls for this. We do thank them, however, for providing the opportunity to kill you without suspicion. Some nut fooling around with explosives, trying to make a statement . . . the bomb goes off prematurely. . . . I'm sure you can fill in the blanks."

Victor was glad he didn't blush, as he didn't want the man to see how he felt. The shotgunner continued, "Our plant allowed your man to get close enough, then gave him the information to lure you here. We saw you both come up, and he's being dealt with as we speak."

Victor felt an emotion he hadn't known in millennia pass over him: helplessness. All of his carefully laid plans taken apart by these fanatics. He looked past his enemy at the two men who were watching the exchange, still hunched over the suitcase-sized box. "You would destroy all this just to kill me?"

"We all do what we must. You have proven a wily adversary, but the hunt is over."

Victor thought about making one final desperate leap at the man to try to put him between the snipers and himself. Before he could move, his ears caught the unmistakable sound of bullets impacting flesh. Seconds later, three dark shapes came hurtling past the two men, the bodies falling soundlessly to the rocks far below.

Victor grinned at the man's expression of shocked dismay. "You're right; the hunt is over. Tonight."

Victor's last words degenerated into a half-snarl as he leapt at the man. The shotgun roared in response. Even from the hip, at ten feet he couldn't miss.

Searing pain ripped into Victor's chest as he felt the pellets pulp his flesh and ribs. Hit in mid-leap, he flew backward, farther out onto the arm of Sitting Bull. The gunman broke the breech of his weapon, dumped the shells, then reloaded. "They were right. Ironwood pellets, by God. We will triumph over you, even if it takes a thousand more years. For now, this is a good start."

Stunned by the impact of the shot and nearly paralyzed from the wood in his heart, Victor could only watch unblinking as the man came toward him. What he was sure were his last thoughts went through his head. *I have failed*. Not that it was going to matter in about three seconds.

Again, no sound was heard when more bullets exploded the gunman's head. His muscles relaxed, dropping the shotgun. A moment later, the body crumpled on the statue's stone arm, leaving a bloody smear on the rock.

His two companions watched the body of their triggerman slide off Sitting Bull's arm to smash against the rocks below. One pressed a button on the device they were leaning over, then both started rappelling down the mountain. All the speed in the world couldn't help them, however, as Victor watched the red dot from Marten's silenced rifle find one, then the other. The two men jerked and hung limply in their mountaineering harnesses, swaying on the rope.

It was then Victor remembered the hunters' mission. Rolling over, he grunted as he felt the wood pellets grate in his chest. A creeping numbness was spreading from there to the rest of his body, a symptom of the wood in his heart. Victor dug the claws of his functional hand into the stone and dragged his body towards the bomb. Foot by agonizing foot he closed the gap until he could almost touch the bomb, which silently ticked toward detonation.

Fourteen seconds left. . . . got to get it. . . . Victor's thoughts were short-circuiting as the numbness reached his head. With one final heave, his arm flopped onto the bomb, his fingers sinking into the plastic explosive. His last conscious action was to heave his body off the statue's arm and begin sliding toward the ground thirty stories below him. A blinding flash of orange light registered on his eyes, then blackness. . . .

◊◊◊

Victor awoke to darkness. He smelled cordite, burned cloth, and rubber. Feeling tentatively around him, his hands encountered metal, and he realized he was in the trunk of a car. Just then he heard the sound of a key in the lock as the trunk lid popped open.

Marten stood over him, a set of folded clothes in his hand. Victor looked down and saw his current garments hanging in tatters on his pale body. There was no sign of injury. He climbed out of the trunk, took the proffered set of clothes, and dressed quickly. He could see the first rays of sunlight creeping over the horizon. Looking around, he saw the car was on a silent country road. Buttoning his shirt, he adjusted his collar and looked at Marten again. This time Victor noticed a large bandage on his forearm. Marten's expression was inscrutable as usual.

Victor leaned against the car. "What happened last night?"

"Actually, it was yesterday morning. You've been out for a while," Marten said."

"And?"

"You saved the monument," Marten said. Victor felt a surge of relief mixed with pride before he suppressed it.

"Okay. How did you get that?" Victor asked, pointing to the bandage.

"Well, when you fell off the arm, the bomb landed a few yards away. You were pretty torn up. I thought you were dead. Well, really dead."

"So you . . ." Victor's gaze fell to the bandage as his voice trailed off.

Marten nodded. "Opening your mouth was the easy part. Getting you to stop was more difficult. Luckily, you couldn't move, so I could get away from you fairly easily. Not totally painlessly, though."

Victor scratched his face even though there was no itch there. It was just something to do while he thought about what had happened. He had never fed from Marten, usually procuring his blood from the criminals he dealt with on a regular basis. He looked at the slim man, who stared back at him in silence. Finally Marten spoke.

"We should be moving on, Victor. The police may be searching for anyone connected with the group, and I may be remembered by someone." Marten walked around to the driver's side of the car, turning his back on Victor.

"Of course," Victor said, still thinking. "Marten?"

The slim man half turned, waiting.

"How did you escape their ambush?"

The only man Victor could call his friend smiled. "Victory through the use of superior technology. I had night vision and excellent training. They didn't. I have skills even you aren't aware of. After all, what good would I be if you knew everything, eh?"

Victor also smiled, somewhat abashed at the realization he had taken Marten for granted.

"Marten?"

Marten stopped, his hand on the car door.

"Thank you."

"You're welcome." Marten got into the car, leaving Victor alone with his thoughts. *That was as close to death as I ever want to get.* He smiled ruefully as he thought of the hunters. *The wood was a nice touch. Too bad for them it doesn't kill us, only paralyzes the body. Of course, unless someone is watching over me, I'm as good as dead anyway if that happens. That's why I have Marten around. Well, one of the reasons anyway.*

Victor turned around to get into the car and stopped. The rays of the rising sun silhouetted the statue of Sitting Bull in a bright halo of light. The car and Victor were protected in the huge shadow of the fabled Native American chieftain. Victor smiled at the sight. *This is what makes this life worthwhile—the fact that Sitting Bull will see the sun rise tomorrow, even if I cannot. However, tonight puts a new twist in the game. The game of cat-and-mouse begins anew, and this time I won't stop until I find them all.*

He walked to the back door of the Cadillac and got in. Immediately he felt more secure behind the heavily darkened windows.

Marten looked back at him. "I thought you might enjoy seeing that."

"You were right. I think our work here is done. Let's go home." Victor pressed a button at his side, raising a mirrored partition that blocked all sunlight from the front. He leaned forward and turned on the radio, tuning it until he got a local news station.

". . . and to recap our top story, seven members of a local racist group were found dead yesterday at the monument of Sitting Bull, which is still under construction. Police found evidence of an explosion on the site, along with evidence of an eighth member who appears to have died when the bomb they were setting off at the monument detonated prematurely. Police are still investigating the incident, but preliminary reports indicate the group was planning to destroy the monument to Sitting Bull, the Dakota Native American chief who defeated Custer at the Battle of Little Big Horn. All known members of the group are currently in custody. A spokesperson for the group has released a statement declaring their innocence. We'll keep you updated on that as reports come in. Stay tuned for the upcoming weather report here on KBBA. . . ."

Victor had frozen, listening to the report. A smile crossed his face for a moment, then just as quickly faded away. *Once again, history does repeat itself. As Cicero commented, those who do not remember the past are doomed to repeat it. Luckily, I don't have that problem. I doubt my enemies have that advantage.*

John Helfers' short stories have appeared in *Phantoms of the Night, The UFO Files, Sword of Ice and Other Tales of Valdemar,* and other anthologies. He is currently editing his own first anthology, *Black Cats and Broken Mirrors,* which will be published in 1998.

Some stories send a chill down one's spine—
a chill that has nothing to do with the cold.

The Drifting Snow

BY AUGUST DERLETH

Aunt Mary's advancing footsteps halted suddenly, short of the table, and Clodetta turned to see what was keeping her. She was standing very rigidly, her eyes fixed upon the French windows just opposite the door through which she had entered, her cane held stiffly before her.

Clodetta shot a quick glance across the table toward her husband, whose attention had also been drawn to his aunt; his face vouchsafed her nothing. She turned again to find that the old lady had transferred her gaze to her, regarding her stonily and in silence. Clodetta felt uncomfortable.

"Who withdrew the curtains from the west windows?"

Clodetta flushed, remembering. "I did, Aunt. I'm sorry. I forgot about your not wanting them drawn away."

The old lady made an odd grunting sound, shifting her gaze once again to the French windows. She made a barely perceptible movement, and Lisa ran forward from the shadow of the hall, where she had been regarding the two at table with stern disapproval. The servant went directly to the west windows and drew the curtains.

Aunt Mary came slowly to the table and took her place at its head. She put her cane against the side of her chair, pulled at the chain about her neck so that her lorgnette lay in her lap, and looked from Clodetta to her nephew, Ernest.

Then she fixed her gaze on the empty chair at the foot of the table, and spoke without seeming to see the two beside her.

"I told both of your that none of the curtains over the west windows was to be withdrawn after sundown, and you must have noticed that none of those windows has been for one instant uncovered at night. I took especial care to put you in rooms facing east, and the sitting-room is also in the east."

"I'm sure Clodetta didn't mean to go against your wishes, Aunt Mary," said Ernest abruptly.

"No, of course not, Aunt."

The old lady raised her eyebrows, and went on impassively. "I didn't think it wise to explain why I made such a request. I'm not going to explain. But I do want to say that there is a very definite danger in drawing away the curtains. Ernest has heard that before, but you, Clodetta, have not."

Clodetta shot a startled glance at her husband.

The old lady caught it, and said, "It's all very well to believe that my mind's wandering or that I'm getting eccentric, but I shouldn't advise you to be satisfied with that."

A young man came suddenly into the room and made the seat at the foot of the table, into which he flung himself with an almost inaudible greeting to the other three.

"Late again, Henry," said the old lady.

Henry mumbled something and began hurriedly to eat. The old lady sighed, and began presently to eat also, whereupon Clodetta and Ernest did likewise. The old servant, who had continued to linger behind Aunt Mary's chair, now withdrew, not without a scornful glance at Henry.

Clodetta looked up after a while and ventured to speak, "You aren't as isolated as I thought you might be up here, Aunt Mary."

"We aren't, my dear, what with telephones and cars and all. But only twenty years ago it was quite a different thing, I can tell you." She smiled reminiscently and looked at Ernest.

"Your grandfather was living then, and many's the time he was snowbound with no way to let anybody know."

"Down in Chicago when they speak of 'up north' or the 'Wisconsin woods' it seems very far away," said Clodetta.

"Well, it *is* far away," put in Henry abruptly. "And, Aunt, I hope you've made some provision in case we're locked in here for a day or two. It looks like snow outside, and the radio says a blizzard's coming."

The old lady grunted and looked at him. "Ha, Henry—you're overly concerned, it seems to me. I'm afraid you've been regretting this trip ever since you set foot in my house. If you're worrying about a snowstorm, I can have Sam drive you down to Wausau, and you can be in Chicago tomorrow."

"Of course not."

Silence fell, and presently the old lady called gently, "Lisa," and the servant came into the room to help her from her chair, though, as Clodetta had previously said to her husband, "She didn't need help."

From the doorway, Aunt Mary bade them all goodnight, looking impressively formidable with her cane in one hand and her unopened lorgnette in the other, and vanished into the dusk of the hall, from which her receding footsteps sounded together with those of the servant, who was seldom seen away from her. These two were alone in the house most of the time, and only very brief periods when the old lady had up her nephew Ernest, "Dear John's boy," or Henry, of whose father the old lady never spoke, helped to relieve the pleasant somnolence of their quiet lives. Sam, who usually slept in the garage, did not count.

Clodetta looked nervously at her husband, but it was Henry who said what was uppermost in their thoughts.

"I think she's losing her mind," he declared matter-of-factly. Cutting off Clodetta's protest on her lips, he got up and went into the sitting-room, from which came presently the strains of music from the radio.

Clodetta fingered her spoon idly and finally said, "I do think she is a little queer, Ernest."

Ernest smiled tolerantly. "No, I don't think so. I've an idea why she keeps the west windows covered. My grandfather died out there—he was overcome by the cold one night, and froze on the

The Drifting Snow   199

slope of the hill. I don't rightly know how it happened—I was away at the time. I suppose she doesn't like to be reminded of it."

"But where's the danger she spoke of, then?"

He shrugged. "Perhaps it lies in her—she might be affected and affect us in turn." He paused for an instant, and finally added, "I suppose she *does* seem a little strange to you—but she was like that as long as I can remember, next time you come, you'll be used to it."

Clodetta looked at her husband for a moment before replying. At last she said, "I don't think I like the house, Ernest."

"Oh, nonsense, darling." He started to get up, but Clodetta stopped him.

"Listen, Ernest, I remembered perfectly well Aunt Mary's not wanting those curtains drawn away—but I just felt I had to do it. I didn't want to but—*something made me do it.*" Her voice was unsteady.

"Why, Clodetta," he said, faintly alarmed. "Why didn't you tell me before?"

She shrugged. "Aunt Mary might have thought I'd gone wool-gathering."

"Well, it's nothing serious, but you've let it bother you a little and that isn't good for you. Forget it; think of something else. Come and listen to the radio."

They rose and moved toward the sitting-room together. At the door Henry met them. He stepped aside a little, saying, "I might have known we'd be marooned up here," and adding, as Clodetta began to protest, "We're going to be, all right. There's a wind coming up and it's beginning to snow, and I know what that means." He passed them and went into the deserted dining-room, where he stood a moment looking at the too long table. Then he turned aside and went over to the French windows, from which he drew away the curtains and stood there peering out into the darkness. Ernest saw him standing at the window, and protested from the sitting-room.

"Aunt Mary doesn't like those windows uncovered, Henry."

Henry half turned and replied, "Well *she* may think it's dangerous, but I can risk it."

Clodetta, who had been staring beyond Henry into the night

FIELDS OF BLOOD

through the French windows, said suddenly, "Why, there's some-one out there!"

Henry looked quickly through the glass and replied, "No, that's the snow; it's coming down heavily, and the wind's drifting it this way and that." He dropped the curtains and came away fromt he windows.

Clodetta said uncertainly, "Why, I could have sworn I saw someone out there, walking past the window."

"I suppose it does look that way from here," offered Henry, who had come back into the sitting-room. "But personally, I think you've let Aunt Mary's eccentricities impress you too much."

Ernest made an impatient gesture at this, and Clodetta did not answer. Henry sat down before the radio and began to move the dial slowly. Ernest had found himself a book, and was becoming interested, but Clodetta continued to sit with her eyes fixed upon the still slowly moving curtains cutting off the French win-dows. Presently she got up and left the room, going down the long hall into the east wing, where she tapped gently upon Aunt Mary's door.

"Come in," called the old lady.

Clodetta opened the door and stepped into the room where Aunt Mary sat in her dressing-robe, her dignity, in the shape of her lorgnette and cane, resting respectively on her bureau and in the corner. She looked surprisingly benign, as Clodetta at once confessed.

"Ha, thought I was an ogre in disguise, did you?" said the old lady, smiling in spite of herself. "I'm really not, you see, but I have a sort of bogey about the west windows, as you have seen."

"I wanted to tell you something about those windows, Aunt Mary," said Clodetta. She stopped suddenly. The expression on the old lady's face had given way to a curiously dismaying one. It was not anger, not distaste—it was a lurking suspense. Why, the old lady was afraid!

"What?" she asked Clodetta shortly.

"I was looking out—just for a moment or so—and I thought I saw someone out there."

"Of course, you didn't, Clodetta. Your imagination, perhaps, or the drifting snow."

"My imagination? Maybe. But there was no wind to drift the snow, though one has come up since."

"I've often been fooled that way, my dear. Sometimes I've gone out in the morning to look for footprints—there weren't any, ever. We're pretty far away from civilization in a snow-storm, despite out telephones and radios. Our nearest neigh-bor is at the foot of the long, sloping rise—over three miles away—and all wooded land between. There's no highway near-er than that."

"It was so clear. I could have sworn to it."

"Do you want to go out in the morning and look?" asked the old lady shortly.

"Of course not."

"Then you didn't see anything?"

It was half question, half demand. Clodetta said, "Oh, Aunt Mary, you're making an issue of it now."

"Did you or didn't you in your own mind see anything, Clodetta?"

"I guess I didn't, Aunt Mary."

"Very well. And now do you think we might talk about some-thing more pleasant?"

"Why, I'm sure—I'm sorry, Aunt. I didn't know that Ernest's grandfather had died out there."

"Ha, he's told you that, has he? Well?"

"Yes, he said that was why you didn't like the slope after sun-set—that you didn't like to be reminded of his death."

The old lady looked at Clodetta impassively. "Perhaps he'll never know how near right he was."

"What do you mean, Aunt Mary?"

"Nothing for you to know, my dear." She smiled again, her sternness dropping from her. "And now I think you'd better go, Clodetta; I'm tired."

Clodetta rose obediently and made for the door, where the old lady stopped her. "How's the weather?"

"It's snowing—hard, Henry says—and blowing."

The old lady's face showed her distaste at the news. "I don't like to hear that, not at all. Suppose someone should look down that slope tonight?" She was speaking to herself, having forgotten Clodetta at the door. Seeing her again abruptly, she said, "But you don't know, Clodetta. Good night."

Clodetta stood with her back against the closed door, wondering what the old lady could have meant. *But you don't know, Clodetta.* That was curious. For a moment or two the old lady had completely forgotten her.

She moved away from the door, and came upon Ernest just turning into the east wing.

"Oh, there you are," he said. "I wondered where you had gone."

"I was talking a bit with Aunt Mary."

"Henry's been at the west windows again—and now *he* thinks there's someone out there."

Clodetta stopped short. "Does he really think so?"

Ernest nodded gravely. "But the snow's drifting frightfully, and I can imagine how that suggestion of yours worked on his mind."

Clodetta turned and went back along the hall. "I'm going to tell Aunt Mary."

He started to protest, but to no avail, for she was already tapping on the old lady's door, was indeed opening the door and entering the room before he could frame an adequate protest.

"Aunt Mary," she said, "I didn't want to disturb you again, but Henry's been at the French windows in the dining-room, and he says he's seen someone out there."

The effect on the old lady was magical. "He's seen them!" she exclaimed. Then she was on her feet, coming rapidly over to Clodetta. "How long ago?" she demanded, seizing her almost roughly by the arms. "Tell me, quickly. How long ago did he see them?"

Clodetta's amazement kept her silent for a moment, but at last she spoke, feeling the old lady's keen eyes staring at her. "It was some time ago, Aunt Mary, after supper."

The old lady's hands relaxed, and with it her tension. "Oh," she said, and turned and went back slowly to her chair, taking her cane from the corner where she had put it for the night.

"Then there *is* someone out there?" challenged Clodetta, when the old lady had reached her chair.

For a long time, it seemed to Clodetta, there was no answer.

Then presently the old lady began to nod gently, and a barely audible "Yes" escaped her lips.

"Then we had better take them in, Aunt Mary."

The old lady looked at Clodetta earnestly for a moment; then she replied, her voice firm and low, her eyes fixed upon the wall beyond. "We can't take them in, Clodetta—because they're not alive."

At once Henry's words came flashing into Clodetta's memory—"She's losing her mind"—and her involuntary start betrayed her thought.

"I'm afraid I'm not mad, my dear—I hoped at first I might be, but I wasn't. I'm not, now. There was only one of them out there at first—the girl; Father is the other. Quite long ago, when I was young, my father did something which he regretted all his days. He had a too strong temper, and it maddened him. One night he found out that one of my brothers—Henry's father—had been very familiar with one of the servants, a very pretty girl, older than I was. He thought she was to blame, though she wasn't, and he didn't find out until too late. He drove her from the house, then and there. Winter had not yet set in, but it was quite cold, and she had some five miles to go to her home. We begged Father not to send her away—though we didn't know what was wrong then—but he paid no attention to us. The girl had to go."

"Not long after she had gone, a biting wind came up, and close upon it a fierce storm. Father had already repented his hasty action, and sent some of the men to look for the girl. They didn't find her, but in the morning she was found frozen to death on the long slope of the hill to the west."

The old lady sighed, paused a moment, and went on. "Years later—she came back. She came in a snowstorm, as she went; but she had become vampiric. We all saw her. We were at supper table, and Father saw her first. The boys had already gone upstairs, and Father and the two of us girls, my sister and I, did not recognize her. She was just a dim shape floundering about in the snow beyond the French windows. Father ran out to her, calling to us to send the boys after him. We never saw him alive again. In the morning we found him in the same spot where years before the girl had been found. He, too, had died of exposure.

"Then, a few years after—she returned with the snow, and she brought him along; he, too, had become vampiric. They stayed until the last snow, always trying to lure someone out there. After that, I knew, and had the windows covered during the winter nights, from sunset to dawn, because they never went beyond the west slope.

"Now you know, Clodetta."

Whatever Clodetta was going to say was cut short by running footsteps in the hall, a hasty rap, and Ernest's head appearing suddenly in the open doorway.

"Come on, you two," he said, almost gaily, "There *are* people out on the west slope—a girl and an old man—and Henry's gone out to fetch them in!"

Then, triumphant, he was off. Clodetta came to her feet, but the old lady was before her, passing her and almost running down the hall, calling loudly for Lisa, who presently appeared in night-cap and gown from her room.

"Call Sam, Lisa," said the old lady, "and send him to me in the dining-room."

She ran on into the dining-room, Clodetta close on her heels. The French windows were open, and Ernest stood on the snow-covered terrace beyond, calling his cousin. The old lady went directly over to him, even striding into the snow to his side, though the wind drove the snow against her with great force. The wooded western slope was long in a snow-fog; the nearest trees were barely discernible.

"Where could they have gone?" Ernest said, turning to the old lady, whom he had thought to be Clodetta. Then, seeing that it was the old lady, he said, "Why, Aunt Mary—and so little on, too! You'll catch your death of cold."

"Never mind, Ernest," said the old lady. "I'm all right. I've had Sam get up to help you look for Henry—but I'm afraid you won't find him."

"He can't be far; he just went out."

"He went before you saw where; he's far enough gone."

Sam came running into the blowing snow from the dining-room, muffled in a greatcoat. He was considerably older than Ernest, almost the old lady's age. He shot a questioning glance at her and asked, "Have they come again?"

Aunt Mary nodded. "You'll have to look for Henry. Ernest will help you. And remember, don't separate. And don't go far from the house."

Clodetta came with Ernest's overcoat, and together the two women stood there, watching them until they were swallowed up in the wall of driven snow. Then they turned slowly and went back into the house.

The old lady sank into a chair facing the windows. She was pale and drawn, and looked, as Clodetta said afterwards, "as if she'd fallen together." For a long time she said nothing. Then, with a gentle little sigh, she turned to Clodetta and spoke.

"Now there'll be three of them out there."

Then, so suddenly that no one knew how it happened, Ernest and Sam appreared beyond the windows, and between them they dragged Henry. The old lady flew to open windows, and the three of them, cloaked in snow, came into the room.

"We found him—but the cold's hit him pretty hard, I'm afraid," said Ernest.

The old lady sent Lisa for cold water, and Ernest ran to get himself other clothes. Clodetta went with him, and in their rooms told him what the old lady had related to her.

Ernest laughed. "I think you believed that, didn't you, Clodetta? Sam and Lisa do, I know, because Sam told me the story long ago. I think the shock of Grandfather's death was too much for all three of them."

"But the story of the girl, and then—"

"That part's true, I'm afraid. A nasty story, but it did happen."

"But those people Henry and I saw!" protested Clodetta weakly.

Ernest stood without movement. "That's so," he said, "I saw them, too. Then they're out there yet, and we'll have to find them!" He took up his overcoat again, and went from the room, Clodetta protesting in a shrill unnatural voice. The old lady met him at the door of the dining-room, having overheard Clodetta pleading with him. "No, Ernest—you can't go out there again," she said. "There's no one out there."

He pushed gently into the room and called to Sam, "Coming, Sam? There are still two of them out there—we almost forgot them."

Sam looked at him strangely. "What do you mean?" he demanded roughly. He looked challengingly at the old lady, who shook her head.

"The girl and the old man, Sam. We've got to get them, too."

"Oh, *them,*" said Sam. "They're dead!"

"Then I'll go out alone," said Ernest.

Henry came to his feet suddenly, looking dazed. He walked forward a few steps, his eyes traveling from one to the other of them yet apparently not seeing them. He began to speak abruptly, in an unnatural child-like voice.

"The snow," he murmured, *"the snow—the beautiful hands, so little, so lovely—her beautiful hands—and the snow, the beautiful lovely snow, drifting and falling about her. . . ."*

He turned slowly and looked toward the French windows, the others following his gaze. Beyond was a wall of white, where the snow was drifting against the house. For a moment Henry stood quietly watching; then suddenly a white figure came forward from the snow—a young girl, cloaked in long snow-whips, her glistening eyes strangely fascinating.

The old lady flung herself forward, her arms outstretched to cling to Henry, but she was too late. Henry had run toward the windows, had opened them, and even as Clodetta cried out, had vanished into the wall of snow beyond.

Then Ernest ran forward, but the old lady threw her arms around him and held him tightly, murmuring, "You shall not go! Henry is gone beyond our help!"

Clodetta came to help her, and Sam stood menacingly at the French windows, now closed against the wind and the sinister snow. So they held him, and would not let him go.

"And tomorrow," said the old lady in a harsh whisper, "we must go to their graves and stake them down. We should have gone before."

In the morning they found Henry's body crouched against the bole of an ancient oak, where two others had been found years before. There were almost obliterated marks of where something had dragged him, a long, uneven swath in the snow, and yet no footprints, only strange, hollowed places along the way as if the wind had whirled the snow away, and only the wind.

But on his skin were signs of the snow vampire—the delicate small prints of a young girl's hands.

August Derleth was a prolific author and editor, and the founder of Arkham House, which published such masters as H. P. Lovecraft, Ray Bradbury, and Robert Bloch, among many others. Some of his books of the macabre include *Not Long for this World, Someone in the Dark, The Lurker at the Threshold,* and *Mr. George and Other Odd Persons.* He was also the author of many mainstream works, including *Wind over Wisconsin, The Milwaukee Road, Bright Journey,* and *Still Is the Summer Night.*